THE VESSEL GAMES

E.J. EDEN

DEDICATION

For the Craftsman Caste that stole my heart.

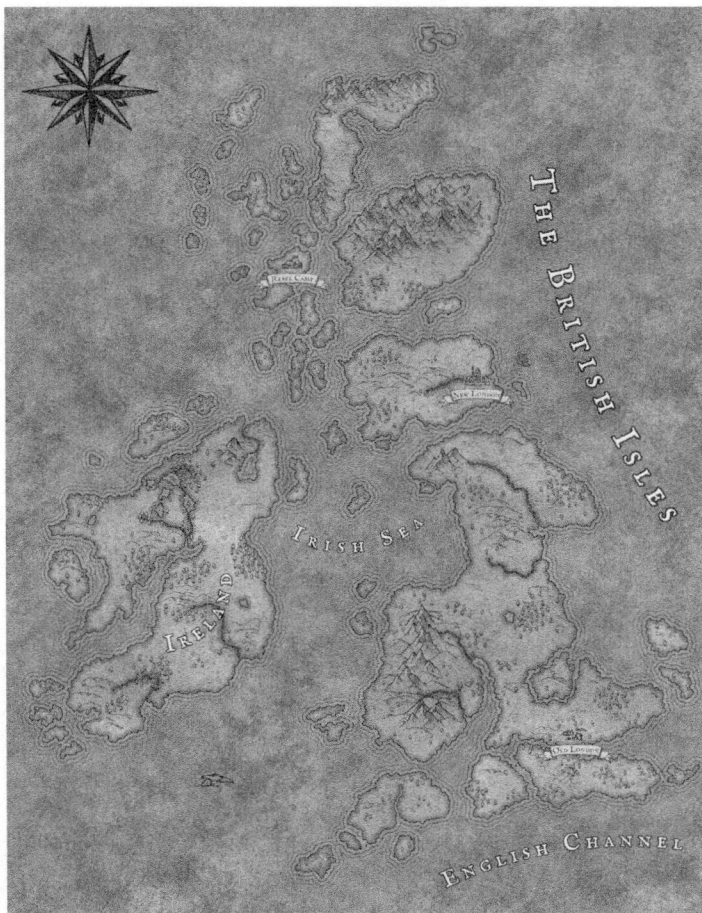

THE BRITISH ISLES

REBEL'S CABLE

NEW EDITION

IRISH SEA

IRELAND

OLD EDITION

ENGLISH CHANNEL

TRIGGER / CONTENT WARNINGS

'The Vessel Games' is set in a dystopian future —a
patriarchal, religiously extreme society.
This is a **new adult** book and not recommended to readers
under 18 years of age.
This book contains:
Graphic language
Graphic violence
Graphic sexual content
Religious extremism
A threat of rape to a MC (NOT carried through)
Mention of domestic violence (NOT on page)
Mention of abortion (NOT on page)

Thank you, dear reader, for coming on this ride.
Now, buckle the hell up.

CHAPTER
ONE

"Bless me, Father, for I have sinned."

"Pray, child, what is your sin?"

Chloe took a shaky breath. She wished she could tell him the truth. She really did. But if she wanted to still be alive tomorrow, then she needed to opt for a more generalized summary of events.

"Lust."

The confessional was so dark she barely saw the rosary beads in her sweaty palms. There was a long pause before Father Jeremiah filled the silence once more. "Do you want to elaborate on that, Chloe?"

"Not really," Chloe said through gritted teeth. "Isn't confessing your manner of sin and saying you're sorry for it enough?"

Father Jeremiah shifted, his face shrouded by the intricate carvings of the lattice wall that stood between them. "Romans, 8:6, Chloe," the father mandated, as Chloe lifted her head to the ceiling, stared at the roof of the confessional, and recited the passage.

"If our desires rule our minds, we will die. But if our

minds are ruled by the Spirit, we will have life and peace," she said, offering the psalm up for penance.

Father Jeremiah was already muttering the prayer of absolution before she'd finished that psalm.

Chloe had always thought it strange that a priest could forgive a sin that, if discovered, would cause her execution. But he didn't know what he was providing forgiveness for she supposed. The hinges of Father Jeremiah's confessional door creaked open, and Chloe sprung to her feet. She wouldn't let him get away. She'd been trying to get him alone for weeks. Chloe burst out of the confessional, intent on catching him before he could scurry off. He'd been avoiding her because he knew as well as she did that it was almost August.

Almost time.

But this year, she had a plan. And she'd decided that he was going to be the one to help her. Father Jeremiah's eyes went wide as Chloe stood in front of him, blocking his way to the safety of his office. He sighed as he seemed to connect the dots. Honestly, Father Jeremiah should have known. After all, she hadn't come to confession in ten months.

"Chloe, tricking someone into granting an audience with you is deceit. God does not look upon that kindly." He moved around her, but Chloe side-stepped and stood her ground in front of him.

"I wasn't deceiving you," Chloe protested. "It just worked out well with me already being here. Two birds with one stone and all."

Father Jeremiah let out an audible sigh. "I have to go."
"Where?"
"There's...gardening I need to attend to."
Chloe didn't miss a beat. "Fine. I'll come with you."

"You cannot kneel in anyone's presence, you know that." Father Jeremiah darted past Chloe toward the rear of the church and into the parish gardens.

Chloe was hot on his heels, her shoes clacking on the stone floor. Her pale pink, empire-waist dress that Lilian, her lady's maid, had picked out today flowed behind her and continued to trip her up in her pursuit.

Damn these clothes, Chloe thought.

The dresses, although designed for beauty, yes, made the wearer catchable. Killable. A shiver that had nothing to do with the church door swinging open trickled down her spine.

Chloe squinted as she entered the blazing heat of the outdoors. It seemed every summer had grown more unbearably hot since the Games had started. It was better than autumn though—that was when the acid rain usually came. Chloe grimaced at the thought of acid rain becoming a real possibility again in just a few short months, but she forced herself to focus. She might not have this opportunity for an audience again. She needed to act now.

Chloe took a shaky breath. "You don't agree with it either. I've seen your face during the Games. Ever since I was first allowed to watch it, I've watched you. And you hate it as much as I do."

Father Jeremiah shoved a trowel into her grasp. "Don't let your father see you on your knees then, if you must help. Or him. He'll tell on you." He turned his head towards where James, Chloe's bodyguard, had followed them outdoors.

"Back inside the church, please, James."

James's immense frame slumped a little as he protested, "But Your Highness—"

"Thank you, James." Chloe responded with the same air

of authority that her father did when he'd decided some-thing and that no one could change his mind. It had always infuriated her, but it came in handy sometimes.

James was six foot eight and amongst the strongest Defender Castes in New London. But he looked every inch the petulant child as he trudged back into the church and shut the back door.

Father Jeremiah turned to Chloe with an incredulous look. "Somehow a five-foot-two blonde, cherub-faced, seventeen-year-old scares me more than he does."

Chloe pushed her dress to the side and began ripping the weeds out of the soil. "Yes, well, the cherub-faced one will rule the country someday."

"She will one day be *married* to the man who rules our country, yes," Father Jeremiah corrected gently, before joining on the grass beside her. Chloe pulled out a particu-larly stubborn weed with an aggression that could only be matched by her father.

"Yes. I'd forgotten all about my brother's death, and how I'm the only useless girl left to carry on the line. Thank you so much for reminding me," Chloe said with icy restraint.

"Your Highness." Father Jeremiah stopped troweling and looked at Chloe with such an intensity that it unsettled her. "You should understand more than anyone that women are the most precious thing on the planet. They carry our ancestry lines on. They keep the human race going. Well, the chosen few do, by God's grace. We must serve and protect them."

Chloe's throat tightened. Thanks to her gender, she'd never get a say in how to serve or protect her people. That job belonged only to kings. Chloe continued to weed with ferocity. "Which brings me to why I'm here." She stopped then and looked him dead in the eye.

"If the church sides with me—if I get my stepmother and other Nobles to side with me and endorse a petition to stop the Vessel Games, then—"

"That would anger your father. He would consider it a betrayal. He'd never forgive you. Besides, no other females besides you or the Queen would be able to sign a petition, anyway."

Chloe's stomach turned to lead when she'd realized she'd forgotten a crucial piece of information whilst making her plan. No other women were literate. It was forbidden for women to read and write. Everyone except her and the Queen relied on their husbands, their sons, and their brothers for that. She was exactly one half of the women who had the ability to sign the petition. None of the noble ladies would or could side with her, which was what she'd been hoping for. The allies she'd hoped for in this movement were...nonexistent.

Sweat had broken out on Father Jeremiah's forehead. At the immense heat or at the thought of siding with her against her father, Chloe did not know.

"The Games are wrong." She snatched a plant that sat beside her and began digging again. "They're unjust and sick and cruel. Why can't the Vessel choose her husband and who she wants for herself? Why do innocent boys have to die?" She thumped the plant into the soil and set its place. "I won't watch another Games. And from the look on your face last time, I don't know if you can either."

"Last year was...different." Father Jeremiah's face had gone slack.

Last year, one of the Clergy Caste had decided he'd wanted to contend in the Games. He'd insisted that God had spoken to him and told him to compete. They'd been close, and the boy's death had not been kind. Father Jeremiah closed his eyes, as if imagining the horrors of the stadium once again. The blood on the sand, the cheers of the crowd as the victor had proposed to his Vessel.

It was supposed to be an honor to battle in the Games. As honorable as going to war for the United Kingdoms. Chloe wasn't exactly sure of what countries remained after the Great War. Even though it had finished over sixty years ago, that was information only men in the King's inner circle of Nobles were privy to. It wasn't the kind of information that a female needed to know, even a princess.

"Chloe." He breathed her name as if it were a prayer. "I'll admit to you and you alone that I don't agree with the Games. But the High Priest does. The Church is powerful, and the people of New London are holy and will follow their High Priest and their King, no matter what. The Games were decided by church and monarchy—it's the only fair way that the Common Castes can get what they want and in a way that also keeps *you* safe."

"But—"

Father Jeremiah held out a hand. "Let me finish, Chloe." His tone made her feel like she was just a child at Sunday school again. "The Uprising was only ten years ago. Some Traitor Castes involved are alive to this day. Many would wish to see you and your father's legacy dead. Your mother wouldn't want you—"

"My mother wouldn't want what?" Chloe snapped. "You'd use her memory against me? She's dead, Jeremiah."

"And now your father wishes to protect you from the same fate. He wishes to protect you from those who harmed your mother. And who would've harmed you, if we had given them the chance."

Chloe's throat constricted. "I'm aware."

He paused, seemingly searching for the words to make the horrors of the Games bearable. "Despite the attack on him and your mother, the King gave them what they wanted, in the fairest way he was able to. These Common Castes...they have the opportunity to be elevated. To gain riches beyond their wildest dreams. They won't get another chance like that. Ever."

He scratched his nose and a bit of mud smeared on his face; it was so dark it almost had a reddish tint.

Chloe threw the trowel down and stood up. She'd had enough. "Why do there need to be Common Castes and Nobles anyway? Why can't we share resources equally? Why do I get a full belly and this"—she indicated to her lavish dress—"while others go hungry?"

"Chloe," Father Jeremiah muttered, "that sort of thinking is very dangerous. We should reward those who are more important in our society for their service to God. Your father is the absolute monarch. He is God on earth; no one can be the same Caste as him or you for that matter."

"Then why won't you do what I ask of you?" Chloe exploded. Only the birds sang in the silence that followed, not understanding what had transpired.

Father Jeremiah's weathered face examined Chloe's coolly.

"I-I'm sorry. I didn't mean it," she apologized.

"That temper, Chloe, be careful of it." Jeremiah's face had turned stony. "You are royal, and therefore I serve you as I serve Him, but you are not a man. You are *not* your brother. He might have succeeded in making such changes, but you will not. Stop now, Chloe, before things become dangerous for you." Father Jeremiah bowed low and slowly.

"Your Highness," he said in parting before heading back to the church door.

As it clicked shut, Chloe felt the harsh sting of tears pricking at her eyes.

You are not your brother.

She certainly was not. Sometimes, she thought it might have been easier on everyone, particularly the monarchy, if she'd been the one to die that day. If he hadn't died in that accident, and if the line of succession had stayed clear, then perhaps the Uprising would never have happened. Perhaps her mother would not be—

Chloe swallowed. She shouldn't have pulled rank on Father Jeremiah. It was the complete opposite of what she'd been asking for the United Kingdoms to become. If she couldn't convince someone of her views without asserting her dominance as a royal, then her argument was all but null and void.

"Your Highness?"

"Not now, James." She wiped the tears from her cheeks.

"It's dinnertime in the banquet hall."

"I don't feel well." She tried to keep her voice as even as possible. "I'm going back to my room; send the King my apologies. I won't be joining him and my stepmother tonight."

She couldn't bear to see the King's face, to have him ask her about her day, as if they were a normal, happy family. Her father had murdered many people in the wake of her mother's assassination. She should hate him for it. And yet...she still loved him deeply. She wished she was allowed a say in what was to become of the United Kingdoms.

But she never would have that.

She'd live out the rest of her days throwing balls, wearing pretty dresses, and producing heirs like a good princess. Chloe couldn't stand the ache in her chest when she thought about the future awaiting her.

James escorted Chloe from the church. She didn't understand why the King insisted James guard her in the inner sanctum. The walls around the center of the city kept the church and palace grounds holy and safe. But these days, the walls were beginning to feel a lot more like a cage and less like a sanctuary.

As she walked toward the magnificent palace, she tried not to look at the arena as she passed it. The arena lay in the exact center of New London. She'd tried many times to forget why it was built and how. To block out the memory of seeing the traitors of the Uprising build it and then be the first ones executed within its walls.

The King had made her watch; she'd been seven years old.

"These people wanted you dead. They killed your mother. They would have murdered you if I hadn't done this. If I did not stop them. I compromised by giving them the Games. I am a kind King. Remember that, Chloe."

Chloe tore her gaze away from the arena and tried not to think about the time she'd be forced to spend within it. She was just as shackled to it as the traitors who'd built it had been.

∼

CHLOE STARED at the ceiling of her bedroom until complete darkness had fallen and the palace had grown silent. She pulled on the long, red wig she kept hidden under the mattress of her bed, as well as the Common Caste clothes Lilian had given her: black jeans and a hoodie.

She slipped them on before sliding the window open

and climbing out as quietly as possible. A knock at the door had her pausing in mid-air. Her breath caught in her chest as she hung halfway out. If she didn't make a sound, they'd assume she was asleep.

"Chloe? Chloe, are you awake?" It was her stepmother, coming to check in on her after her absence at dinner tonight.

"I-I'm tired, Mary, and unwell. I'll see you tomorrow." Chloe's muscles cramped at the exertion of staying so still in such an awkward position.

"Ok, good night, darling heart." As the footsteps faded, Chloe sighed in relief. The Queen must've thought Chloe was just moments from letting oblivion take her and falling asleep.

Chloe wished that were the case. She continued her task and scaled down the building with skill; after all, she'd done it a thousand times before.

It was time to sin again.

CHAPTER
TWO

K arina had been waiting for hours. She shuffled in her seat as she watched Noble girl after Noble girl emerge in tears. It did nothing for her nerves.

The man's voice echoed in the silent waiting room, "Karina Roberts."

Karina's head snapped up. Her heart raced in anticipation of what awaited her.

She was going to be sick.

"You've got this." Elaine grabbed her hand and squeezed so hard that it hurt. Karina nodded at the man in acknowledgment and stood. He'd just assessed her with a distaste that unsettled her. He probably hated testing Commons — especially Traitor Castes.

"I'm ready."

Karina shuffled through the waiting room, fidgeting with her dirty t-shirt. Her ripped jeans seemed out of place amongst the dresses and pearls of the Nobles. "In your own time, Miss Roberts." The man glanced at his watch.

"S-Sorry. Nervous," she replied.

The man flung the door open and strode in, waiting for

her to follow. In it were the following bits of furniture: a hospital bed, a monitor, and a desk. There was an array of awful looking silver contraptions laid out. She hoped to God that they wouldn't be part of the telling.

The sharp, tangy aroma of cleaning products filled Karina's nose. She breathed in the familiar smell and tried to imagine that she was at work. Her body seemed to know better. The man indicated toward the blue patient gown that lay waiting for her on the bed.

"Right. Clothes off. We don't have all day."

"What do I -"

But he'd already left, the door slamming behind him. He was a doctor, so he'd be in a Noble Caste. Only the Noble men had the "prestigious" jobs like doctors, law-makers, and business owners. Some Noblemen were so wealthy from their titles given to them by the King—the Lords, Counts and Dukes—they didn't even need a job. It was a stark difference to Traitor Castes by deed that weren't allowed to work after they'd been found guilty of a crime. Being banned from work at all was effectively a death sentence.

Karina stripped her ripped jeans and baggy t-shirt from her skinny frame. She threw off her shoes and shivered when her feet touched the icy floor. Tiptoeing up to the hospital bed, she took her place.

"You can do this." Karina told herself, breathing out a whoosh of air in an attempt to calm her frazzled nerves.

The doctor burst in again and stomped toward her. Karina winced. "Right, ultrasound. Show me your belly."

She pulled up the gown she'd been given, exposing her lower abdomen. The man squeezed jelly on her that was so cold it made her jump in surprise.

She opted to look at the ceiling instead of at the monitor. She pushed down the irrational glimmer of hope that was buried inside of her. Once, many years ago, lots of Commons could bear children. Common Castes were most of the population, after all. But now? There hadn't been a Common Vessel since that Defender Caste girl over seven years ago. She'd been the first and last Common Vessel to be competed for in the Games. And from the glimpses Karina had seen of her in the Noble District, with one eye left and chains around her hands and feet, that hadn't exactly gone well for her. Karina had heard that she'd tried to run away. She couldn't imagine why the Defender Caste girl would have wanted to do that. After all, Vessels were the highest rank of Noble.

If she became a Vessel, well, then Karina would've had everything she ever wanted and more.

But Karina knew deep down that she'd be no different from the other girls. She would be a Barren, just like everybody else had been over the last few years.

Natural selection, some Noble woman had jeered at her once as she cleaned their toilet. *Our Lord God wants only the great and those of noble blood to breed and carry our ancestry lines on.*

Karina hadn't bothered to argue back. If all the Common Castes died out, then Nobles would have to farm the land for the little food that was left.

Karina was flung out of her reverie when she glanced at the doctor. His hand was shaking with his strange contraption frozen over her belly, his eyes wide.

"What Caste are you, Karina?"

"I'm Traitor Caste."

The doctor's face was drained of all color.

"By blood or by deed?"

"By blood." Karina swallowed, remembering back to the

day her father had been executed and her family declared traitors. "Why?"

"I... I need to double check. I'm required to do an internal examination. Open your legs."

"What do you mean?"

"Open your legs." He repeated, a new pair of latex gloves already on his hands. The doctor grabbed one of the horrible-looking silver contraptions. "Relax a little," he suggested, launching the contraption between her legs.

As the cold steel hit her most intimate of parts, Karina's face burned in equal parts embarrassment and pain. She wriggled up the bed, trying to get away from the awful feeling.

"Stay still." He ordered.

Karina's lip wobbled, and tears sprung to her eyes. There was a terrible grinding sound as he opened the contraption. It felt like he was ripping her apart from the inside out. What was he doing to her? She felt... violated. She lay there, staring at the ceiling with tears running down the side of her face and onto the bed below her. He took some sort of stick out from his desk drawer and pushed it inside her. As he poked and prodded her, Karina tried to imagine she was elsewhere. She tried to imagine she was back with her Pa, that they were laughing and playing. When he finally released the contraption and tugged it out of her, she let out a breath of relief.

She prayed to God that the worst part was over.

"What was that?" Karina asked.

"Nothing." He grunted, removing his gloves. "I needed to do an internal exam. As I suspected, you are Barren. Collect your identification card from the desk."

Before Karina opened her mouth to thank him for his time, the man had disappeared.

~

"So, we're both Barrens, then." Elaine said, as they walked out of the Telling clinic.

"It's nothing we weren't expecting." Karina said, shrugging a little, "How did your telling go? My doctor was a bit... on edge."

"Mine was fine." Elaine shrugged. "No Traitor Caste has ever been a Vessel, which only confirms what the Nobles already think of us. We're damned." Elaine made her fingers into claws and bared her teeth as if she were some kind of wild animal. "Satan on earth."

Karina chuckled and placed her new identification card that read "BARREN" in her bag along with her Caste papers. The clinic they'd been assigned to attend was in the Noble District. So now, Elaine and Karina had the pleasure of being stared down by several Nobles as they made their way home.

As they hurried through the Noble district, she admired the beautiful mansions and pruned-to-perfection gardens lining the streets, with pavement so clean Karina could practically eat off them. Karina watched in awe as two stunning Vessels came closer toward them on the street. At their necks was the golden "V" sigil necklace, a sign of their status as the highest Caste of Noble.

The women looked at her and Elaine with distaste, whilst quickly crossing the road to avoid them. Although Karina had known she'd end up being a Barren, it would've been nice to become a Vessel. Having a mansion, status, and as much food as you wanted wouldn't be so bad, she suspected.

A pair of Defenders in their riot uniforms emerged from around the corner.

"Crap," Elaine swore, seeing the threat march toward them.

As one, Karina and Elaine turned on their heels and walked the opposite way.

"Stop where you are." A Defender ordered.

"Damn it. This is the second time this week," Karina muttered, swiveling around to face them.

"Papers." The other Defender said, his gun pointing right at them.

Both Elaine and Karina reached for their bags as slowly as possible. No sudden movements; they'd learned that the hard way.

"We've been at the clinic, officer." Karina said, her voice tight.

"I didn't ask where you've been, you stupid bitch. I asked for your papers."

Karina shook with anger. She knew this game. "I'm a documented citizen of New London. I'm no Shadowlander. Or is it because I look different to you?" Karina gestured to her dark brown skin. They'd always targeted her because of it.

"Shadowlanders infiltrate and pose as Common Castes in New London all the time. We need you to prove it." He shoved his gun further into her face. Karina collected Elaine's papers and passed both sets to him. He snatched the papers from her grasp, "Commons aren't allowed to be in Noble Districts unless they are working. You don't have any uniform on. I'll have to fine you for trespassing."

"That's ridiculous." Elaine scoffed. "We just told you we've been at our telling—"

Karina threw Elaine a warning stare, interrupting her. "Yes, officer."

The Defender glanced over at the papers and made a

low whistling sound. "Commons. And Traitor Caste at that. One by blood and one by deed. Well, I can see what you did." He motioned to Elaine's deformed hand, sniggering in a way that made Karina want to punch him.

She'd become a Traitor Caste through deed—by committing a crime. Elaine's dad had died in the Uprising, like Karina's. Their mum had died in childbirth, and Elaine was the eldest, so it'd been up to Elaine to provide for her family. In desperation, she'd stolen a loaf of bread and been caught quickly after.

When the Defenders sentenced her, she was still under-age, so they'd taken three fingers instead of her hand. *A mercy,* they'd said. They'd told her to give thanks to God. But now, as a Traitor Caste by deed, she was no longer eligible for a legal job. So, she'd had to find other—more illegal—ways to make money. Karina hated that Elaine had to do... those sorts of things to survive. But it was *Madame Butterfly,* the brothel in Hell's Gate, that always seemed to be the one place where Defenders never arrested anyone for illegal activities.

Karina pursed her lips.

"If you wanted to come past *Madame Butterfly* tonight, I could... make alternative arrangements... if you waive that fine." Elaine batted her long eyelashes, her hazel eyes looking almost amber in the evening light. She took a step closer to them and angled her body to give them... well, to give them a good view of her voluptuous frame. Karina's stomach roiled. "That would be... more enjoyable for you. You won't see a dime of that trespassing fine. It'll go straight to the Crown. But if we call it a day..."

The Defenders glanced at one another with grins on their faces. "You've got yourself a deal. Will she be joining us, too?" He stepped toward Karina, his hot breath tickling her face. He stunk of cigarettes and sweat. She tried not to shrink back when he caressed her hair, "You'd be quite nice to ride."

"She's not for sale," Elaine snatched Karina out of his grasp, angling her body in the way of her friend's. "I'm working from eight o'clock on; drop by whenever."

Karina stood there, horrified at what her friend had agreed to.

"Come on, Karina." Elaine growled under her breath.

When Karina was sure they had gone, she snapped her head toward Elaine. "What the hell, Elaine? Why did you do that?"

"You need the money. I said I'd work off the fine, but I didn't say doing what, did I? I plan to give them the worst head of their life. I'll make it super toothy. Really bitey." She lifted a brow, "Their dicks will be sore for weeks."

Karina let out a surprised giggle, "Elaine!" She scolded, but she didn't stop laughing all the same.

"Don't mention it. That year you fed us? We owe you." They'd made it to Hell's Gate, the entranceway to the slums.

"You owe me nothing." Karina shrugged. "Oh, I almost forgot!" She dug around in her bag and couldn't wait to see Elaine's face. "I was so distracted by our tellings before that I didn't give you this." Karina grinned when her fingers scraped against the smooth wood and leather string. "This is for you."

Karina dangled the necklace in front of Elaine. She'd worked on it all month, grinding down the precious piece of oak she'd bartered for at the Craftsman district to a perfectly shaped heart. She certainly couldn't afford a metal chain for the pendant; the piece of leather string had been expensive enough.

"Happy eighteenth birthday, Elaine."

Elaine's eyes widened, "That's... that's too much, Rina."

"Don't be silly." Karina's lips curled into a smile. She could tell that Elaine loved it as much as she did as she'd been crafting it. She wished she'd been born into the Craftsman Caste.

Karina was good with her hands and probably could've made a decent living.

"Let me put it on you," Karina offered.

Elaine's eyes sparkled with tears as she lifted her ebony hair out of the way so Karina could tie it around her neck. The necklace looked perfect on her, just like Karina knew it would.

Karina embraced Elaine fiercely, "Love you."

"Love you too." Elaine's face was buried in her shoulder. "Thank you. For everything."

"No matter how shit things get, I've got you. And you've got me, okay?" Karina grasped either side of Elaine's face. Karina hated what Elaine had to do to survive. She wished she could do more—give her more. But a necklace was all she had.

"Okay." Elaine sniffled.

"I'll see you tomorrow?"

"I'll see you tomorrow," Elaine confirmed, and with a wave, they parted ways.

Karina looked around her. Now that she'd made it to Hell's Gate, she noticed how it was a stark contrast to what she'd just seen in the Noble District. Beggars lined the streets; people yelled and cursed at one another. But what Karina hated most was the smell; it was putrid.

Anyone who'd committed a crime that hadn't been sentenced to death? They were Karina's not-so-friendly neighbors in the Traitor slums now. The sinners. The worst of the worst.

And of course, since they all needed to be punished for their sins, they were all being denied food and water as much as possible. It was penance.

After all, Karina thought darkly, *struggling to stay alive distracted you from fighting back.*

~

"KARINA, SNAP OUT OF IT."

She lifted her head from her plate to her mother's dark brown eyes. "Hmm?"

"You're elsewhere."

"Sorry, Ma. I guess I'm just..." Karina glanced at her measly rations, "disappointed."

"Of course, you are, baby," her mother's eyes shone with concern.

Karina swallowed, considering whether she should ask what was really on her mind. "How was it? Giving birth?"

"It was the best day of my life. And I'm sorry you'll never get to experience that."

Everything had changed during the Great War. Just sixty-five years ago, humans could breed normally. After the nuclear fallout of the Great War, however, the survivors fled to the safe walls of New London. They'd been forced to pledge fealty to the King and Church upon entrance, and then fertility declined.

At first, it was so subtle that the people of the United Kingdoms barely noticed. Fewer and fewer children played in the streets until only a handful of women each year were giving birth. Schools shut, becoming a relic of the past. Common Castes began to vastly outnumber the Nobles.

And then, Nobles began to seduce the fertile Common Caste women, promising them a better life. Promising riches beyond their wildest imaginations. Karina's mother had been one of the few who had married for love and not riches. She'd married a Craftsman, content with her choice.

But then the same thing kept happening and unrest built in the city. Common Castes hated that they had nothing to offer these women, that they had no way to have children of their own, purely because of their status. Others hated the Nobles getting the lion's share of the rations— that the Nobles didn't have to toil in the fields. That *they* didn't have to risk death by acid rain. The Noble district had metal barriers on every house to shield them from weather events, far superior to anything in any of the other districts in New London.

That's when the Uprising started. The Uprising had then resulted in the death of the Queen and the beginning of the Vessel Games. The King had given them exactly what they wanted: a shot at a Vessel wife in exchange for peace. The lives of the Uprising leaders, of course, had been forfeit that first year.

Karina swallowed, a lump forming in her throat, as she remembered her father among them.

"Could you... be a Vessel, Mum? Now that you're no longer married to Dad?"

"I'll always be married to Dad." Her eyes sparkled with emotion. She looked down then and continued picking at her food. "Besides, it's too late for me now."

"So, you can't have kids anymore?"

Karina's mum frowned, changing the subject, "Where's your brother? That boy will get whipped in the streets if he's not careful."

"That hasn't stopped him before."

Marcus took after their father in all the wrong ways. He dreamed of a better life, of revolutions, and of destroying the Vessel Games. Karina already suspected that he was part of an underground rebellion group. The amount of times he'd snuck out of their bedroom and the seemingly endless number of cryptic messages he'd been receiving and hiding from her under his worn mattress had made this fact easier to figure out.

As if on cue, Marcus strode into the kitchen.

"Where have you been, Marcus?" Mum challenged, her eyes narrowing. It wouldn't surprise Karina if her mum knew about his membership in the rebellion as well.

"Just working. What's for dinner?" Marcus has always been a terrible liar.

"Is that so?" their mother responded, her lips pinched together.

"Mhm." Marcus set his jaw, looking at his mother unflinchingly.

Karina glanced between her mum and brother, who now seemed to be competing in a staring competition. "I'm going to bed."

She pushed her chair away from the table, the floor screeching in protest as she did. Karina couldn't be bothered to play the role of mediator tonight.

"If you've been at work," her mother said with ice in her tone, "then where has your paycheck been for the last few weeks? We're up to our eyeballs in bills."

Marcus stilled, his eyes darting around their dark flat for an excuse. Candlelight flickered, making his face seem almost ghoulish. Karina wondered if they'd ever be able to afford luxuries like electricity.

"Okay. You caught me. I lost my job," Marcus admitted quietly.

Karina's mother took a steadying breath, as if she'd already known.

"Then where have you been?"

"Trying to find a new one," he snapped. "No one is taking Traitors by blood anymore."

"What are we going to do then, Marcus? Karina's cleaning job won't cover what needs to be covered. If you don't get a job soon, we'll be out on the streets!" Her mother grimaced at the thought, a worry-line appearing between her dark eyebrows. "How could you be so careless?"

Karina knew what would happen to her if they ended up sleeping on the streets, and her mother did too. A pretty, young girl begging on the streets in the Traitor district? She'd be attacked daily. Not to mention when the Shadow-landers raided New London, the three of them would be out in the open with nowhere to hide and no protection.

She'd be...

Karina's mother must have sensed her panic and placed a hand over Karina's. "Karina, we'll figure it out. Your brother," she shot him a look, "has a responsibility to protect you."

Karina hated that she even needed protecting. She snatched her hand from her mother's grasp. "Goodnight." She muttered.

She trudged up the rickety stairs that led to her and Marcus' tiny bedroom. The floorboards were dusty and falling apart. Her squab lay on the floor, next to Marcus'. Her blankets were sprawled carelessly across it. She used to make her bed, but she'd given up on that. A shit-hole was still a shit-hole, no matter how much she'd tried to deny it. A mouse sat in the corner, squeaking in surprise when it realized it had company.

"Don't you have anywhere else to go?" she asked the mouse.

The mouse squeaked again before retreating to a hole in the wall.

"Yeah, me neither."

Behind her, the door hinges creaked as it swung shut. Karina frowned, a tingle running up her spine. She had the strangest sensation come over her. It was as if she could feel someone watching her.

And then a hand covered her mouth. A deep voice, one she didn't recognise, whispered in her ear. "If you scream, I'll kill you. Go to the window and climb out."

Something was sticking into her back. A thick fog of panic enveloped Karina. If she went with this man, it was likely terrible things would happen to her. It was certain death if she followed his instructions. That weighed against a potential death if her brother could save her. Karina had only a second to decide. In that moment, she decided on the latter. She rallied her courage and let out a blood-curdling scream.

"Stupid bitch!" the assailant shouted.

Just as Karina had hoped, he didn't kill her. Instead, the man forced her toward the window at a faster pace.

Footsteps sounded up the stairwell. Karina dragged her feet, but the intruder thrust her onward. The door burst open; Marcus' eyes were wide with fear when he saw what lay before him. In his hand, he held a kitchen knife.

Karina spun around and saw what the man had been pressing into her back. He had a gun. She launched herself toward the man and screamed like a banshee. He seemed entirely shocked and taken aback that Karina wasn't too frightened to defend herself. The gun flew out of his hand, skidding on the floor behind them. Karina then hurtled herself toward the gun.

She didn't know how to use it, but if she could just get hold of it—

The man tossed Karina aside like she weighed no more than a ragdoll. Her head slammed against the wall with force, and Karina saw stars. Everything blurred and slowed. Karina's head was foggy.

"Get your hands off of my sister!" Marcus growled, prowling toward him.

Now that the assailant was disarmed, Marcus made his first move. He was a good fighter—their father had taught him well.

Marcus grunted as he thrust his knife toward the man's abdomen, but the man dodged it with such skill that a ball of lead collected in Karina's stomach. Even with a black balaclava restricting his vision, the intruder moved with speed and deadly precision. Karina knew he was lethal. Karina crawled across the floor toward the gun again. A piercing pain at the top of her head had her collapsing on the floor. Hot blood trickled down her forehead, blurring her vision.

"Don't hurt her!" Marcus had a strange stoic expression as he slashed wildly at the assailant, hoping to find purchase.

The assailant continued to duck and evade Marcus' knife. Finally, a stab hit home in his arm. The assailant yelled in pain but quickly pulled the knife from where it sat, now lodged in his arm. He turned it on Marcus, his own sticky blood still marring the steel. Marcus' eyes widened in fear.

Karina barged toward him, trying to push, shove, or do anything she could to get his attention diverted from her brother. He still blocked every blow with ease. One move was too slow and had Marcus crying out in pain. Marcus clutched his stomach and fell to his knees, blood pooling and spilling from his hands.

"Marcus!" Karina screamed.

"Upstairs!" the muffled voice of her mother yelled.

Footsteps thundered up the stairs. Her mum must've gone to their neighbors for help. The assailant seemed to realize he was about to have a lot more company. He sprinted toward the broken window, now his only way of escape.

"I'll find you! I'll kill you for what you've done to my brother!" Karina shouted at him, still barely able to make his figure out in the darkness of her bedroom.

"Good luck, my lady." The grin on his face was feral. He turned on his heel and launched out of the window.

Karina crawled toward her brother, who was now unconscious. "Marcus...."

Her mother and her neighbors burst into the room, weapons brandished as they yelled wildly. Her mother screamed at the sight of her brother lying on the floor in a pool of his blood.

"Get him to the hospital!" Karina ordered. Her mother glanced at her, checking to see if she were hurt too. Her head pounded, but she said, "I'm fine. I'll follow you. I just need a second. Go!"

The men carried Marcus together out of the bedroom.

Karina took a shaky breath. What the hell had just happened? She looked around, unsure how such her room could have born witness to something so shocking mere moments ago. And then—

Something caught her eye in the shards of glass now scattered over the floor.

A ring.

She shuffled through the shattered glass and bent down to inspect the ring. The sigil on it was one she didn't recognise. It was... a picture of some sort. Karina gripped the ring tightly, glancing back toward the broken window now letting in the starless night. The wind shifted, sending a blisteringly cold breeze toward her.

The man might have fled, but Karina had a strange feeling that this was only the beginning.

CHAPTER

THREE

William Albridge was mad as hell.

Louis, his deadbeat boss, had been avoiding the site for days. He knew that most of his workers had been looking for him, and that they were all pissed.

Will hammered in his final nail of the day with grim determination. Every single muscle in his body ached. He'd worked eighty hours this week. They'd been reinforcing the boundary walls of New London. There'd been too many Shadowlander raids recently.

Will remembered what his teachers at school had told him: if you venture past New London's walls, you won't come back. The savage Shadowlanders will kill you. Them or the extreme temperatures with no shelter and a lack of food. Or the acid rain that came to fry your skin from your bones every so often. All were terrible ways to die beyond the city walls.

Climate disasters didn't happen too much these days, but still occurred often enough for Will to never want to be caught outside of New London. No matter how bad shit got in the city itself.

The King also had ordered reinforcement walls around the only other remaining city in the United Kingdoms: Manchester. That was the High Priest's domain. Some said that its rules were even stricter than those of New London.

Will jumped from the scaffolding with ease. "Later, boys. I'm off to collect my paycheck."

"Good luck with that," Julian scoffed.

"It's been three weeks. Our rent's due, and Mum needs more meds. If Louis doesn't give me what I'm owed, I'll quit."

"And do what? Go work at *Madame Butterfly*?" Julian jeered. The other boys still working guffawed with laughter. "There's no other company with the volume of steady work that Louis brings. All that gambling pays off. He's got tons of contacts in the Noble circles."

"I'll quit." Will insisted.

Louis' reputation for gambling away his workers' earnings should've been enough to deter Will from taking this job. But he'd needed the steady money to afford his mum's medication, so he'd taken the risk. But another missed paycheck would mean eviction from their flat. And that was not something that Will could afford to happen.

Will had an inkling that Louis would be gambling away his paycheck at Hell's Gate tonight. Will planned to start at *Madame Butterfly's* and make his way around those God forsaken alleyways until he found his erstwhile boss.

Hell's Gate was treated like it just didn't exist. After all, the rich and the powerful needed somewhere to fuck around where their wives couldn't see. Clergy Caste had come in about five years ago and tried to "cleanse" it of its sin, but riots had ensued. The King wasn't aware of how bad it had gotten again recently. And the Nobles that frequented it... well, they were determined to keep it that way.

In Hell's Gate, people made their own rules.

It took Will over an hour to walk from the boundary walls of the traitor Slums and into Hell's Gate, and by the time he made it, the balls of his feet had begun to ache. Will arrived at the Gate and cleared his throat at the sleeping guard.

"Identification, please," the Defender slurred, drunk.

Will grabbed his I. D. from his pocket. The Defender shone a torch on the I. D.—checking that it wasn't a fake—and handed it back to him. Will paid the one pound entrance fee and then the Defender waved him through the drawbridge and onto the roads of Hell's Gate. He paused in shock as he surveyed the scene before him. He'd never been here on a Friday, and to say it was anarchy would be an understatement. Men had already begun drinking, brawling, and even fucking on the streets.

Will frowned in distaste but kept his head down. He'd come here to reason with Louis. If his boss didn't hand over his money, then Will promised himself he'd leave the job for good. Will was so lost in his thoughts that he didn't notice the girl walking in the opposite direction. He knocked into her, and she fell onto the concrete with a thud. Her bag went flying, its contents spilling across the dirty street.

"Watch it!" She yelled at him from the ground.

"I'm so sor—" Will stopped short, his breath hitching in his chest.

The girl's copper brown skin perfectly complimented

her dark eyes. Her hair plunged past her shoulders in loose, midnight black waves. Her lips were so plump and sultry that Will could barely keep his eyes off them. His hands grew sticky, and he forced his gaze away from those perfectly shaped lips and to those rich brown eyes.

Holy *shit.*

She was the most beautiful woman he'd seen in his entire life.

"Sorry." He finished.

He held out his hand to help her up, which she took, even as distrust was etched over her gorgeous features. Much to his surprise, her palms were callused, just like his own. She'd known hard labor. She wasn't a Noble then, but he hadn't seen her around the Craftsman district. Will was certain. He would've remembered a face like that. Perhaps she was a Farmer Caste?

Her build was slender, and she had baggy, dirty-looking clothes on, but Will could imagine that she'd be a perfect hour-glass figure underneath those clothes. He shook himself. He shouldn't be imagining... things like that about a woman he'd just met.

He scampered over to her bag, picking it up. A few things had fallen out of it, and he got a glimpse at her I. D. card. *Traitor by Blood* it read in angry, red letters. His eyes widened in disbelief. The girl snatched the card from him, stuffing it away.

"I'm Will." He said dumbly, holding out his hand.

"Karina," she said, surveying him but ignoring the handshake.

Instead, she dug through the bag, searching for something. "Damn it. *Damn.*"

"What's wrong?"

"I had a ring in my purse. It's not there anymore. I... I needed it."

"I'll help you." He offered with what he hoped was a friendly smile. "It was really my fault, so it's the least I can do."

The distrust on her face still didn't fade, but she nodded in agreement. They scanned the streets, much to the chagrin of all the passersby. Most yelled at them to get out of the way. One even threatened to pull a knife on them. Karina raked her fingers through her long, dark hair, a line of worry etched between her brows.

"You should go. I'll keep looking." Will offered, feeling guilty that he'd made her lose something of such value.

"No. No. Don't worry. I just... I got attacked last night in my house. I remember what the ring looks like, and I'd be able to describe it to someone, but it was the only clue I had."

Will's eyes widened. "Attacked?" He knew the Traitor slums were dodgy, but being attacked in her own home? It must've been worse than he thought.

"Yeah. Don't worry." A realization flickered over her face. "Shit. I'll be late. I have to go." She glanced over at *Madame Butterfly*.

Will followed her gaze, and his curiosity got the better of him. "Late for what?"

"A job interview," she said, one eyebrow arching.

Will's face felt hot under her gaze.

"Right." His eyes darted to the floor.

"I have to run. Thanks for the help, Will." Karina ran toward off down the street without another word.

His gaze tracked her movements down the pavement. She kept her head down and her hood up, he noticed. Her beauty probably garnered the attention of many, so she'd learnt to conceal it.

When Will was sure that she'd made it inside *Madame Butterfly's* with no trouble, he continued his search for the ring. The quest took him another hour, two potential brawls, and a drunk man throwing up on him, but it was worth it. Because there, in the gutter, was the ticket he needed to see Karina again—the ring.

∽

KARINA DIDN'T LET herself think about what she'd have to do in the brothel. Instead, she pushed her way through the crowded streets, keeping her head down, and headed resolutely for *Madame Butterfly's*. Karina's legs shook with nerves, but she carried on. What choice did she have, really? This was her only option. If she didn't get another job, then they'd be on the streets come winter.

Karina yanked open the heavy wooden door and stepped inside. A strong musk of alcohol, cigarettes, and sweat greeted her. Smoke plumed around the entire reception area, giving the dark space an air of mystery. The women were clad in provocative clothing, and she assumed would be her coworkers soon. Still, they ignored her. Karina wasn't surprised in the least. After all, she looked like a nobody. Her attire screamed that she was poor and of no consequence. Large bodyguards flanked the girls, and their lustful eyes assessed Karina keenly.

"Fresh meat, looks like," one of the guards said, clutching Karina's arm. "Fancy a kiss, love?"

Karina pulled away from him. "Thanks, but no thanks." She muttered. Karina tilted up her chin and strode toward the reception desk. "I'm here to see Madame Butterfly, please."

"Through there." The receptionist grunted, barely looking up at Karina.

She'd pointed to a room away from the main lobby, shrouded by a gauzy curtain. Karina swallowed and pushed it aside, ready to meet her fate.

An older woman, skin sagging with age, glanced up from the large oak desk she sat at and considered Karina. She scanned her up and down, looking not the least bit impressed. Madame Butterfly wore a luxurious fur coat that overwhelmed her tiny, frail frame. A gold chain hung from her neck. Karina marveled at how a Traitor Caste afforded such luxuries. The woman's eyes were dark, almost black — Karina couldn't discern the pupil from its iris. The effect it gave was... unsettling.

"Karina, I assume?"

Karina nodded, too nervous to say anything.

"I'm Madame Butterfly." Her lips tilted upward into a toothy smile, but it looked more like a snarl to Karina.

Madame Butterfly strutted over to where a grand fireplace sat in the middle of the room. She looked at the hungry flames devouring the wood and threw another log in. The fire spat up, and Karina felt its heat from where she stood. Despite her fear, Karina took a step forward. She loved being close to fire — the array of colors would be such fun to paint, and she loved the heat of the flames prickling at her skin.

"Take off your clothes." Madame Butterfly instructed without taking her eyes off the dancing flames.

"W-what?"

"I need to see what I'm working with."

Karina quickly removed her top and her jeans.

"All of them." Madame Butterfly instructed sharply.

Karina's stomach coiled in shock and fear. A lump had formed in her throat. She removed her bra, her nipples pebbling at the sudden cold, and slid her underwear down her thighs, revealing her body in its entirety.

Madame Butterfly stalked toward her, circling her like a piece of prey.

"Lovely." She said, as if she were assessing a piece of chicken at the market. "Skinny, I'll admit, but you've got a lovely face." Karina's head hung low, but Madame Butterfly took Karina's chin in her grasp and pushed it up. "You'll do nicely."

As soon as Madame Butterfly turned her back, Karina knelt on the floor, gathering her clothes as quickly as she could.

"So, I've got the job?" Karina asked.

"You have one more task." Madame Butterfly said, moving back to her desk. "Come in, Percy."

The bodyguard from outside strode in and Karina gathered her clothes in front of her in fright, horrified.

"Leave the clothes off, darlin.' We can have some fun without them." He smiled, showing a few missing teeth.

Madame Butterfly instructed, "Pleasure him." Karina flinched, her lip trembling. She didn't move toward the man. "Did you not hear me?" Madame Butterfly's tone had sharpened.

"I don't know how to." Karina said, her voice barely a whisper.

"There's a myriad of ways, my dear. With your mouth. Your hands. But this time, I'd like to see you fuck him."

"I can't..." Karina said, shaking her head. She backed away from both. "I won't."

"Oh, come now. Once you've done it just once, it's really not that much of a big deal, is it Perce?"

Almost in response, Percy stalked forward, rubbing his hands together and Karina cowered in the corner.

"Please..." Karina's eyes prickled with tears. This is what Elaine did every night? How could she stand it?

As if Karina had summoned the woman herself, Elaine burst into the room. Her lip fell into a thin line as she assessed the scene before her.

"Get your clothes on, Karina," Elaine said. Karina had never heard Elaine like this— so hard and unyielding. She shoved Percy away and stood to block Karina from the man. Her head snapped to the old woman. "What the fuck, Butterfly? I told you that you needed to send Karina Roberts away when she got here. That she's *not* to work here. Ever."

"El—" Karina began.

"Not now, Karina." Elaine hissed.

Madam Butterfly assessed her nails, clearly bored already. "I'm not sure if you've noticed, Elaine, but you're not the boss here. I am. And I *own* you. I can do whatever I want and that includes seeing your little friend for an interview. One she failed, by the way."

"I don't give a *fuck* who you think you own, but it's *not* Karina. We had a deal." Elaine bit out. "Did we not?"

"We did." Madame Butterfly waved her hand in dismissal. "Fine. I don't care either way, Elaine, but I *will* get my pound of flesh. Fuck off then."

～

ELAINE DRAGGED Karina out of the brothel and onto the street. "Ow, Elaine—"

"What are you playing at, Karina? This isn't some little

game. Those people could've really hurt you. They would've hurt you whether or not you wanted them to."

Karina's lip wobbled. "I didn't have a choice. Marcus lost his job. We've got no money."

"I know, Rina." Elaine said, clutching her face in her hands. "Marcus told me. He thought you'd do something like this. Play hero, try to fix things. He asked for my help to stop you. I'd told that bitch she wasn't allowed to see you for any 'auditions.' I made a deal that—"

"What deal, El?" Karina said, her eyes widening.

"It's nothing."

"I call on the truth pact." Karina grabbed Elaine's hand, squeezing it hard.

Elaine sighed, "That's not fair."

"I don't care, El. Tell me." Karina's eyes searched Elaine's.

"I told Butterfly not to see you. She was told to kick you out of the building. I told her I'd give her one hundred percent of my wages this week in exchange for the favor."

"El—" Karina's mouth popped open in shock. "You shouldn't have—"

"It doesn't matter, Rina. It doesn't. All I want is for you to lose your virginity to someone you love, someone kind. I want it to be lovely and fun and—" Elaine was flushed as she spoke, her expression bright with excitement.

It was as if... as if she knew what it felt like to be loved in such a way. Karina narrowed her eyes, "Have you... have you met someone, El? Is there something you're not telling me about? Maybe someone?"

A fellow worker yelled Elaine's name from inside the brothel. "Look, I can't talk about it right now, but I'll find you tomorrow. I'll come to your house, okay?"

"Okay." Karina embraced Elaine tightly. "Thank you," she kissed her hair, "thank you for protecting me."

"You're breaking my ribs," Elaine mumbled, and Karina snorted with laughter.

"Now, get out of here," Elaine ordered, "and keep your head down and your hood up."

Then, her friend disappeared back into the brothel that now owned her for the week, leaving Karina alone once more.

CHAPTER
FOUR

Will knelt down, examining the golden ring he'd recovered with curiosity. It was unlike anything he'd ever seen before, with some sort of symbol in the middle. A triangle with a... was that an eye in the middle?

It looked valuable.

Will considered the possibility that Karina might have lied to him, and that this ring was, in fact, stolen property. She was a Traitor Caste, after all. There was no way someone of her station would have received something as valuable as this without getting their hands on it illegally.

But despite his reservations, Will pocketed the ring and walked toward *Madame Butterfly's*. He'd almost forgotten why he'd come to Hell's Gate before he strode past a bar window and glimpsed Louis. As predicted, his boss was drinking and playing poker, his fat belly rubbing the edge of the poker table. A cigarette dangled out of one side of his mouth.

Will's eyes narrowed. He should forget about Karina

and demand his wages back from Louis now before the bastard could slip away again.

Louis was large, but Will had a muscled physique from years of hard labor and could handle himself in a brawl. Will looked between *Madame Butterfly's* and the bar window, considering his options. He shook his head. It was *his* fault Karina had lost the ring in the first place. He needed to return it to her, and after that, he'd collect the money Louis owed him. With his mum being so sick, he'd done all those extra hours to pay for her meds and not so this fat bastard could gamble it away.

He strode toward the rickety-looking inn that was *Madame Butterfly's*. Will flung open the double doors and entered the looming darkness of the brothel. Several women greeted him, eager to touch him in places that made Will blush. He jumped out of their reach.

"You're a handsome one, aren't you? Very *exotic*. I thought they'd blown your lot in China up in the Great War."

"I'm British." Will bit back, swallowing his temper. China had been one of the first countries to fall in the Great War. His ancestry lines came from there, so Will appeared to be half-Chinese and half Caucasian. He had the olive complexion, the dark hair, and eyes of his Ma, but he had the large, burly build of his Pa, as well as his towering height.

His Ma wasn't allowed to practice her religion here. *Buddhism*, he remembered her whispering the word to him, knowing it was a sin to talk of such things. He wouldn't dare even mutter that word in public. That had been the rule when she'd been given refuge inside the walls of New London. Forsake your other beliefs and trust in God; for God, the King, and the Clergy had saved you from certain death. If they found anyone practicing another religion, they'd be burned at the stake. The High Priest had enforced that rule again after his studies of Mary Tudor, the first devout Catholic Queen and daughter of Henry the Eighth.

Will pushed through the hordes of women toward the reception desk. He tapped his foot with impatience. It might be another two damn weeks before Will tracked Louis down again. In front of him, waited a tiny red-headed girl.

"A room, please." The red head said to the receptionist in a flat voice.

There was something so familiar to him about that light lilting voice. It had an air of authority about it, as if it were a voice that was used to being listened to. There were two others trailing behind the red head—one olive-skinned brunette girl about Will's age and a man with a mop of sandy blond hair who looked a little older. They both shifted behind the petite red head, glancing around the room warily. Will's eyes narrowed. Those three looked guilty somehow, which was unnerving. After all, there were many sins that occurred daily at *Madame Butterfly*'s, and Will wondered what these three were up to that would make them all so on edge.

"Would you like a partner for each of your companions up there to greet you too, Miss? I can get a lady for our gentleman and two men for you and your friend." She grinned. "Rooms and workers are rented by the hour."

"No, thank you. Just the room. We'll all go up together. We need it for three hours."

"Three hours? With none of our workers in there with you?" She narrowed her eyes at the other two behind the red head. "I'll have to admit, that's a rather unusual request, love."

The red head slipped a one-hundred-pound bill across the desk. "That's for you to accept my peculiar request and for your *understanding* that this stays between us."

Will balked.

He'd never seen that amount of cash in his life, let alone in just a *single* bill. She'd *have* to be a Noble to be throwing that kind of cash around. The woman pocketed the money, licking her lips.

"Room 101," she muttered, slipping the red head a key.

The crimson-headed girl spun to face Will—she was wearing a large pair of sunglasses. *Inside.* Will didn't have time to assess the strange girl any longer. He was next in line.

"Welcome to *Madame Butterfly's*. Which of our ladies would you like to book tonight?"

"Look, I don't have any money. I–"

"We don't do credit here." She waved at the two bodyguards, and they placed a not-so-subtle hand on Will's shoulder, a sign for him to leave.

"I'm looking for Karina."

"She doesn't work here. She refused to... perform in her job interview."

"Do you know where she is?" Will pressed.

"No. Bugger off."

Then, the bodyguards began pushing him back harder. The prostitutes who had once surrounded him backed away like he was an unpleasant smell.

"Please. I need to find her, I have something of hers." He insisted.

"Karina?" Someone said at the top of the stairs. "I know her. She's my best friend." He spun to see a girl about his age in a black corset, fishnet tights, and heels. "He can come with me to my room for ten minutes. I have a spare shirt for you. You're covered in vomit. I'll hear what he has to say."

"You're working, Elaine," the receptionist said.

"Well, consider this my break," the girl snapped, descending the stairs and grabbing Will's arm. "This better be worth it." She grumbled, pulling him back up.

～

CHLOE BURST through the door of room 101 with her two comrades not far behind her. "Do you think anyone noticed us?"

The room was dark and smelt of something rather pungent, but it was the only place the three of them could meet in private. There were too many eyes on them out in the open.

"I think we're safe." Tiffany waltzed over to the bed and flopped down on it. She didn't seem to have much of a problem with the putrid stink in here.

"Honestly Tiff, how can you sit on that?" Chloe wrinkled her nose, pointing to the bed. "Knowing that the sheets probably have never been cleaned?"

Tiffany rolled her eyes, "Chlo, in my seventeen years on this earth, as a *lowly* Craftsman Caste performer, I've slept in places a lot worse than a stinky bed."

A wave of guilt washed over Chloe. She'd been so sheltered from the world. "Sorry. I'm such a..." Chloe frowned as she searched for the right word. "A brat."

Tiffany tipped her head back and let out a laugh that was so joyful Chloe couldn't help but grin. "At least you're aware of it, Chlo." Tiffany nudged Chloe playfully with a knee.

"Can we get the bloody hell on with it?" Tommy

glanced around his shoulder and back at the door.

"All right, don't get those knickers in a twist, Tommy. I don't have long either." Chloe said, pulling the red wig off. That thing was always so damn *itchy*. "But I thought a little practice was better than no practice, right Tommy?"

Tommy examined Chloe from the doorway, rolling a golden coin through his fingers. It disappeared completely every so often and then reappeared.

Tiffany shot him a glare. "I thought you were the one with the brains, Tom. Close the damn door. Someone will recognise her."

Tiffany and Tommy were both Craftsman Caste and part of the troop of artists who often came and performed at the palace—that was how Chloe had met them. Now just look at how far they'd come, Chloe mused.

"If someone recognised her," Tom said, "then she'd get a wrap on the wrists and Daddy will tell her off. If someone recognises *us* and *her* and *what we're doing,* Tiffany. You and I are the ones who will both be dead. They'll say that we convinced her to practice in *sin,* even though it's the other way around." Tommy ran a shaking hand through his greasy, golden hair. "I can't believe I let you two con me into this."

"Hey. That's not true and you know it, Tom. She's risking a lot to be here." Tiffany protested.

If anyone knew what they were doing here. Chloe'd be in serious trouble. And that wasn't even considering the *other* little secret she was hiding from her family... if *that* secret came out, all hell would break loose.

Tommy secretly practiced what Chloe knew to be called illusion magic. Before the Great War, people would travel for hours and pay thousands of pounds to watch illusion shows. David Copperfield, Criss Angel, and long before that, even Harry Houdini. All of them—illusionists pre-Great War.

"I still don't know why you wanna learn this stuff, princess." Tiffany lifted a brow.

Chloe's palms grew sticky when Tiffany reminded her of her station, regardless of it being in jest. *Princess.* She tried to forget that she was one of those as regularly as possible.

"I don't know. My brother used to love it. He'd play card tricks with me, and it always seemed so magical. When I do these lessons, it makes me happy. It makes me forget who I am, and what I have to be." Chloe added, "And you never know. The magic, illusions... that sort of thing could come in handy."

"Yeah, learning card tricks and sleight of hand are going to be *real* handy for a princess, I'm sure." Tommy said with a disbelieving tone. He was well aware of the risks, even more so than Tiffany, who had conned him into giving Chloe the lessons to start with.

But they'd traded in secrets.

That had been the agreement. If Chloe ever revealed Tommy's identity, and the fact that he practiced the now-banned illusion magic, Tommy could reveal the secret that Chloe had whispered in his ear a few months ago.

The one that'd get her executed.

Not to mention, in exchange for her lessons, Chloe was paying both Tiffany and Tommy a handsome price. Chloe had no access to the royal coffers. But she had her allowance, so she gave them as much of that as she could without it being too obvious where the cash was being siphoned. But the real value exchange that was going on here?

Illusion magic lessons for insider secrets about the

Vessel Games.

That was what Tommy could sell off at a steep price.

Chloe figured it was fair. The Nobles had such an advantage all the time... why shouldn't she give them any information she could find on that year's Games? About what the Vessels that year wished for in a man, so a Common Caste could get a special vote, or even make the public root for a particular couple and score highly in the popularity segment?

As far as Chloe saw it, she was just evening on the playing field. And maybe... just maybe... she hoped if the Games swung in favor of the Common Castes this year, then she'd be able to convince the other Nobles to put an end to the Games, once and for all.

It was the only power she had. It wasn't much. But she'd wield it as much as she could.

"Okay. So, we went through levitation tricks last time..." Tommy sighed. "Show me what you've got."

Chloe glanced over at Tiffany, who nodded. "You've got this, Chlo."

Chloe returned the smile that Tiffany had offered and began her lesson.

∾

"Go on in. I won't bite." The young woman said, opening the door. It had gold numbers on it that read: 102. Will glanced toward room 101. That was where the mysterious red head from downstairs had gone with her friends.

"Hurry," the girl urged, and he jumped inside. "I'm Elaine, by the way."

"Will." Will shifted on his feet. "Aren't you gonna lock the door?"

"We don't lock doors for our own safety. We need to get out and call security downstairs if anything goes wrong," Elaine explained. Something felt tight in Will's chest. Will glanced at her deformed hand and put the pieces together: *Traitor by deed.* Elaine moved her fist behind her back, away from his gaze, and considered him coldly. "What do you want?"

"Karina. I bumped into her on the street, and this came out of her bag." Will handed the ring over to Elaine, who inspected it herself. Her face went pale.

"Where did she get this?" Elaine whispered.

"Karina mentioned a man attacked her last night and—"

"Attacked? Why didn't she tell me?" Elaine's hand shot to her neck, where a pretty, wooden pendant hung on a string. Will wondered if the pendant was something tying the two of them together. She frowned and fiddled with it as Will said, "I–I don't know. All I know is that she was heading here just before."

"Thanks for your help. I'll return it to her after my shift."

Will understood that as his dismissal and turned on his heel to leave.

"See ya around." Elaine shut the door in his face.

He thought little of it. She must meet assholes of the first order. He traipsed down the hall, surprised that he felt a twinge of disappointment at the prospect of not seeing Karina tonight. Maybe he'd see her around the slums and then he could—

An ear-splitting scream sounded through the corridor. Will snapped his head back to where it had originated. It came from room 102.

Elaine.

47

FIVE

Will sprinted back to room 102 and wrestled with the rusty gold knob, but the door wouldn't move an inch.

Will cursed and tried to barge through the locked door. Still, it didn't budge. Crashes sounded, and it seemed a lot like objects were flying and glass was shattering behind the door. At least from the commotion he heard.

Whatever was happening, Elaine was putting up a hell of a fight.

"Get out of the way." Said a harsh voice behind him that made him jump. It was the red head from room 101. She unclasped a pin in her hair and worked on the lock with an intense ferocity.

"You can pick locks?" He asked. Will had thought with the amount of money she'd handed over downstairs that she wouldn't need this kind of skill set.

"I've been breaking out of places my whole life," she muttered. "Hold on!" she yelled to Elaine. "Keep fighting, we're coming!" The bobby pin clicked, and the door swung open.

Unfortunately, the red head held no weapons on her either; Will realized this fact with dread. With a grim nod to each other, Will and the red head burst into the room.

An immense man, dressed in black and with a balaclava covering his face, dragged Elaine toward the window. Elaine tried to stick her heels into the wooden floor, slowing him as much as she could, even as her shoes made an awful screech across the floor.

Will stood still for a second, overwhelmed by the scene before him. But the red head didn't hold back. She launched at the man, kicking out at his knees. A crack sounded, and he groaned in agony as she hit home. But even injured, he continued to drag Elaine toward the balcony. Elaine's face was etched in terror.

Will lurched into action, grabbing onto Elaine's outstretched hand and tugging her back. She only moved a few inches, but it was progress.

"Hold on to me!" Will shouted.

The man's pace increased now, dragging Elaine away. Elaine clung on to Will tighter, her nails digging into his flesh. Her expression was desperate, and Will noticed that wooden, heart-shaped necklace hanging around her neck bouncing wildly as she tried to free herself.

A soft thud sounded behind him, and Will snapped his head toward the source. The red head lay sprawled on the floor, knocked out cold. His stomach dropped. It was up to him to save Elaine now.

Another hooded man slammed the door shut and suddenly he was surrounded by two men much larger than and clearly more adept at fighting than him. The second man began striding toward Will, who still held on steadfastly to Elaine's arms. The second intruder, however, held a rusty, three-armed candelabra in his hand. It must've been the weapon he'd used to knock red head out.

Will looked back at Elaine in panic, his eyes wide. He was outnumbered, and they both knew it. Maybe someone downstairs had heard the tousle—

"Will!" Elaine gasped.

She was looking down at the man who held onto her torso. And on his finger was a replica of the ring he'd just returned to Elaine. Whoever had come for Karina had also ventured here for Elaine.

"Will," Elaine gasped, the terror in features turning into something else: resolve.

"The ring. Tell Karina—"

Everything went black.

～

WILL WOKE WITH A START. He was drowsy, and his head hurt like hell. The red head was awake and inspecting the window that the attackers must have taken Elaine through. The two men had escaped with Elaine, and it had gone unnoticed by anyone else.

"Who the hell was that?" Will asked.

"I'm not sure." The girl watched the busy streets below, massaging her temples.

Things started clicking into place, "The ring."

"What ring?"

"The ring. The one I came here to give Elaine. They also attacked her friend, Karina, last night. But Karina got away. This man had the same ring on his finger, same strange sigil on it."

"Who's Karina?"

50

"A Traitor Caste girl. We should visit the Defenders' headquarters; we need to report this."

Will started towards the door, but her hand shot out, holding him back. "Will... if you report this, you'll be in danger. You know how the Defenders are. You're a Common Caste at the scene of the crime. You've got her DNA all over you, and you're the easy win for them to close the case." The strange red-headed girl pulled her hood around tighter, as she looked around the room. "They'll hang you first and ask questions later."

"But she's been abducted," Will protested. "We have to do something."

"I'll fix this. But I need to get back to the P—" She stopped herself mid-sentence. "I need to go," she finished quietly.

"We need to fix this now! Someone's been abducted. Karina might be next." Will ran his hands through his hair and winced in pain when he reached the spot where they'd hit him.

"I *will* fix this. You have my word."

"A stranger's word means nothing to me." Will said. "Come with me. If we can go to the Defenders together, there's less chance of..."

"I can't do that." She surveyed Will in a strange way, a soft one at that. "You know, you remind me a lot of someone. Your spirit. The way you move... you even look a bit like him, too."

"Who?" Will frowned.

"My brother." The red head's lips curved into a smile, and her eyes glazed over, as if traveling far away for a moment. She shook her head and was back in the room. "Don't tell anyone about the fact you saw me here tonight, okay?"

The girl began backing away from him, already trying to flee from the scene of the crime. If he had any sense left in him, he should, too.

"How are you going to do that? I don't even know your name." Will wanted to learn more, to understand what the hell had just happened, but she'd already disappeared.

CHAPTER
SIX

No matter what she did, Karina couldn't seem to stop crying.

"Karina," Marcus reached out his hand, wincing at the exertion, and placed it on her shoulder. "This won't help."

The Defenders refused to allocate resources to print missing posters, so Karina had used all of her savings to buy some paper and pens. She'd been drawing Elaine's face on each one of them all morning, since she'd heard the news. Karina didn't look up from her task, blinking through her tears to finish her sketch.

She'd always been a talented artist. Whenever they had enough money left over for Christmas gifts, her mum and Marcus would buy her a few, new coloured pens. When Karina drew, she felt safe. She felt like she was in control.

Karina's mind wandered back to a few days ago, to the attack.

Good luck, my lady. That's what he'd said to her. *My lady?*

What did he mean by that? Was he some sort of insane person? A small voice tugged at Karina, telling her softly that guess wasn't it. And after Elaine went missing last night? More puzzle pieces. Clearly, there was something darker at play here. She just needed more pieces to fit together with the rest.

"You don't think it was a Shadowlander attack, do you?" Marcus asked, cradling his abdomen.

He'd been lucky, they'd said. The knife hadn't ruptured anything internally. Her mother hadn't had the money to take him to see a proper doctor, but luckily, they'd found a Traitor by deed that was previously a doctor before his crimes and he'd stitched Marcus up.

Karina shook her head, "You know they attack in groups. And they don't mask their faces like that if they attack. Or carry guns. It has to be a New Londoner. And why attack Elaine, too? They come for resources to loot, not for... girls." Karina's pencil dug a little too hard into her latest drawing of Elaine, ruining the shape of one of her eyes. "The Defenders can't say it's a murder case when they haven't found a body, can they? It's a missing person's case. But they're doing nothing to find her." Karina flung the picture and her pencil aside and stood. "I'm going for a walk."

Karina's mother watched warily as Karina stormed out of the living room, nursing a hot drink that Uncle Frank had given her. Uncle Frank was one of their neighbors, and her dad's best friend. He'd been one of the neighbors to come to Karina's aid.

"Rina, it's best if you stick close to here. We don't know if that nutter is still on the loose," Uncle Frank said.

He'd become something of a leader in the small community in the Traitor slums. Everyone respected him, even looked to him for guidance. Karina often wondered if her mum would remarry him, but she never had.

"No one else is looking for her," Karina said, snatching up her pile of her sketches of Elaine and stuffing them in her bag. "So, if no one else will do it, I guess I'm going to have to."

Together, they all jumped at the knock that rapped on their front door.

Marcus reached into his pocket. It must have cost him all his savings, but he'd bought a gun after the attack, one off the black market. Karina hadn't seen him without it since.

"I'll get it," she said.

Karina couldn't put her finger on why, but as she trudged through the dark hallway, a nervous flutter sat in her stomach. She needed to snap out of this; no one would come and attack her in broad daylight.

Karina flung open the door to see fifty armed Defenders scattered across the streets before her. She stumbled back in fright with her eyes wide as saucers.

A gentle face popped out from behind the front Defender. "Don't be frightened, dear."

The woman had glossy raven hair with tight ringlets of curls. Every line and angle of her face was sharp, yet seemed perfectly crafted. Her nose, jawline, and cheekbones... She looked like how Karina imagined a runway model might've looked like before the Great War. Ma used to tell her stories before she went to bed about beautiful women who graced the runways and wore gorgeous clothes as their *job*. Karina couldn't imagine such a thing. Her job mostly consisted of scrubbing toilets. But this woman would have fit in among the models of old. She was beautiful, including her skin, which was a darker brown than Karina's, and her eyes were an immense and depthless black.

But none of that was what had made Karina balk. Oh, no. It was the most prominent thing the woman wore. For there, sitting on her intricate up-do, was a sparkling golden crown.

The Queen.

Karina's eyeballs almost popped out of their sockets. She was in the presence of holiness. Karina didn't know how to curtsey or bow, so she settled for the next best thing —she fell to her knees.

"Forgive me, Your Majesty. I didn't recognise you."

The Queen chuckled, ducking past the Defender who was standing in front of her and touching Karina's shoulder. "Sorry about all this fanfare, my darling. The King wouldn't let me visit without a battalion of his highest trained Defenders." She rolled her eyes at the inconvenience of it all. "Men are *so* protective."

Karina said nothing, just kept her eyes glued to the floor.

"May I come in, darling heart?"

"O-of course," Karina stammered.

Queen Mary glided past Karina, through to the dark corridor of the flat. Her perfume smelled like sugar and berries... it was so sweet that it made Karina blink in surprise. Karina sniffed her own armpits, checking to ensure she wasn't smelling too bad herself. Traitors had strict rations of both food and water, and if it came to either drinking water or bathing in it, she'd opt for the former.

A glass smashed in the other room, and Karina hurried into the lounge behind the Queen. All of Karina's family were on their knees too, trembling. They'd stripped Marcus of his gun. The smashed glass, no doubt dropped in shock, was sprinkled across the gray carpet.

"Apologies for the abrupt call in." The Queen said,

assessing the tiny apartment with displeasure. The golden dress she wore looked rather out of place in their dingy flat. She snapped her perfectly manicured fingers, and three more Defenders entered the room, carrying a golden chair. They placed it behind the Queen at the exact moment she sat. "I can't ruin the dress, you see."

She seemed almost embarrassed at the grandiosity of it all.

Almost.

"Karina, sit down, please. I have some news that I felt was rather necessary to deliver myself," Queen Mary added.

Karina eyed the Defenders, who were assessing Marcus. He didn't break their gaze once. She noticed that Uncle Frank had tucked her mother behind him.

"Sit!" Queen Mary commanded again. This time, annoyance laced her voice. Karina doubted the Queen had ever had to tell someone to do something twice.

Karina dropped onto the sofa as quickly as she could.

"Karina. There's been a terrible mistake. I came here on behalf of the crown to apologize," the Queen said.

Karina half-wondered if the Queen was about to inform her that Elaine had died, that they'd found her body. But there was no way any royal cared about what happened to a missing Traitor Caste girl.

"When you were tested," Queen Mary added. "The doctor was incorrect. He read the data wrong."

Karina frowned, her mind swirling with confusion, unable to put the pieces together.

"Karina, my darling," The Queen said, "God has blessed you with the ultimate gift, one that other girls would die to have for themselves. You are a Vessel."

SEVEN

The room was silent. "I-I'm a... what?"

"You're a Vessel." The Queen said again. She smiled, but it didn't touch her eyes.

Marcus let out a hoot of exhilaration. Uncle Frank hugged Mum, whose eyes were welling with tears of happiness. This is what every Common Caste and their family prayed for, what they *dreamt* of.

But Karina remained still. "That doesn't make any sense. Why was the doctor incorrect? They do hundreds of the tests each year, when we all turn eighteen. No one's ever gotten it wrong before."

"An unfortunate mistake." The Queen waved her hand in casual dismissal. "But this is going to work a little differently from the past. There's never been a Traitor Caste Vessel, you see. Some say that this is God's way of punishing your people's sins, but Karina, He has chosen you. Praise be to God on high."

"Glory to Him," All the Defenders barked, making Karina jump.

"What do you mean?" Karina said, her mind still reeling.

"It is customary for the victor's families to be upgraded from whatever Common Caste they are. The same rule applies for Vessels, although there haven't been many Common ones in the ten years since the Games started," Queen Mary said.

Karina understood this was a big reason Common Caste men competed. If they won just a single round in the Games, it would lift their family out of poverty, and they'd get anything their heart desired.

Before the Great War, there was the lottery. Now, there were the Games. Some were desperate or foolish enough to risk death for the chance at a better life.

"Yes. Once the Games are over, then my family can come and live with me and my husband." Karina swallowed at the thought of marrying someone in just a few weeks' time.

"No, Karina. You are a Traitor Caste. Well, you know this. Very few Common Castes have been Vessels over the past few years." She shrugged. "That wild Defender Caste was our most recent, and that didn't go well."

Karina had heard whispers about the Defender Caste that had been discovered as a Vessel about seven years ago. She'd been difficult to tame, to say the least. Some rumors said she was so unhappy she'd tried to run away. Some said she'd even tried to kill her own husband. She'd lost her eye for that. Defender Castes were the highest-ranking members of the Commons, and even *she* hadn't been able to make it work.

But a Traitor Caste by blood as a Vessel?

The Games had been going for ten years, and Karina had never heard of such a thing.

"However, the Church will not condone moving your family to the rank of Noble. I tried to convince the High Priest and the king for you. But they both agreed that sinners living in the Noble District among true God-fearing men is unacceptable."

Karina couldn't believe it. What was the point of being elevated in rank if her family starved? "Your Majesty, with all due respect, my family are not sinners. My dad made a mistake, and they punished him for it. But my family hasn't committed any crime. We're traitors by blood only."

"The High Priest insists that sin runs in the blood," The Queen said, standing and patting her humongous dress back into shape. "You must do so much more than any of the other Vessels. You need to prove to the public that you are good, godly, and worth dying for." She stood up and began walking away, her duties done.

"No one should die for me," Karina bit out.

The Queen stopped, her back still facing Karina. The silence was deafening. Uncle Frank and Karina's mother's eyes were wide with shock, as if not quite believing what she'd just said to the Queen. The Guards rounded on Karina, pressing forward.

"You besmirch the Games?" one of them asked, "That's blasphemy." They prowled toward her, but Karina did not balk.

Her mother stepped in between Karina and the Defenders. "Forgive her, your majesty. She is in shock at the news. You know, women are creatures that... cannot handle such things due to our delicate nature."

"At ease," The Queen commanded her guards, and just like that, they fell away again.

Now, the Queen faced Karina directly. Her eyes were as cold as her tone, "But they *will* die for you, Karina. And happily. The question is: will you be worth it? God has deemed you pure and worthy to bear children. Praise Him." The Queen made the sign of the cross in the air, and then the Defenders around her followed suit. "But you do not have a choice in this, darling heart. Pack your belongings. You'll be staying at the palace until the Games are over. I'll be waiting in the car." The Queen turned on her heels, her dress whooshing with the movement, and as quickly as she came, she was gone.

"I can't go," Karina said, shaking her head. "Why does everyone else get to have their families come, but mine can't?" Karina was breathing hard now, tears blurring her vision. Her mother caught Karina's arms and pressed her chin toward her. "Go. God has chosen you, Karina."

"What if I don't?"

"There's never been an unwilling Vessel before, except for that Defender Caste girl. They took everything from her, Karina." Uncle Frank said. "I suspect they'd do just about anything to make you willing, starting with hurting Claire and Marcus." Uncle Frank placed a protective hand on her mother's shoulder.

Karina rose to her full height. "I'll do my duty, Frank."

Frank nodded, as if comforted by this fact, knowing that her mother would be safe as long as Karina had breath in her lungs.

"But I will find a way." Karina promised. "I'll convince them to let you come with me. I promise." Karina pressed her forehead to her mothers, "I swear it."

～

KARINA SAT in the vehicle's backseat.

"This car is bulletproof," the Queen informed her from

the front seat. "So, you're safe here. No Shadowlanders, Traitors, or anyone else can hurt you. Not anymore."

Karina hadn't thought about that. Since the Uprising and his previous wife's death, the King had taken no risks with his family's safety. Karina needed to think like this, too. She was a target. A commodity. Something of value.

"All the rest of the Vessels this year are Nobles. You're sure to love them." The Queen said, "I'll teach you all how to be Vessels of the highest order. It's my favorite queenly duty."

"I can't wait, Your Majesty." Karina hoped Queen Mary couldn't sense the apprehension in her voice. A flash of inspiration hit Karina. "Your Majesty, my brother... I'm sorry to ask you... but he recently lost his job. If you aren't able to promote them up to a Noble Caste, could you please help them pay their bills until he finds a new one?"

The Queen looked at her with softness. "It's done," she said, leaning forward to tuck a strand of hair behind Karina's ear.

Karina's eyes welled with tears of joy and gratitude. "Thank you, Your Majesty."

She marveled at how a *woman* was able to have such power. What would Karina have had to do to get hold of that money? Karina remembered that night at *Madame Butterfly's*. She shivered just thinking about it. But it was all over now.

"How many Vessels did you discover, your majesty?" Karina asked.

"Four. Plus you." Just five girls who turned eighteen this year could bear children. Karina shuddered at what this meant for the future of humanity.

"What will happen when we run out, Your Majesty?" Karina said.

"Of what?"

"Of Vessels."

"2 Corinthians 4:1-15, Karina. 'But we have this treasure in earthen vessels, that the surpassing greatness of the power may be of God and not from ourselves.'" The Queen gave her a tight smile. There seemed something else there, in those depthless eyes.

It looked a lot like fear.

Karina was unsure how the biblical quote about Vessels answered her question, but the Queen continued then, "God will provide. Vessels were always meant to be a treasure. This is God lifting His mighty hand on us and helping us find the way."

It seemed a lot more like science than God, from what her dad used to whisper to her in bed at night. He'd said that the Great War and nuclear events had caused radiation. That the radiation had continued to affect humans as they'd lived generation to generation after the war.

But Karina simply nodded.

"We're here!" the Queen said, shifting the conversation from such heavy topics. "The entire staff, royal family and Vessels are lining up in front of the palace waiting to greet you." She squeezed Karina's hand. "I organized it especially."

"Thank you." Karina said. The Queen meant well; Karina was sure of it. She wanted her to feel welcome here, no matter her Caste. The Queen needed this to work as much as Karina did.

"Praise Him for you are with us. Oh, and I hope you don't mind, but I invited the media, too."

Karina's heart lurched into her mouth. *Media?*

The media covered all aspects of the Games, so everyone knew what was happening at all times. Everyone in New London looked forward to the latest news about the royal family. Wives would ask their husbands to stay up and read them the latest newspaper articles about the Games. Considering every other form of entertainment was considered improper, the Nobles lived for it.

"I'm not dressed properly." Karina objected, motioning to her scruffy t-shirt and torn jeans.

"Don't worry about that," the Queen said with a wink, "Besides, everybody loves a Cinderella story."

~

THE QUEEN EMERGED from the car as camera flashes assaulted her from every direction. She smoothed her dress and smiled serenely at the press before her. "This year, we have experienced something unprecedented. We discovered a Vessel in the Traitor Caste."

There were audible gasps from the media, and even from Karina's place inside the car, she saw them peering around at one another, as if some sort of scandal had occurred.

"This is unprecedented, yes. But I don't want her treated differently from the other Vessels. From now on, we have elevated her to the rank of Noble. This is also what we do with all our male winners, and you will treat her accordingly. Am I understood?"

The press was ruthless, and the Queen was ensuring they wouldn't ask her uncomfortable questions. Karina breathed a small sigh of relief.

"Out you come, Karina," the Queen instructed.

Karina stepped out of the car to the humidity of midday. Before her lay the palace with an entire line of people waiting to greet her. The other Vessels looked on from afar, and she felt a strange excitement to meet the others. But first, she had to survive the press.

"Karina, is it?" A man with a hooked nose and blond, curly hair asked. Karina nodded. "Just to be clear. Why are you a Traitor Caste? Did you commit a crime? Do you think this is God showing you He forgives you for your sins?"

"M-My father was in the Uprising ten years ago," she answered. More gasps ensued. "None of my family knew about it or helped, though. So, we were Caste down instead of executed." Karina remembered herself. "Praise be to God," she added quickly, the words tumbling from her mouth.

"Are you excited about finding a husband? Do you think more Common Castes will fight in the Games now? Seeing you elevated may have given them hope they can be Caste up too. "

"I-I'm not sure." Karina hoped not.

In the ten years since the Uprising had started and the Games had begun, the contest had become a rite of passage for the Nobles. They'd had the upper hand before the Uprising, seducing Vessels with the promise of the fortunes they held. Nowadays, Nobles endured training for the Games every day with the best trainers that money could buy. They only had a couple of years of opportunity to compete from the year they turned eighteen to twenty. So, with all that preparation and training, the Nobles still held the upper hand for the Games as well.

"Thank you for your questions. Any press regarding Karina will go through me," the Queen said.

She eyed them all, daring them to argue. They bowed toward the Queen and moved away, sensing that their work was finished. Queen Mary linked arms with Karina, and together, they strode toward the palace steps. Karina had never seen it up close before. As a Traitor Caste, she wasn't allowed in the inner sanctum that contained the palace and church; she'd had to worship at the tiny Traitor Caste church on the outskirts of the city.

"You'll be living with us while the Games are going on. When they are over, we'll provide you with your own house and a protection detail," Queen Mary said.

"T-thank you." Karina said, marveling that her arm was tucked into the *Queen's* arm. When they reached the steps, the Queen stood in front of a portly man in a gray suit and then even she bowed low to the ground. Karina followed her lead.

"Hello, my dear. It seems you found a sinner who has been forgiven of her sins."

"It's a miracle," the Queen said, whilst patting Karina's shoulder.

Karina did not lift her head. She'd copied the Queen's curtsey, but she hadn't centered herself properly and her legs wobbled.

"A genuine miracle," the King said, assessing her.

A light voice interrupted the exchange. "Father. Can't you see she's struggling?"

Someone pulled on Karina's arm, helping her up. "I'm Chloe."

The girl grinned. The only way Karina could describe this girl was angelic. She had a heart-shaped face, porcelain skin, and a small button nose. Her ice-blue eyes shone with intelligence. They considered Karina now with something that looked like kindness.

She must have been the princess.

"I'm Karina, Your Highness." Karina went to bow again, but Chloe caught her arm.

"None of that nonsense, I insist," Chloe said, wrinkling her nose and waving her hand on dismissal.

"Come on. You must meet the other ladies." Chloe linked arms with her in the same way the Queen had. "You don't mind if I introduce her, do you Step-Mamma?" Chloe asked.

"Of course not, darling heart. Run along, you two."

Chloe dragged Karina over to where the other four girls stood, waiting to greet her. They all wore dresses in different shades of blue and in distinct styles. Each of them also wore a pearl necklace that had a large golden "V" as a pendant.

Karina had remembered seeing that pendant in a mansion they had assigned her to clean in the Noble district. Karina's mum once told her that Mary Tudor had one just like it, and Queen Mary, a descendant of the original Queen Mary, the ardent Catholic child of Henry the VIII, had decided it would be a good way to identify the elite Vessels.

It stood as a mark of royalty.

"This is Sarah," Chloe said.

"Your Highness." Sarah curtseyed.

This time, Chloe didn't insist she should get up. Sarah's red curls fell in front of her face.

"Sarah is, how do you say? I guess, she's the pack leader," Chloe said to Karina, not taking her eyes off Sarah. That ice in her gaze had turned cool—cold, even. "You'll all be very kind to Karina, despite where she hails from, won't you, Sarah? I won't hear of any cruelty?"

"Of course, Your Highness." Sarah bowed lower, but Karina saw the rage in her eyes as they flicked up to meet Chloe's. "We're always kind to new girls."

Sarah's gaze now turned on Karina, assessing her. Sarah wore a sky-blue dress that puffed out so widely that it was a wonder she could fit through doorways. Her breasts practically spilled out of the tightly corseted dress. Karina had to admit, however, that the hue of her dress complimented her fiery red hair and the smattering of freckles over her cheeks and nose.

"This is Anne," Chloe pointed out next.

A girl with an olive complexion, brunette hair, and hazel eyes curtseyed deeply. Anne wore a midnight blue dress that was much less ostentatious than Sarah's. It flowed down simply, highlighting her naturally curvaceous figure. Anne glanced up at Karina briefly, and then her eyes immediately darted back down to the floor.

"N-nice to meet you." She stammered, her eyes flicking back and forth between Karina and the Princess. "Your Highness..." Anne curtseyed so low it looked like she was about to fall over, but Chloe had already moved on with Karina in tow.

"And these two, are the twins. Louisa and Rachel," Chloe finished.

The two girls had black hair and ebony skin. They didn't look identical but were still very similar.

Chloe's nostrils flared. "Well introduce yourself then," she ordered.

One of them wrinkled their nose up. "I'm Rachel, that's Louisa. And you need a bath."

Karina's eyes widened at the accusation. The other Vessels sniggered, and the servants in earshot shifted uncomfortably. Karina's cheeks flared with heat. The sad thing was, though, that it was probably true. And now she'd been in the presence of royalty smelling like a dung heap. She turned to apologize to Chloe, but the princess was looking at one of the twins instead of at her.

"And *you* need to learn some manners. Don't let me catch you talking to Karina in that way again," Chloe said.

The twin that had been speaking—Rachel—curtseyed. "Apologies, Your Highness. I was only trying to help my fellow Vessel. We need to look out for one another." Her tone was saccharine sweet, but Karina could hear the bite.

"I see," Chloe said, her head tilting slightly. "Come along, Karina, and I'll introduce you to the servants." Chloe strode off ahead of her.

"Yes, go meet the servants. Where you *really* belong," Rachel muttered quietly enough for Chloe not to hear her. Her eyes roamed over Karina, and she smirked.

Maybe Karina had been foolish to hope that Noble girls would be kind to her just because she was a Vessel as well. It was clear that to them, she wasn't worth the dirt on her shoe.

Karina examined Rachel, trying to think of something to say. The way her hair glistened in the sunlight reminded her of Elaine's.

Elaine.

Karina's stomach dropped.

She'd been so swept up in this whole ordeal that she'd almost forgotten about the attack. Elaine was missing. Karina's steps faltered a little as she tried to catch up with Chloe.

Chloe examined her with worry, "What's wrong?" she asked, frowning.

Karina assessed her options. Chloe had been kind to her. And she seemed...pretty normal for a princess. Perhaps Chloe would help her find Elaine. "Can we speak in private?"

"James, my bodyguard, needs to be with me at all times. That's about as private as you'll get here." Chloe rolled her eyes. "Come on." Chloe took Karina's hand and pulled her down the steps toward the palace's grand gardens. Once Karina was sure that no one was in earshot, she spoke. "My friend is missing."

Karina glanced behind her and noticed a large hulk of a man had been following them, but he remained at a respectable distance. She lowered her voice further. "I'm not sure why, but I think it's connected to me, too. There's something weird going on."

"What do you mean?" Chloe asked.

"Well, there was another attempted kidnapping. On *me*."

Chloe's eyes widened.

Karina continued, "A few days ago, I was notified that I was Barren at my telling. Elaine was too. But the doctor looked odd when he told me the news, and his face went pale... as if he were frightened of something. The next day, someone broke into my house and tried to take me, but they failed. My brother fought him off and the neighbors in our community helped us. But now Elaine's been taken too."

Karina knew it was a risky move to tell Chloe this information, but Princess Chloe was a friend to the people. Although she was barely seventeen, at every opportunity she had, she'd be out among the masses, helping the hungry, the poor, and the sinners. She was well known and loved for her charity work. She'd even insinuated in the newspaper that she wanted to get rid of the Games. The next day, the newspaper had an article directly from the King, retracting that quote. Karina wondered how much trouble she'd gotten into for that.

Chloe assessed Karina in a way that unsettled her. Karina had always been very good at reading people. She had a knack for knowing exactly what people were thinking. Her dad had called her an empath. And when she'd told Chloe about Elaine...

Chloe didn't look surprised.

At all.

A tingle ran up Karina's spine. Chloe had known about the attack—she was sure of it.

"That's odd." Chloe swallowed. "How do you know she's not just missing? Have they found a body?" Chloe's voice was tight.

Karina grimaced but shook her head.

"Sorry, but I had to ask," Chloe said. "Murders still happen often in the Traitor slums, but Defenders quickly find bodies after the fact. Even murderers don't venture outside New London's walls. They're too scared of the Shadowlanders."

Karina shivered at the thought of running into a heathen Shadowlander outside the city walls. Or inside. The Shadowlander attacks had become more and more frequent.

Chloe continued on, "Someone going missing though.... that *is* rather strange. We need to find her."

Karina almost wept with relief. "Well, princess—"

"Chloe, please. If we're going to be friends, I can't have you calling me that," Chloe said, grimacing a little.

"Well, Chloe." Karina gulped, hardly believing her life right now. She was on a first name basis *with royalty.* "No one was looking for her. Not even the Defenders. If I could return to the slums and look for her myself..."

Chloe shook her head. "The king would never let you. It's too dangerous, and you're far too valuable. Your face will be in the papers by tonight, and people will recognize who you are. People could try things." Karina shivered at the thought. "James?" Chloe called to the burly man.

"Elaine, you said? What was her last name?" she trailed off, looking at Karina.

"Stephens," Karina answered.

"Elaine Stephens," Chloe continued, "is missing. What do you know about that?"

James looked rather apprehensive. "I know very little, Your Majesty."

"I happened to be asking you about open cases in New London just this morning. Why didn't you tell me about this one?" Chloe's eyes narrowed.

James shrugged, shuffling his feet. "There's been more Shadowlander raids as of late. I thought it more apt to inform you about them."

"But a *missing girl* is important, James. Surely the Defenders are looking into that." Chloe's face was flush with anger.

"They didn't even try to look for her or give out missing person posters." Karina's eyes were bright with tears. "I had to make them myself."

Chloe's mouth turned into a thin line.

"James," she said as evenly as she could manage, "go down to the Defender headquarters and insist upon a proper investigation. *And get Elaine's missing posters out.*"

James shuffled next to her. "Your Highness, I did just receive word while you were greeting the lady." He indicated toward Karina. Karina started in surprise—she was a lady now. "The Defenders have already been in contact with me about this case."

"And?" Chloe snapped.

"They've found the culprit. He had Miss Stephens' DNA all over him. Scratches on his arms, which show a struggle.

72

Security cameras have spotted him in the crime's vicinity. They've taken him in for questioning."

Chloe's face had gone utterly white, "What's his name?"

"William. William Albridge."

EIGHT

The punch that hit home on Will's face was agony. He'd gone to the Defenders' headquarters, ready to help find whoever took Elaine. After a restless night, he'd convinced himself that the red-headed stranger was wrong. If he gave the Defenders the information they needed, he'd be on his way. There were processes to be followed. There were witnesses at the Headquarters station, seeing him give his statement. Not all Defenders could be so corrupt and act so improperly that he'd be in danger for simply reporting a crime.

He'd been desperate to help Elaine, and he'd thought that just maybe he might see Karina there. She'd be able to vouch for him. Or perhaps the red head who had helped him had been a Defender Caste and had connections here. They couldn't just *pin* a crime as serious as this on someone without due process.

How wrong he'd been. They'd already been looking for him when he turned himself in.

A surly Defender stood in front of him. "Admit what you did, and we can all go home, son."

"Except I won't go home, will I?" Will spat out the blood that had welled up in his mouth. Will knew he'd made a massive mistake by coming here. "You'll kill me no matter what."

"Well, we've got evidence of you meeting with Elaine and being the last person seen with her. Her DNA is under your fingernails, and the trashed room at *Madame Butterfly's* had your fingerprints everywhere, too."

The Defender rattled off the list, as the lump in Will's throat thickened. He was screwed. He thought of his mum. Who would look after her? Who would be able to provide for her? He was an only child and her only support.

"All we need is a confession. We can finish this today."

"Finish what?" Will asked.

"You. Your execution." The man assessed his fingernails. "We'll make your death as quick as your confession. If you confess today, you'll have a painless bullet to the head. Done in a second. If you don't, you can expect night after night of torture during the trial. And an even more painful death. Perhaps you'll get a stoning. Maybe you'll be hanged or even drawn and quartered. No jury on God's green earth is going to believe you."

Will's heart beat faster, as the Defender looked at him with a bored expression. "So, do you want me to get my tools to pull your teeth and fingernails out, or are you going to talk?"

∼

CHLOE'S sick feeling of dread only increased as she paced around her bedroom. She'd tried everything to escape from the palace today before Karina had arrived with her stepmother. She'd also tried to talk to James—who was aware of all Defender business—and make him spill that Elaine had gone missing.

If he'd told her that, then she would've been in a position to move the investigation with Elaine forward. But if Chloe knew about Elaine going missing *before* James told her, then it would've been clear Chloe'd been out of the palace. And then her father would lock her down and make it even harder for her to escape. That was something she couldn't afford to do right now—not with everything that was at stake.

She'd hoped that the Defenders would have at least *tried* to find the right culprit. But Chloe had known it last night; Will was the easy suspect. As long as someone paid for sins in New London, it didn't always matter who or even if they were actually guilty.

Chloe flung her door open, she'd had enough of thinking this through. She needed to take action.

"James."

"Your Highness."

"Take me to William Albridge."

"But—"

"*Now.*" Chloe's tone offered no room for argument.

She hurried down the grand marble staircase, through the large French doors, and jumped into the front seat of the car. James barked an order for the other two Defenders watching the doors to accompany them. Chloe could barely sit still; she felt so anxious.

Chloe remembered back to that night. That boy, Will, had really tried to save Elaine. He couldn't be much older than she was. Her brother's toothy smile flashed into her mind... Will couldn't be executed for a crime that he didn't commit.

Not while she was around to stop it. She just hoped to God that she wasn't too late.

~

WILL'S screams echoed around the interrogation room. The Defenders just kept going and going. He couldn't hold on any longer. But if he gave in, if he said what they wanted, then he'd be killed today. He'd be killed regardless; he realized bitterly. The Defenders decided that Will had been the one to murder Elaine, and nothing he said would change their minds.

"The ring! I told you already about the man with the ring. What about Karina? Find Karina and bring her here. She was attacked by the same people, too!" Will argued.

The man ripped another fingernail from his nail bed, and Will screamed in agony.

Half delirious with pain, Will almost swooned as his mother's face swam into his mind. With Will dead, there'd be no one to look after her anymore. She needed her meds. She needed support. The door slammed open, and a huge hulk of a man stepped through. Through Will's blurry vision, he saw a blonde figure emerge, one who had a golden crown placed on her head.

She looked... familiar.

"Step away from the boy," the girl ordered with quiet authority.

The torturer looked rattled. "But, Your Highness, I was only told that–"

"Step away from him!" She exploded, her rage palpable.

"James, it was my understanding that torturing suspects had been abolished. You will write me and my father a full report on how this happened and who is responsible."

"Your Highness..."

"What?" She snapped.

"When you lobbied to stop torture in interrogations, your father agreed in the interim only. But the High Priest disagreed with you. Your father had no choice but to reinstate it. He didn't tell you as he thought you'd be upset."

"Well, he was correct." Chloe's hands balled into fists. "William is coming with me to the palace. Unshackle him now."

Will's pain subsided a little. His fingers still killed him, but the Princess' face had started to take shape in his mind.

The redhead in Madam Butterfly. Will realized everything with a start.

What the hell had a princess been doing sneaking around *Madame Butterfly's*? He frowned and opened his mouth to say something, but she shook her head in warning.

Her panicked face told him all he needed to know—that it wasn't public knowledge.

She lifted him up and whispered in his ear. "I know you remember me from that night. Don't. Say. Anything. I'll get you out of here alive. But you can't tell them I was there, okay?"

Will nodded numbly. Whatever the princess was doing at *Madame Butterfly's*.... She'd been in disguise. And it was likely she'd get into serious trouble if her trips were revealed.

"Come on," Chloe ordered Will.

He staggered to his feet. "Where are we going?"

"To see my asshole of a father."

~

CHLOE STORMED into her father's chambers with a rage in her belly that rivaled Henry VIII's temper. The other Nobles snapped their heads toward the door she'd just slammed open. They all sat around a long table with papers, maps, and building plans splayed out in the middle.

"Chloe. I'm in a meeting," the King said, sensing her anger. "Can this wait?"

"No," she burst out. "No, it cannot. You bought back torture in interrogations without telling me?" Chloe's eyes sparkled with tears at the betrayal.

"Darling. The High Priest insisted sinners would not be honest until—"

"Until what? You hurt them so much they admit to a crime they haven't committed to stop the pain? That's what Will was likely to do, anyway."

The King tapped his pen on the table. "Who's Will?"

Chloe stomped back outside, and it was silent for a moment. She stormed back in with Will in tow; he was still shackled. They wouldn't allow him to travel with her otherwise. Blood dripped from his hands. Chloe tried to give him a confident smile, tried to let him know she knew about the game that was afoot.

"This," she gestured to him, "Is Will, William Albridge. Who *did not* commit the crime that the Defenders accused him of. In fact, there was little to no proof at all." The Nobles looked away from the heated exchange, unsure of where to avert their eyes. "Lord Coddington, Duke of Northumberland. Please watch this." Chloe addressed the room, "Because I want you *all* to think about how Will's ruling can affect *you*. If we set this precedent, with no proof needed, and then torture suspects until it's too much to take, and they confess regardless, then how will you fare?" Chloe eyed each nobleman. "You all have many enemies in New London. Enemies that would wish to see you dead, too. If this becomes how we treat all suspects... what's stopping you from being next?"

The Lords shifted in their seats.

Chloe's father had turned purple with rage.

"Give me his file James," The King barked.

James jumped at his name, scuttling over to the King and producing Will's case file he'd taken from the Defender headquarters.

The King read the file through his spectacles. He snapped it shut. "Chloe, there is evidence here. Plenty of it."

"But you've got the wrong man!" Chloe exploded. Will flinched next to her, his shackles clinking.

"Lower your tone, young lady." The King warned.

Chloe saw sense then—screaming at her father and embarrassing him in front of the other Nobles was probably doing nothing to help her cause. But as she watched the other Nobles in the room, she saw that what she'd said was already haunting them. Some Noblemen's eyes had glazed over, already thinking about what was at risk if Chloe's prediction came true. She knew most of them would do at least something that was illegal. If the Defenders caught the people doing their dirty work for them and then they caved and gave up the Nobles' names to save themselves, then higher, richer heads would roll.

Chloe took a calming breath, "Your Majesty, I apologize for my outburst," Chloe said, eyes lowered in a sign of submission. "But Will did not commit this crime."

"How can you be so sure?" the King asked, flipping the case file open and assessing it again. "There is evidence that points to the contrary here."

"Because...." Chloe searched for the words. She steeled her spine as resolve set in. "Because I was with him."

The Nobles gasps of horror echoed around the chamber. The King turned yet another, deeper shade of purple. "What?"

"Not like that, Father. I'm still pure; I promise you."

"And you can prove that?" He hissed.

Chloe swallowed. "Of course."

"W-What were you doing outside the palace walls?" The king looked terrified that his seventeen-year-old daughter had outsmarted every security measure he'd put in place to protect her. "There could've been a Shadow-lander attack! You know they've been happening more often! You could've been killed, and the monarchy ruined! Do you have any idea how many people in this city want you dead?"

"I-I'm so sorry. It was the first time I'd ever done it." The lie slipped off her tongue. "I just wanted to have some fun. And then I saw the abduction happen."

"At *Hell's Gate*?" The King roared. The Nobles glanced at one another in shock. Chloe kept her head down and nodded in assent. "Yes. Will tried to help Elaine. I swear on my life I'm telling the truth."

"Forgive me, but your honesty does not mean much right now." The King scoffed.

The King's eyes darted around the room to the other Nobles. There was no way that the King could execute him now. Not with the Nobles as witnesses to her testimony. Chloe had to admit it; she felt rather pleased with herself. It had been a massive risk to admit she'd been there, but this could be a huge win for her.

She might even get some Nobles on her side now and take down the Games for good.

"Will Albridge," The king began, "you've broken the law by not handing yourself in. You had Miss Stephens' DNA all over you, and your case file also mentions testimony that witnesses at *Madame Butterfly's* said you were there and *on edge*. And despite my daughter's protests, you were with her..." He glared at his daughter. Chloe felt the urge to sink away and disappear into one of the grand paintings behind her under his hard stare. "There's no footage to prove this. All the clues point to you, but if you attest that it was not him, Chloe?"

"I do," Chloe said.

"Then I will not execute him."

Chloe moved toward her father, relief spreading throughout her body. "Thank you, Father -"

"I was not finished." The King put his hand up to Chloe, who fell silent.

"The Defenders are still convinced he committed this crime, and my daughter has deceived me already. She could deceive me again for her own wicked means. But, William, only God may judge you now. He will prove your innocence or guilt."

He turned on his heel and walked toward his desk. "So, your sentence must be one that only God can save you from," the King said. Chloe and Will glanced at one another in confusion. The King then barked out, "I sentence you, Will Albridge, to the Vessel Games."

"No!" Chloe screamed, "You can't do that!"

The King returned to where Will and Chloe stood with incredible speed for such a large man. "I'll do whatever I please. I am the *King*. I am God on Earth." He rose to his full height, and Chloe almost cowered back from him—almost —she didn't recognise her own father in this man. He was a stranger.

A cruel, hard stranger.

"Chloe, you best go pray your sins away to Father Jeremiah at confession, before we make sure that you are still pure. If you are not," his pudgy finger pointed at Chloe. "May God have mercy on your sinful soul."

Chloe stared around her at the other Nobles, hoping for someone to help her father see sense. She'd played the game all wrong. So much for her delusional thoughts of her political prowess.

What he could do as the chosen conduit of God on Earth... this was a perfect opportunity to show the other Lords how powerful he was. To show exactly who ran this city. The king continued, "If he is indeed innocent, as you say, God will protect him during the Games. If he survives, then God has proven that he has not sinned, and I'll absolve his record of any wrong-doings." Her father had the power to sentence anyone to death. When he wanted, where he wanted.

After all, he was King.

It was a power that Chloe would never have. She was a woman and unfit to rule. Someone deemed *lesser*. The man her father chose for her to marry would have more authority than she would, despite her bloodline, and all because of her gender. Every Noble in this room wanted their son to be her husband, to be the future King. They would never side with her she realized with horror. Not while they wanted his favor. Not while they wanted the throne for themselves.

"If he is guilty, however, the Lord's might will be just and swift," the King added.

Chloe could not hold back her tears any longer. Her father had betrayed her. The tears ran down her face in torrents, but she refused to wipe them away. "You know he hasn't got a chance in hell. This isn't justice. God won't decide Will's fate! *You've* decided."

Chloe's eyes went wide when she realized what she'd done. She'd insinuated her father and God were not one and the same.

Blasphemy.

The room was still for a moment, the shock of what had just come out of Chloe's mouth palpable amongst everyone here.

"Watch yourself, daughter," the King said with quiet rage.

Another agonizing moment came as the King decided what to do next. With his audience—the Nobles—here, it was a tricky game for him to play. What Chloe had just said was unforgivable from anyone else.

"Your brother would be ashamed of your behavior." The King hissed. Chloe reeled back as if his comment were a physical blow. "If you spent more time following instructions rather than ignoring them, perhaps he would be here still."

Chloe's eyes burned. It was the worst thing he possibly could've said. Chloe had always blamed herself for Arthur's death... if she'd just gone and gotten help... if she'd thought faster... The tears now fell down her face in torrents, her lip trembling with emotion.

"Father... I'm sorry—"

"Get out of my sight," the King barked at her. "Wait for your repentance. Father Jeremiah will come to deliver it to you. Not even a princess can escape her duty to God."

Chloe curtseyed low before looking up at her father. "I'll never forgive you." She hissed.

The King knew how much Chloe hated the brutality of

the Games, how much she wanted them to end. This punishment was as much hers as it was Will's.

"Go." The King waved her away, holding his temples and closing his eyes. "And James, take our new contestant to a cell."

CHAPTER
NINE

Chloe sat on her bed, awaiting her punishment. They'd already tested her purity, as her father had insisted upon. Chloe thought she'd had her father cornered. She should have known that he'd been playing this game for much longer than she had, and he was more skilled at it. Now, Will was bound for the Games.

Will would die because of *her*.

The Games had grown in popularity over the past ten years, and Nobles trained for years before they competed. Will was just a Craftsman Caste. Even if Will managed to get into a lower round with a weaker group, the King would have plans in place to stop him from surviving. Hell, he might even plant Nobles in Will's round and pay them off to kill Will first. The King had given this punishment to Will because he knew Chloe would hate it, and he'd been right.

But Chloe wasn't going to let her father win this without putting up a fight. She just needed to think of a plan. Chloe almost jumped out of her skin when the knock on the door sounded. Father Jeremiah peered around the corner of the door.

"You're here to make sure I do it, aren't you?" She asked, and his eyes were sorrowful as he nodded.

"Chloe—" Father Jeremiah began, but Chloe stopped him.

"Wait outside. You'll be able to hear it from out there." Chloe murmured.

Father Jeremiah looked like he wanted to say more, but he nodded pensively and clicked Chloe's bedroom door shut again.

Chloe sighed as she unbuttoned the front of her dress. Then, she peeled off her underclothes, trying to ignore the thick fog of dread that enveloped her. She could see her reflection in the mirror as she picked up the whip.

"We must pay for our sins in flesh," Chloe said, loud enough for Father Jeremiah to hear her outside; she didn't want to do this bullshit a second time.

She recited the High Priest's prayer, confessed her sins, and took a deep breath. Chloe knew Father Jeremiah would come to check the marks on her, so she'd have to do this correctly.

She'd have to make it hurt.

"Daddy said it's dangerous for you to go to the river swing alone." Chloe said, her nose tilting up at her brother. "He and Mamma said that if you ever went back there without them, I'm to be a good girl and tell on you."

Her brother's ice-blue eyes met her own, a naughtiness sparkling in the depths of them. "But if you tell on me, how will you ever go on the swing yourself? I know you want to. And I'll bring you with me. We won't be alone. We'll be together, see? It'll be fun."

"But Mamma said the rope won't hold—"

"The rope will hold. Mamma is being a worrywart. If you come with me, I promise to show you that card trick. It's not

really magic like I told you. It's an illusion." Arthur reached over to Chloe's ear, and from nowhere, a coin appeared. Chloe's eyes widened.

"How did you do that?"

"Well, I'll show you later if you come. But you can't tell Mamma and Pappa about my magic tricks either. That sort of thing isn't allowed." Arthur arched one eyebrow in question. "So, are you with me?"

Chloe looked behind her, to where James, her bodyguard, sat talking to Arthur's bodyguard. They were both completely distracted.

"Just this once." Chloe grinned.

"Come on!" Her brother grabbed her hand, as they darted through the palace gardens.

Chloe always followed her brother anywhere he went. But she'd never gotten to go with him to the river swing before. That place had always been for his friends and him only. Until recently, when the Duke of Northumberland's son had fallen and broken his leg; that was when Mamma and Daddy had forbidden it. Still almost despite them, Arthur ran on, over-taking her. She could see the long rope with the plank of wood seat dangling in the cool breeze and the river bubbling angrily below.

"I want to go on it first! I'm six now. You should let me," Chloe moaned.

"No. I'm the oldest. Me first." Arthur jumped onto the swing, glancing back at her with mischief dancing on his features. "I'll only be a second."

I'll only be a second. That's what he'd said.

Arthur ran at the swing and jumped onto it at pace. He laughed louder as he flew higher in the air. Chloe gasped, marveling at how high he'd gone. He must have been far braver than she was. Arthur clung tightly to the rope on his way back *down. But the rope snapped, and Arthur flew through the air, his arms outstretched, as if hoping to grab onto something.*

"Arty!" Chloe had cried.

Arthur fell further, and as he descended, so had Chloe's stomach. He was falling from such a horrible height. Another crack. Chloe flinched and shut her eyes in fright. When she dared to open them again, a large rock in the river was painted in blood. Arthur's motionless body was face down in the river and being pulled relentlessly away from her by the current. Chloe tried to move her limbs, to scream for help and run toward him.

But she remained motionless, frozen in shock and fear.

"Arthur!" her mother screamed, appearing and pushing past Chloe. But Chloe had known it then—her mother was too late.

The last King of their line had died before he'd even lived. And it was all her fault. She'd done nothing to save him. If she'd only followed instructions... if she hadn't disobeyed her father's wishes...

Chloe shivered at the memory and picked up the cat-o'-nine-tails. Her back tingled despite there being no lashes there yet. And now, because of her disobedience, an innocent boy would suffer the same fate as her brother. And all she'd be able to do was watch from the sidelines. Again. A single tear trickled down her face as she gazed in the mirror.

"Forgive me." But as she went to work punishing herself for her sins, it was not God she was asking forgiveness from.

~

WILL WAS HUDDLED in a corner on the freezing concrete floor.

They hadn't given him a swab to sleep on in the cell.

His head hung low as he sat against the wall, legs pressed into his chest. His mum would wonder where he was by now—he'd never even gotten to say goodbye. Will swallowed at the thought of what awaited him once the Ceremony was over. Once the rest of the boys were selected to compete the Games would begin, starting with the Ranking.

Will knew deep in his heart that he didn't stand a chance at winning. Nobles trained relentlessly for a chance at a Vessel wife. Nowadays, it was almost a rite of passage for them. Any Common Castes that competed tended to be so desperate that they were dangerous, or they'd been training from a young age too. Boys could only compete between the ages of eighteen and twenty years old, and Will certainly hadn't intended to sign up to compete. Most Common Castes knew it was a death sentence if you did, so they avoided it at all costs.

His cell door swung open with a creak, and two hooded figures moved into the cell.

"Thank you," a light voice said to the guard who had accompanied them, placing cash in his hand. "You have my protection if anyone finds out. But they'll only find out if you tell them. Understood?"

The man nodded, counting the money she'd placed in his hand.

The figures lowered their hoods, and it shocked Will to see Princess Chloe and Karina standing before him. "K-Karina." Will stuttered, still put on edge by her beauty. "I... I looked for you."

"You found the ring?" Karina said, her eyes widening.

"Yeah, and the man who took Elaine had the same ring on," Will said.

Chloe nodded, as if this had been what she suspected.

Chloe produced a piece of paper and a pencil from her pocket. "Can you draw it for us, Karina?"

Karina sank down to the floor and shivered. "God, it's freezing in here."

She took out her pencil from her pocket and sketched. She was a talented artist. She might have done well as a Craftsman Caste.

"My mother," Will said, remembering himself. "She's got severe arthritis, and can't do much with her hands. I've been hiding her condition from the other Craftsman around, no one knows how bad it's gotten. She'll be wondering where I am. Is it possible to get to her?" He looked in hope toward Chloe, who shook her head, chewing on her lower lip.

"I'm.... grounded," she said. "These cells that you're in are still in the inner sanctum. The walls now lead to the outer city and the districts, and they're all guarded. *Especially* from me."

"I don't want her to reveal herself. If people find out..." Will trailed off. Common Castes that suffered with similar afflictions tended to disappear in New London and were never seen again.

"I'll go," Karina said, looking up from her sketching.

Will met Karina's soft eyes, "Thank you. And after the Games, when I'm gone..."

"No. That's not going to happen." Chloe shook her head. "That's why I bought you two here. I've got a plan." Will rocked back on his heels in shock. The princess had a *plan*? To help *him*? He leaned closer. "If the evidence is insurmountable, and if we find evidence that proves you didn't harm Elaine, then my father will *have* to relieve you from the Vessel Games. He wants God to judge your innocence or guilt. So, we *need to prove your innocence first*. We need either a confession from the perpetrator, or we need to find Elaine and get the full story. Then, she can tell the King herself you didn't do it. And he'll *have* to free you from competing."

Will couldn't help but feel a little deflated at this grand plan of Chloe's. It seemed like a horrendously difficult task. To find a girl who'd been kidnapped or to find the real perpetrator behind these attacks. Will couldn't see how the three of them—a Vessel, a competitor, and a grounded Princess—could pull something like that off.

Karina paused in her sketching from the floor. "You want to find Elaine? What if...."

"She's not dead. You told me when you got taken that the man didn't even hurt you. They wanted you both for something. And that ring... that ring is our first clue."

Will didn't understand why, but despite his reservations about Chloe's plan, a strange warm feeling bloomed in his chest. The Princess was fighting for him. She believed him, a nothing Common Caste. Maybe this world wasn't so screwed after all.

Will looked at his newfound comrades with something that felt a lot like hope.

"That's the first piece of the puzzle we need to figure out, but we've got to work fast," Chloe said. "We only have a few days until the Ceremony, and then a few days after that, the Games start. It's all downhill from there. So, let's get to work."

CHAPTER
TEN

Karina understood it was going to be a hard sell. But she didn't expect the Queen to be so... cold about it.

"Please, Your Highness. I knew Will before the King sentenced him. His mum will worry about him. I just want to check to see if she's okay."

"Vessels cannot leave the palace under any circumstances other than to watch the Games. It's for your safety. Too many things could go wrong. Unloyal Common Castes, Traitor Castes... Shadowlanders..." The Queen shuddered, not looking up from her desk.

Karina felt entranced as she watched the Queen scan the pages on her desk. She wondered what it would be like to read an actual book.

"I can take a full protection detail." Karina pressed.

"It's far too dangerous for someone of your importance. Besides, you'll miss your deportment lessons, darling heart. Today is dance class. We have a ball straight after the Ceremony. You'll do well to remember it's only a few days away."

A few days away. Right. Karina tried not to ignore the hopelessness that threatened to engulf her. After the Ceremony and the Ranking, the Games would begin. And depending on what round Will is ranked in... they needed to find Elaine before his round.

"But, Your Highness—"

"I said no," she replied sharply. "See you at dance class in two hours."

It took all of Karina's restraint to nod in assent and leave quietly.

Chloe waited for her outside, leaning up against a wall, as she examined her nails with a bored expression. Karina strode past her so quickly that Chloe had to jog to keep up.

"So, I'm guessing that was a no," Chloe said, lifting her skirts higher in pursuit of Karina.

"How do you not go insane? They won't let us go anywhere," Karina said. "Will's mum'll be going out of her mind with worry. No one's even bothering to tell her 'oh by the way, your son is being forced to compete in the Vessel Games by the King thanks to him trying to teach his daughter a lesson in humility.'"

"Welcome to my world," Chloe said, a tightness in her voice.

Karina avoided Chloe's gaze—she'd let slip what Karina had been holding in from Chloe— that Will's sentence was just a tactic to teach Chloe a lesson. To force her into submission. Because of that, Chloe clearly felt responsible for Will, and Karina understood exactly why. She'd gotten him into this whole mess in the first place.

"Sorry, Princess. I didn't mean..."

Chloe shook her head. "The only thing you need to be sorry for is calling me 'Princess.'" She placed a hand on

Karina's shoulder. Chloe stopped then, a roguish grin spreading across her face. Karina followed her gaze—the palace's laundry van hummed by the gates, ready to head out to the Craftsman District. There was a young raven-haired woman folding laundry behind the van. "You see her?" Chloe nudged her head at the raven-haired girl. "That's Tiffany, my friend from the outside... she helps me... with some lessons. I reckon she'd be able to get you out to see Will's mum."

"Damn, you're always looking for escape routes, aren't you?" Karina grinned back.

"I'd take that one if I could, but there are too many eyes on me. My prime time for escape is in darkness," Chloe said, not taking her eyes away from Tiffany, who carried laundry into the back of the van.

"Why do you sneak out anyway?" Karina asked, curiosity getting the better of her.

Chloe averted her gaze, her mind elsewhere, an expression of deep sorrow spreading across her face. She then seemed to notice that Karina was assessing her, trying to figure her out.... Chloe's mask clicked back on, firmly in place.

"It's like you said: this palace can be a prison. Sneaking out gives me something that feels like... freedom."

Karina couldn't help but think there was something Chloe wasn't telling her, but she let it drop.

Chloe and Karina nonchalantly strolled toward Tiffany. Tiffany's eyes lit up when she saw the two girls. "Chlo!" Tiffany said, jogging toward them. Chloe shook her head a little, as if reminding Tiffany exactly where she was. "Oh... yes, um, hello Princess." Tiffany fell into a clumsy curtsey. "My lady." She then curtseyed to Karina.

"I have strict instructions from the Queen on exactly how the Queen likes her sheets," Chloe said, a little too loudly. "Come here." When they were all firmly behind the van and hidden from the other servants who moved about the courtyard, Chloe finally let her strict veneer drop. "Hey Tiff," Chloe whispered, her eyes dancing with excitement. "I've got a job for you. You need to help my friend Karina get in and out of the palace today, okay?"

Tiffany's eyes widened in disbelief. "Are you *insane*, Chloe? Do you know how much trouble I could get into for that?"

Karina looked between the two girls. There was such comradery, such ease between the two of them, that it almost shocked Karina. Chloe was just so... incredibly... *normal.*

"C'mon, Tiff. I'll owe you. I'll cover for you back here, Karina," Chloe added. "Take this same van back into the palace. They shouldn't be longer than two hours, right Tiff?"

Tiffany glowered in response.

"Go!" Chloe ordered. She gave Karina a tiny shove and spun on her heel. Karina surveyed the scene. Palace staff were around, so Karina couldn't see how she'd be able to get inside the van undetected until—

"What on earth is this?" Chloe's voice feigned disbelief.

All eyes were on the princess, and Karina seized her chance. She launched herself into the van and found a laundry basket large enough to fit her whole body into. Tiffany helped pile clothes on her, making sure she was hidden completely.

"Don't say a word." Tiffany hissed. "Or we're both screwed. Got it?"

Tiffany moved out of the back of the van and slammed

the doors. The thunderous crack of the van door made her palms slick with sweat. There was no going back now. Karina's fear was palpable, but as she peered out the van window, she locked eyes with Chloe. The royal looked like a perfectly demure princess taking a stroll in the courtyard. But Karina saw the excitement, the hunger in Chloe's eyes when she glanced at Karina's hiding place. It took little imagination to know that Chloe was wishing it'd been *her* instead of Karina moving off into the unknown.

Escape must have been what Chloe lived for.

~

KARINA'S NERVES were taut the entire journey into the Craftsman District. As soon as the van shuddered to a stop, she heard Tiffany yell: "I'll get it!"

Tiffany yanked open the sliding doors. "Be back here in ninety minutes. *Go!*"

Karina launched herself out of the vehicle and made a run for it.

"Thanks," she breathed to Tiffany as she whooshed past her.

Tiffany just rolled her eyes. She was no doubt very familiar with Chloe's schemes if she knew her well, and Karina suspected Chloe had perhaps pushed her friend a little too far this time.

Karina had commandeered a jacket from the laundry pile that had that sharp tang of sweat, but it was large enough to hide her fine dress and her Vessel necklace underneath it. Karina glanced back to see a woman scratching her head in confusion at the van's open doors. Karina pulled her hood up. No one gave her a second glance as she trotted through the streets. *She'd done it.*

The Craftsman District had always been her favorite place in New London. The streets bustled, and people moved through the District with purpose. Unlike in the Traitor slums, the Craftsmen around here all looked busy.

Farmer Castes were here too, selling the little wares they had left after the Nobles took their cut. Karina thought back to the obscene amount of wealth in the Noble district, and what a contrast it was to what she'd witnessed in the palace so far. At her first dinner with the Vessels, for example, the other Vessels had picked at their plates, barely eating anything. Karina made up for them, though, eating so much that she'd felt ill. The maid had said that the food would be thrown away if she didn't, and Karina couldn't bear to see it go to waste.

As she scanned the Craftsmen walking through this district, she noticed that this Caste was hungry, too. She knew that empty look; she understood it well.

"Coming through!" A flower boy shouted.

Karina fished in the coat's pocket she'd commandeered and was pleased to find a handful of coins. "Can I buy one?" Karina asked.

"Sure, lady." He examined her. "Have I met you somewhere?"

"No, nowhere," Karina said.

She flung a coin at him to catch and snatched a rose from his cart. *Damn.* She'd forgotten that her entrance to the palace had been filmed. Most people would have tuned in on the large TVs that had been set up around New London, especially for the Games. Karina kept her head down to the floor after that.

～

KARINA LOOKED TOWARD THE SKY, trying to remember the instructions Will had given her. He'd seemed more worried about his mother than he did himself. When Karina had looked into his eyes, she'd seen... a softness. Kindness.

Karina kept her head down as she waded through the busy street. When she'd made it, her heels were dirty, and the bottom of her dress was sopping wet. She was going to have a hard time explaining how she'd gotten dirty upon her return. She shook off the thought. Will's mum would be worried sick about him, and that was more important. She'd figure out the rest later.

The van would return to the palace soon, and that was her ticket back into the inner sanctum. Karina knocked at the door of the flat, but it swung wide with a creak, unlocked. "Li Jing?" Karina called. "Li Jing, are you here?"

The house was dark.

Karina stalked down the hall and into the kitchen. Every single drawer was open, their entire contents splayed out on the grimy floor. A piercing scream had Karina spinning on her heels in fright. The woman brandished a candlestick—despite her disfigured hands—-and swung out at Karina. Karina ducked, dropping the flower she'd bought for Will's mother in fright, and getting out of the way just in time.

"Who are you?" The woman screamed, swinging out again. "What are you doing in my house?"

"I'm Karina!" Karina ducked away from the next blow. "I won't hurt you!"

"You're taking me away to hurt me, aren't you?"

"No!" Karina caught the candlestick as the woman went to hit her again.

She swung her leg out, and, rendered unbalanced, the woman tripped. Karina threw the candlestick to the side and looked down at Li Jing, who was now sprawled on the floor.

"I'm not trying to hurt you! I know where Will is."

"My William? You know what's happened to him?" She scrambled to her feet. "I've been worried sick."

"I'm Karina, and I'm a friend of Will's, He told me to visit you, told me to tell you, *"Wǒ ài nǐ."*"

Li Jing blinked at Karina rapidly. *"I love you."* She whispered. Karina guessed that what she'd just said was *I love you* in Li Jing's mother tongue. There was a sudden tightness in Karina's chest. Li Jing sank to the floor. "I'm so tired. But I can't sleep, I'm in such pain, Karina." Will thought she'd say this. He'd thought of everything—he'd told Karina where to find her pain medication so she'd be able to get some rest.

"I know Li Jing. I'm going to help you with that. Sit tight, okay?"

Li Jing shrugged and slumped onto the floor. Karina glanced at her hands, twisted, and unable to help her cook, clean...Karina wished that she could stay here and look after her. "Will...is he home soon?"

"Yes." Karina lied, not knowing what else to say. "Something's come up and he'll be away for a few weeks." Karina rifled through the contents of the house for what seemed like an eternity. Finally, she spotted a small pill container. Karina found a glass and filled it with the small amount of water ration that remained in their fridge.

"When's your next water ration due?" Karina frowned.

"I don't know. Will looks after that stuff."

Karina handed the pill to Li Jing, who took it. Then, Karina worked on the apartment. She did her best to make the place look clean and somewhat respectable. It was marginally better than her family's flat in the traitor slums. And twice the price, she noticed, as she put one of Will's rent bills back into a kitchen drawer. Karina ushered Li Jing to the ruined couch. The sleeping pills had worked, and she'd grown drowsy, so Karina placed a blanket over her.

"That's better now. Thank you." Li Jing whispered.

"Will—he'll be back soon. Someone will come over to help you take your pills until then. They'll make sure that your water and food rations get delivered, okay?" Li Jing's snore reverberated around the room in response. Karina couldn't just... leave her. Li Jing was so panicked when she'd arrived, and with Will gone, someone needed to stick around and make sure she was okay.

Karina had to get back to the palace before anyone realized she was gone. But she'd have to find another way back into the inner-sanctum. She knew that she'd miss Tiffany and the laundry van now, because there was one more thing she needed to do.

She just hoped no one would recognise her.

~

KARINA WAS RUNNING out of time—she had a grand total of thirty minutes to figure out how to get from the slums, back to Hell's Gate, through the Noble district, and into the palace undetected. But Karina couldn't bear the thought of leaving Will's mum there all alone.

"Karina!" Marcus' eyes bulged as he opened the door. "What are you doing here?"

"I don't have much time," Karina said. "Where's Ma and Uncle Frank?"

"Working. I'm still trying to find a new job. But we got some money sent to us. I have a funny feeling that was thanks to you," Marcus said, slumping against the doorway with his arms crossed.

"It is. Now, are you gonna let me in?" she asked. He stepped aside, and she pushed her hood down, giving him a quick hug. "Marcus, there's a woman called Li Jing in the Craftsman District. My friend, Will, wrote the address for you." Karina handed it to Marcus, feeling somewhat icy about the fact he simply glanced down and read it with such speed. Will had to repeat the directions to her over ten times. He'd given her the sheet of paper with the address on it, and Karina hadn't bothered to correct him that it was all but useless to her. "She's got bad arthritis, and she needs to have her medication every day."

"Okay?" Marcus said, taking the note that Karina held out toward him and examining it. "They usually Craftsman Castes that can't work with their hands..."

"Disappear. I know. I'll get the money for her next round of meds. You need to make sure she takes them every day. Okay?"

Marcus nodded, pocketing the piece of paper. "Why are you doing this?"

"Will is a friend." Karina paused. "Have you heard anything about Elaine?"

Marcus shook his head, a worried frown on his face. "It's like... she's just... disappeared into thin air."

"I'm working with someone to figure out what happened to her. I'll keep you updated." Karina grabbed Marcus and he enveloped her into a tight bear hug. She breathed in her brother's familiar scent. The next time she saw Marcus, she'd be at the Ceremony. She gulped at the thought.

~

KARINA JOGGED through the Traitor slums as fast as her heels would allow. The first step to return to the palace undetected was to get past the guard at Hell's Gate. She waited a few moments, watched his movements, and then, when she thought he was sufficiently distracted, she slipped past.

"Oi!" The yell forced her heart to leap into her mouth. She continued walking toward the other side of Hell's Gate —her entrance to the Noble District—as casually as possible.

Who was to say he was yelling at her?

She could still make it. A rough hand landed on her shoulder. *Oh.* So he *had* been yelling at her. Maybe he hadn't been as distracted as she'd hoped. She needed a sleuthing lesson from Chloe.

"You need your I. D. card to get through Hell's Gate, Miss." The Defender sneered.

"I-I've lost it," Karina said, her eyes wide.

"Too bad. Anyone without an I. D. card will be taken to Defender headquarters for questioning." He looked at her with a hungry lust that made Karina's knees go wobbly. It was common knowledge that there were no cameras at headquarters. They did whatever the fuck they wanted, with whomever they wanted.

Karina *had* to get away from him. But she couldn't tell him who she really was. She shuddered to think of what the Queen would do if she found out about her little expedition. She couldn't reveal she was a Vessel. Not without damning herself.

A scream erupted from across the alleyway.

Karina's head snapped around to the source in panic. Figures scattered around Hell's Gate had removed their hoods. The black markings around their eyes stood out against their sharp features. They reached under their cloaks—swords, bows, and axes emerged.

"Shit," the Defender said, releasing her from his grasp.

Karina didn't have time to feel grateful that she'd evaded him. She was in the middle of a Shadowlander attack.

CHAPTER
ELEVEN

"Shadowlanders!" The man next to her screamed, "To your stations, Defenders!"

Karina threw off the Defender's hand from her shoulder and made a run for it.

The streets were already bathed in blood.

Much to her relief, it wasn't long before the sound of gunshots boomed and cracked across the streets. There might have been fewer Defenders here, but they possessed the upper hand. Shadowlanders didn't use rifles. They mustn't have had access to that sort of thing beyond the walls of New London, so they opted for more savage options—knives, bows, and axes. Mostly edge weapons, easily fashioned and hidden.

But the Defenders sure had higher caliber firepower on hand. Literally.

A woman sat on the pavement, rocking and praying. A Shadowlander slit her throat with a grin that made Karina's stomach drop to the floor in dread. Karina stared in shock, her muscles unable to move for a moment. The man was looking at her now, sizing up his next victim.

He cocked his head in an animalistic motion and stalked toward her. Karina backed away from him, her eyes wide. She bumped into something then. Something hard. Something unyielding.

She turned to see another Shadowlander man grinning at her.

"Pretty thing," he said in a strange, thick accent. He caressed her face with a hunger that made acid build in Karina's gut.

Karina kneed him in the balls as hard as she could. But it was no use. When he collapsed in pain, the man behind her had already caught up to them. He grabbed hold of Karina, and despite her kicking and screaming, none of the Defenders fighting came to her aid. They were all too distracted by killing the Shadowlanders rather than protecting those caught in the crossfire.

"Please!" she screamed as the men began dragging her away to a dark corner of the street. "Please help me!"

Karina begged, a muffled cry escaping her throat as the man holding her placed a hand over her mouth. They chuckled at her screaming, crying, and begging, even as they dragged her back farther still.

Karina saw one Defender look her dead in the eye, but he turned away, opting to protect the bags of grain and meat that the Shadowlanders had already begun hauling away toward the outer wall. He'd seen her. *He'd looked straight at her.* But Karina's life was less valuable to him than a bag of grain. Karina sobbed in desperation, her bladder giving way in her fright, wetting her dress.

The men who were holding her cackled as they noticed her incontinence—she'd almost been dragged all the way to the corner. They threw her on the ground, unbuckling their belts, leering over her. They'd use her and then dispose of her.

But Karina had one last hope.

She kicked out as hard as she could and clambered away from the shadows of the corner.

"I'm a Vessel!" Her scream rang out, and a Defender at the watch tower turned toward her. "Look!" She ripped the pearl necklace from her throat, the necklace that held her status and her value to the Kingdoms. She dangled the golden "V" in his view. "Help me!"

The Defender on the watchtower aimed for the man who had seized her, and the Shadowlander fell limply to the ground as the gunshot rang out. Another Defender sprinted toward her and lifted his riot mask. He couldn't be much older than she was.

"My Lady! Are you alright? Why are you not in the Noble District? It was locked down after the attack began."

Of course.

The reason there were so few Defenders in Hell's Gate was because most had moved to defend the Noble District. That's where all the Vessels, victors, and their young families lived, after all. The future of the human race was not in Hell's Gate.

"I-I..." Karina stammered. "I've yet to be married. I'm going to be competed for in the next Games, and I'm staying at the palace."

His eyes widened in shock. "You mean to say you aren't married to a victor who can protect you? I need to return you to the palace immediately. Let me get my superior." He motioned to the man in the watchtower that had come to her aid. "We'll take you back."

The Defender turned and fired a few shots at the

retreating Shadowlanders, keeping Karina well covered behind him.

"No, please don't tell anyone I'm out here. I'll get in trouble." Karina begged.

"I'm sorry, My Lady, but we must report this."

Karina sighed, resigned to her fate. She'd gone against a direct order from a monarch. She was going to have hell to pay.

~

CHLOE COULD DO nothing but watch as Karina shuffled into the magnificent throne room. Her dress hung off her, tattered and dirty. Her Vessel necklace hung limply in her hand. Her cheeks were streaked with tears, and her dress was wet below the waist. Chloe's step-mother sat on the throne next to her, tapping her long nails on the throne's armrest.

The King barely looked up from the newspaper he was reading. Karina approached the dais and curtseyed. Chloe noticed her hands were shaking.

"Your...Your majesty, I..." Karina started.

"I did not permit you to speak." The King's voice was icy with rage. Karina fell silent. The Queen launched herself from her throne and went to Karina.

"Are you hurt?" The Queen asked as Karina shook her head, her lip trembling. The Queen patted at her arms, fussing over her. "You could've been killed in that attack. You are the most precious thing to this country, Karina. I told you not to go. Why would you disobey your Queen?"

The final question came out with a sharpness that Chloe hadn't heard her step-mother use before.

"No, I..."

The Queen's mouth became a thin line. "Karina, darling. You've violated a direct order from me. And therefore, God himself."

Chloe's hands balled into fists with the effort of keeping her mouth shut. If Chloe said anything that defended Karina's actions, then even more of her freedom might be taken from her. Perhaps she'd get confined to her room entirely. And that was not something she could afford right now. She needed to move around the palace freely; it was the only way she could figure out what happened to Elaine and save Will from the Games.

But it didn't make it any easier to witness Karina taking the fall for something that had been her idea. Chloe cursed her recklessness. The Queen was right; Karina could've been killed, and it would've been all her fault.

"The people adore you,." the King said. "You are quite the... distraction from their daily drudgery, Karina. It's so exciting for them to see someone like themselves elevated. You've won the genetic lottery. And I will give you riches beyond your imagination. But *they* feel like they've won too. That's good for contentment levels in our Kingdoms."

Karina didn't look up from the floor.

"What is not good for New London, however, is if anyone found out you escaped out of the palace with neither permission nor purpose. To go against God's wishes and have no consequences. If anyone knew.... well... you could start another Uprising single-handedly, Traitor." He spat the word. "Then you'd really live up to your father's legacy."

"Your Highness," Karina whispered, "I'm sorry, my intention was to..."

"Who else did you meet?" the King asked.

"No one."

"Karina, tell me the truth," the King ordered.

"Only my brother. I... missed him. That's all."

"Is this true?" the Queen asked the two Defenders who had rescued her. "Did anyone else other than you two hear that she was a Vessel?"

The men bowed. "No, your majesty. If anyone else had heard, they would've dropped everything to get her to safety."

"You've served the United Kingdoms well." The Queen stood and glided over to them. She collected the young boys' faces in her hands, assessing them both in turn. "Handsome, too."

Chloe held her breath for what she knew was to come.

"James? Execute them both and throw them over the outer wall."

"No!" Chloe screamed in horror. "They did nothing wrong!" Chloe marched down toward the Queen. "Admit them both to my personal guard. They'll never leave the palace anyway, then. They'll have no opportunity to tell anyone what happened with Karina."

Both men were on their knees, praying and shaking.

"And what then, Chloe? What if they sold that information to the highest bidder? If people knew how easily Karina escaped, many would see us as weak. Will see that we can be *touched*. That we are vulnerable." The Queen shivered.

"She's right," the King said, "Have you not learned anything from your history lessons? King Louis XVI. Charles I. The goddamned Tsar of Russia. You give the common rabble an inch, and they will take a mile." Her father turned to the two men. "Your families will be well looked after."

"Please, Father," Chloe begged in earnest now. "This

isn't who you are. This isn't who you were when Mamma was alive."

The slap that landed on Chloe's face echoed around the room with a cruel finality.

"I was weak, and because of that, they killed your mother. I will never be weak again. Not while I have you to protect."

The King looked at James. "Do as the Queen ordered, James."

The hulk of a man behind Chloe walked toward the men. Karina slumped to the floor and began crying.

"Never disobey me again," the Queen snapped. "Do you understand?"

"Yes, yes. I understand." Karina whimpered, tears flooding her face.

"I'll spare your brother this time," the King said, returning to his throne. "But if you disobey the crown again, he will suffer the same fate. Do you understand me? You must tell him not to speak a word of your visit."

Chloe stood, her horror warping into rage as she heard the screams of the men outside the throne room. They were begging for mercy, pleading with God to save them.

But they don't realize, Chloe thought bitterly, as she tore her crown off her head and threw it on the floor.

This was a godless place.

CHAPTER

TWELVE

"Karina, darling. *One,* two, three. *One,* two, three. You're missing the first beat completely," the Queen chastised.

After Karina's ordeal yesterday, the Queen had insisted she get *back on the horse* with her deportment lessons and continue on with the ballroom dancing lessons she missed out on the other day.

There were five girls, and when the other Vessels had been told to pair up, the twins grabbed one another's hands. Sarah and Anne looked at each other and grinned.

So, Karina had to dance with the Queen. Karina frowned at the Queen who waltzed with such ease and grace. She didn't even seem to *remember* the terrible events of yesterday, which would be forever burned in Karina's mind. There'd been no further mention of the two guards that had saved her from the Shadowlanders and been murdered for it.

Karina stepped on the Queen's foot for what felt like the thirtieth time.

"Sorry!" Karina said yet again.

Karina was useless at dancing; it was as if she had two left feet.

The Queen examined her with an unimpressed sigh. "Okay, Karina. I think you need a man to guide you; they have much less delicate feet than I. I'll see if one of the King's Noblemen is around, and maybe they can come and dance with you for a bit." She smiled, an expression of kindness painted on her face.

Karina knew it was just a farce though—these royals were cruel and cold—even Chloe. Karina was furious she'd let Chloe convince her to leave the palace without a guard, that everything would be fine. Now, two men were dead. And they'd almost *killed* her brother for what she'd done.

The Queen sped out of the room, her emerald dress flying behind her, with a bit of a limp in her step. Karina sighed with relief, but that relief quickly morphed to dread when Sarah and Rachel stopped dancing and turned toward her, ice in their expressions.

"You don't belong here," Sarah blurted. "We've all been talking about it. You don't deserve to marry another victor."

Karina stood, shifting from one foot to another. "Well, I can bear children, like you, so I think you'll find that I do deserve to marry a victor."

"I think they made a mistake," Rachel said, prowling toward her.

"Rachel..." Louisa warned her sister.

"You'll never be accepted into Noble society. No one will ever take you seriously. You're just a prized mare, nothing more."

Karina swallowed, forcing the stinging tears that begged to be released down. Sarah joined Rachel, circling Karina as if she were prey.

"Rachel's right, you know," Sarah said, flicking her fiery

red hair over her shoulder. "A victor may win you, but no lady of society will have you at their parties or balls. You won't be one of us. You'll simply be useful to the victor, so he can put a baby on your belly. And then, when you're no longer of use to him or to New London, you'll be put out to pasture." She leaned forward and whispered in Karina's ear, sending chills up her spine, "And shot."

"They... they wouldn't shoot me." Karina said, backing away. The Queen had assured her she was a Vessel too, that she was an equal.

"The Common Castes love that someone like them is a Vessel, that someone like them can be worthy of holiness." Karina's voice trembled as she spoke, despite her efforts for it to remain certain.

"Sure, you're the new exciting thing for now," Rachel said, her fingers tracing delicately up Karina's dress sleeve. "But they'll soon forget about you. When they get hungry again or when the acid rain comes in autumn, or the drought next summer. You'll mean nothing to them again. And you'll mean nothing to society or to your husband."

Karina gasped as Rachel ripped at the seams of Karina's sleeve. She jumped back in fright.

"Rachel... Stop being cruel to Karina," Louisa warned, more harshly this time. "The Queen will be back soon."

"And Karina," Rachel spat the name like it was an insult, "Will be long gone, won't you? I'll say you felt... unwell."

Sarah grabbed the other sleeve of Karina's before she could dart out of the way and ripped it, too. "You're a Traitor Caste, and you always will be, and no fame, pretty dresses, or a lovely face will change that, Karina. You may look sweet on the outside. But you're rotten on the inside, and all the Noble women know it. Everyone I've spoken to plans to refuse to include you in any high society functions after the Games. You and your victor will be ousted from society."

Karina's tears came hard and fast then, and Sarah's lips curled up into a smile when she'd seen she'd hit the nerve that she'd wanted to. Karina spun on her heel and ran out as fast as her legs could carry her. Karina could barely see in front of her own face. When Karina reached her bedroom, she didn't leave again for a long time. She ignored the knocks from Chloe, begging for her forgiveness. The knocks from the Queen, who said she was sorry that Karina was feeling ill and hoped she would feel better soon. She even ignored the tentative knock of Louisa, who apologized for her twin sister's cruelty and swore that she would invite Karina to every function she held with her future husband.

All these Nobles are the same, Karina thought.

They might pretend to be kind and caring on the outside, but they were as ruthless and as cold as the Shadowlanders that Karina had escaped from. Karina found herself wishing to talk to someone kind, to someone who understood how terrible these Nobles really were. She found herself... wishing to talk to Will.

∾

CHLOE SAT on the altar next to Father Jeremiah, gazing up at the grand statue of Mary. They sat in comfortable silence, listening to the scuffle of footsteps as the younger Clergy Castes moved about their business. They'd been like this for hours, finding comfort in one another's presence. Chloe often turned to Jeremiah and to God when she was feeling rotten. The whole Karina saga had all been Chloe's fault, and now, two men were dead. She shook herself, desperate to wipe their faces from her mind's eye. She knew deep down that it was useless—their expressions before they died would be imprinted on her mind forever.

Chloe shuffled the playing cards in her hands. Inspiration struck her, and she turned to Jeremiah, as excitement sparkled in her eyes. "Pick a card, and I'll guess what card you've got."

"Chloe, that's against the law." Jeremiah frowned, not looking up from his Bible passage.

"It's not illusion magic; it's just a little card trick. I promise."

"Chloe." Jeremiah sighed, placing his book down and swiveling to her. "That is *still* illusion magic. No one should have the power to perform miracles and confound reason but *God*. Why do you push me so?" His tone was resigned, but Chloe could hear the bite there, the anger.

The Games must have him at the end of his tether, just like Chloe. Dark circles ringed his eyes, and his skin tone had turned pallid, almost sickly.

"I'm sorry, Father." Chloe placed a hand on his arm in apology and pushed the deck of cards away deep into her pocket. "I didn't realize it was a sin in the same way that illusion magic is. Arthur used to do them. He loved card tricks." Chloe smiled to herself, thinking of his cheeky, freckly face—it grew harder to remember each day. "I didn't know."

Jeremiah softened. He must've noticed the guilt etched in Chloe's expression, knowing that she truly hadn't wished to alarm him. "It's fine, my child. Be sure to come to confession soon." Jeremiah stood, dusting off his trousers and collecting his Bible.

"Where are you going?" Chloe said, panic lacing her voice. Without him, the immense dread of the Games and guilt over those guards threatened to engulf her. "Before you go, I've been meaning to ask you..." Chloe dug in her pocket for the drawing of the ring.

She'd had no luck with finding anything in the palace library that even resembled the ring of Karina and Elaine's attacker. She'd been working day and night, and if she didn't find something soon...

She was running out of time. Chloe handed the piece of paper with the sigil drawn on it to Father Jeremiah. "Do you recognise this pattern? Have you seen a ring like this before?

Frowning, Jeremiah assessed the paper. "I can't say I have, Princess."

"This piece of paper... it's going to help me save William Albridge."

"Is it now?" Jeremiah stilled. "Well, what's your plan?"

"I thought you had to go?" Chloe asked, lifting a brow.

"I did. But to have the honor of hearing one of my princesses' many schemes?" Jeremiah bowed mockingly, leaving Chloe to snort her amusement. "Whatever I have to do can wait a little longer."

THIRTEEN

It took all of Chloe's self-control to offer a tight smile to the roaring audience as she entered the arena. She trailed behind her father and step-mother, who waved to the thousands gathered in the stifling afternoon heat. Like every year they'd forced Chloe to watch the atrocities of the Games, they sat in the royal box. It elevated them from the rest of the audience and shaded them from the sweltering heat by a gauzy canopy.

They'd designed the arena as a replica of Rome's Colosseum. Her father did always have a flair for the dramatic, she noted bitterly. She scanned across the sea of bodies, with flags of the United Kingdoms waved by Commons throughout the crowd of thousands. Cheers sounded as they handed out food to the Common Castes that was available to them: cheeses, sweets, and cured meats.

Commons dumped as much as they could into their pockets for later.

The sharp tang of alcohol in the air made Chloe crinkle her nose in distaste. Alcohol had been prohibited, except at the Games, of course. Cameras were dotted around the arena, accompanied by an enormous screen, so everyone had a perfect view of the action that would unfold on the sands below. The royal box housed only the King's closest, his inner circle. Nobles who weren't lucky enough to be considered as such sat lower down in the stands. Many of them continued to glance up toward the royal box, distaste painted on their features.

If there was one thing Nobles hated, it was being lower than others.

Chloe examined the crowd below and glimpsed Father Jeremiah wringing his hands together. She wondered if the arena reminded him of the horror of last year's Games. She caught Father Jeremiah's eye and nodded, a pounding in her ears that had nothing to do with the roars of the crowd below. His face looked as grim as hers.

Her father stood before his throne, and Chloe took a seat at his right, while the Queen was on his left. The outfit set out for Chloe to wear today was a cool shimmering silver with a matching tiara that sparkled in the late afternoon sun. The entire stadium came to a hushed quiet.

"My people," he addressed them. Chloe fought the urge to roll her eyes. "After the royal family gave you shelter from the bombs and gave you safety in these walls... After I protected you from Shadowlander attacks, from horrific weather events...You still lusted for more. Ten years ago, you betrayed me. And by betraying me, you betrayed God himself."

A few Common Castes in the crowd bowed their heads in shame.

"But like God," the King said. "I am forgiving. I listened to your plight. You wanted an equal chance to have descendants, just as the Nobles received. Despite your rank, you wished for child-bearing wives of your own, to touch God through your Vessels. You wished for heavenly miracles and for children. Despite what you did to me and my family, I granted this to you. All Common Castes; Defender, Craftsman, Farmer, and even Traitor. I have given you *all* the opportunity to rise above your station. Remember, *I* gave that to you." He let that sink in, and the Queen nodded somberly at his side. "You may be Common Caste, but nothing is out of your reach if you have the courage to take it. I present to you... this year's Vessels!"

The crowd roared in pleasure as a gate opened at the bottom of the arena to reveal five figures. Chloe ground her teeth when she glimpsed Karina in the company of the other Vessels. Karina had refused to speak to Chloe since her escape two days ago. Chloe had had little luck without Karina's help in searching the library books for signs that resembled the sigil on the ring, which was their only clue so far in Elaine's disappearance. Chloe clenched her hands; she needed to get a lead.

After the Ceremony, came the Ranking. And soon after that, the Games would begin.

Chloe looked down at Karina—the girl looked stunning. They'd chosen a lilac dress that complimented her dark skin, eyes, and ebony hair. The tight corset accentuated her curves in all the right places. They'd styled her hair in an elegant up-do, with purple gems dotted throughout. The unmistakable mark of the Vessel, the thick pearl necklace with a golden 'V" pendant hung tightly at her throat.

The Vessels each stepped onto a podium on the sand. A close-up shot of all of them played on the screen with their name and their Caste. Karina shuffled uncomfortably on the podium, but her head remained high.

"Good evening, New London!" A woman in a pink suit and bow tie entered the arena, performing a cartwheel.

Chloe couldn't resist rolling her eyes. The woman, Penelope, was acting like she was at a goddamn circus, not about to watch boys die for no reason.

The Duke of York's daughter, Penelope, had always wanted to be a star, and even though she was Barren, her father had pulled a lot of strings to get Penelope the hosting gig.

"I'm Penelope, daughter of the Duke of York, and I am your host for this year's Games!"

Then, Penelope interviewed each of the Vessels, asking them about the type of boys they wished would fight for them. Sarah was up first, and she started prattling on about her wish for a strong, muscular husband who could defend her against all the savage Shadowlanders getting into the city.

Chloe rolled her eyes. *Real original, there.*

Chloe leaned over toward her father's ear. "You remember what we discussed, Father?"

"Hm." The King grunted.

"Dad," she said. The King's head snapped around at that. She never called him "Dad." Not anymore.

"Remember what Father Jeremiah advised you? You need to give Will an equal chance. As equal as anyone's got here. If people know that he's a criminal, that'll affect his Ranking score and then God can't judge him fairly, like you wanted. No one can know you sentenced him to play," Chloe said this loud enough that the other Nobles surrounding his throne would hear. Most of them had been at their disagreement and knew that Will had been sentenced to the Games.

If the public knew Will was a criminal, that would affect the popularity vote, which contributed to each competitor's Ranking score. How the boys were ranked would be crucial for his survival. She'd tried to ensure that even if she failed at finding Elaine, the at least Will would have a fighting chance. Chloe gulped at the thought; she'd been unable to find any leads about the sigil ring in the library, despite her many late nights there this week.

"I say we should have just executed him," Lord Dartfield said with a sneer. "My boy Caleb is going to compete in the Games this year. That Craftsman doesn't stand a chance."

"It is not for you to decide one's innocence or guilt; that's only for God." There was a hard edge to Chloe's voice as she spoke, but Dartfield didn't appear to be rattled.

"As agreed with Father Jeremiah, no one can know this is his sentence," The King said with a tight nod. "We must not tip the scales ourselves. You're right on this issue, Chloe. Only God can judge him."

Father Jeremiah had agreed to advise the King to keep Will's criminal history a secret from the public. Sometimes, she thought idly, Father Jeremiah would make a better father than her own. No father who truly cared would have used a boy's life to punish her for her insolence. Chloe shot a final, dark look at Lord Dartfield before settling back into her seat.

But the princess froze entirely when she glanced down at his hand.

"What is it, my darling? You've gone pale," Queen Mary said, assessing her with concern.

Chloe forced her gaze away from Dartfield and smiled in a way that she hoped was somewhat convincing. For there, on Lord Dartfield's hand, sat a ring with a strange symbol on it.

The ring she'd been looking for.

The same ring that Elaine's captor and Karina's attacker had worn.

~

WILL's gaze darted across the arena from where he stood. The interviews with the girls had almost finished. One twin, Rachel, was going into great detail about her thankfulness to God that He'd selected her to be a Vessel. That had given Will some time. He just hoped it was enough.

Will had been released from the cells just an hour ago. There Chloe had greeted him and explained how she'd convinced her father to give him a fair shot at the Games. The Ranking was in equal parts a popularity and skills contest. She'd known that if they'd revealed him as a criminal, his popularity score would have plummeted, and he'd be placed into one of the more dangerous rounds.

The crowd wanted to see those they loved win, and those they hated lose. Painfully.

After they'd released him from his cell, he'd half considered making a run for it. Maybe he'd get his mum, and they'd escape and...

But where could he run?

Everywhere within the walls was monitored. Outside, he had radiation, harsh deserts, acid rain, and Shadowlanders to deal with. They wouldn't last two days.

"Ma!" Will's voice shook as he saw his mother sitting in a row toward the bottom of the arena.

"Will!" She looked... healthy; it surprised him to see.

Will had been worried sick, and although Karina had promised she'd see her, Karina hadn't been back to visit him in the cells since. He'd just assumed she hadn't been permitted to leave the palace. Will tripped his way over to his ma and embraced her. She smelled of lavender and home. He'd missed her so damn much.

"Where have you been?" Tears trickled onto her cheeks,

and Will wiped them away gently. "I was so worried about you."

"I... It's a long story," Will said.

A boy on the brink of adulthood sat next to her and assessed Will.

"Who's this?" Will asked.

"This is Marcus. He's been coming to visit. Making sure I've got my meds, and I've got my rations. Such a lovely boy!" She smiled down at him with a fondness that made Will's heart squeeze a little.

"I'm Karina's brother." He held out his hand.

"Thanks for looking after my ma," Will said thickly.

Marcus leaned in and spoke under his breath, quiet enough for only Will to hear, "Karina got into some serious shit for helping you out. She told me I needed to keep her visit to your ma a secret. Otherwise, I'm in danger."

Will's mouth went dry. He couldn't believe Karina had been so brave, and that she'd sacrificed her own safety to make sure his ma was okay. He looked toward her, standing serenely on the podium.

"Ma? I have something to tell you." Will took a shaky breath, "I have to enter the Games this year."

"What?" She gasped. "Will, you'll be killed!"

"I don't have time to explain. But I have a friend. She's working on...getting me out. I think." He embraced her again, knowing his time was running out. "I love you, Ma."

Penelope's nasally voice echoed through the arena. "Now, we've heard from the Vessels. We invite those who wish to compete to come forward."

Will strode down the stairs without looking back. He didn't know if he'd have the courage to keep walking if he did; her wails for him to return echoed around the arena. When he made it to the entrance gate of the arena, Will straightened his shoulders and glanced around at the other competitors.

The competitors all stood anxiously, awaiting their turn. All of them looked massively well built with hardened lines of muscle, and cold eyes. They all looked older than he did, although the rules of the Games were that you could only be between eighteen and twenty to compete.

Most of the Common Castes here looked like Defenders. The rest were Nobles, and they'd likely been training to get a Vessel wife since they were old enough to hold a sword. There were maybe three boys he recognised from the Craftsman District, and one slight boy he'd seen at the Farmers' market. All were risking their lives for glory, God, and, of course, money.

They all stood by the Gate and were ushered into the arena by the Defenders. Will's hands trembled as he looked up at the royal box. Chloe was there in all her sparkly glory, her face giving nothing away. She gave a tight nod, unnoticeable to all but him. Chloe had made sure no one knew he was a convicted criminal. He was grateful for that, at least. That might help his Ranking score, and that score would determine the order that they'd fight in.

"Let's welcome our competitors this year!" Penelope said in a shrill voice. "Come on in, boys!"

The roar from the crowd was nothing short of feral.

The surrounding boys jostled for a position at the front as the gate opened. One boy shoved others out of the way with a force that had others stumbling. His blond hair was slicked back, his jaw looking like it could cut glass. He appeared angelic, almost, but Will noticed a dangerous glint in his eye. Will prayed that he didn't end up in the same round as the blond.

Soon, the boys stood on the podium, opposite to the

Vessels. Penelope marched up and down the line, like a drill sergeant at dawn.

"I count forty of you strapping young lads." She grinned. "If my calculations are correct, eight of you will compete per round if you all survive the Ranking task."

A one-in-eight chance of winning.

Will could see why boys risked their lives to compete. A one-in-eight chance of winning the lottery and getting everything you ever wanted. You just had to kill seven people to get there.

"What's your name, handsome?" She addressed the blond boy Will had noticed at the gate earlier.

"Caleb Dartfield. First son of Lord Dartfield. Whoever my Vessel is, she'll become a true Noble with a great bloodline. Can't say that for most." He flashed her a grin. The Noble houses chuckled in response, but the Common Castes remained in stony silence.

"You seem confident that you'll win a Vessel, Caleb," Penelope said, one eyebrow hitched.

"I will. I've been training for this since I was eight. I want to be in round one, so I can have the first choice. I want only the best." He gave Penelope a perfect movie star smile, and her cheeks flushed at the intensity of his gaze.

Some of the Vessels looked impressed. Sarah flicked her bright red hair over her shoulder in a way that Will thought was supposed to look seductive. Rachel was practically licking her lips. Will's gaze moved over to Karina—she just looked bored. To Will's surprise, a swell of relief surged in his chest.

"And why are you competing this year?" Rang out before him.

It took a few awkward seconds for Will to realize that

Penelope had the mic pointed at his own mouth. "Ah. I... I um..."

"Camera shy, how sweet!" Penelope teased. "Let's hope you don't get stage fright when you're back here fighting in just a few weeks. That would not bode well for you." She placed a finger on Will's nose, and the audience howled with laughter. "So... have any of the ladies taken your fancy, Camera Shy?" She used the nickname in a derogatory tone and Will's heart rate fluttered in panic.

His palms sweating and vision blurring, he said the only thing that he could think of:

"Karina."

The audience gasped.

"You like the look of Karina?"

Will nodded.

"She's exquisite, isn't she?" Penelope asked the audience. The crowd hooted in approval.

"She's... beautiful, yes. But she's more than that." Will murmured. "I knew her before today, and... her heart is beautiful. She's kind. That's not something I see a lot these days." The words spilled out of Will's mouth before he was able to control them.

The crowd fell silent at the candidness of the answer. It seemed to have struck a chord because after a few beats of quiet, the audience seemed to sigh collectively and "aws" echoed around the arena. Will looked at Karina then, and he mouthed the words, "Thank you."

She'd given up a lot for him, and he would never forget that kindness. Karina's face was stony, but her lips quirked upwards for just a moment.

"Well... Camera Shy is not love shy! Give it up for Will Albridge!"

Cheers and hoots sounded, and then Penelope had

moved on to the next boy. As she did, Will glanced at the rest of the boys, letting out a sigh of relief that his turn was over. But Will noticed someone staring right at him.

Caleb.

The Noble would've hated the fact Will had just won the audience over with such ease. Caleb had said that he'd wanted to be the best. And then Will had beaten him at something. Will gulped.

He'd just made himself a threat.

CHAPTER
FOURTEEN

The Vessels had an entire room to themselves to get ready for the ball. Karina wished the Queen hadn't insisted that they all prepare for the ball together, but here they were. She was thankful there were too many others present for the Vessels to do anything cruel again. Her palms were still damp with sweat, and her knees bounced as another Noble painted her face with make-up. Karina marveled at the feeling of the make-up being plastered onto her skin—no other caste was allowed to wear it.

A Duchess who had taken a special liking to Karina was musing about who the Vessels would end up with. "Between you and me, despite the fact that Will is dreamy and his confession about your *kind heart* was to die for, I think you'll end up with the blond in the end. What was his name? Caleb."

Sarah's head snapped up. "No one cares what you think, Margaret. Besides, why would Karina end up with Caleb?"

"Because she's the most beautiful," Duchess Margaret

said, unabashed. Karina wished the Duchess wouldn't say things like that. She didn't like the look in Sarah's eyes when the duchess did. "And I've seen all the media; the Common Castes love Karina. It's their very own Cinderella story."

"Well, I disagree," Rachel said, examining her nails and occasionally swotting away other Nobles who were attempting to tend to her hair. "Caleb's of Noble blood, he wouldn't want some dirty Common to bear his children, no matter how pretty she may be—"

The Queen burst into the dressing room, and everyone stopped what they were doing to curtsey. She clapped her hands. "Come girls, it's time for you to take your places."

Karina practically jumped out of the make-up chair. They made their way through the palace corridors, and she lined up outside of the ballroom with the other Vessels to await her turn. They were entering the ballroom one by one to rapturous applause. Karina wrung her fingers in her hands, a ball of nerves collecting in her stomach. She'd have to dance at the ball. In front of everyone. She was fucking terrible at dancing.

A shimmering silver in the shadows caught her eye. "Pst!"

Karina blinked a few times, trying to make out the figure in the darkness. "Tiffany?" She said, frowning in confusion. "What are you doing in the dark?"

The last time Karina had seen Tiffany was the day Tiff had helped her escape. Karina shuddered at the memory of it.

"I'm not allowed to talk to Nobles when I'm working..."

"When you're working?"

Tiffany popped her head out of the shadows, and now

Karina understood what the shimmering silver was all about. It was a leotard. "I'm performing as a dancer tonight at the ball."

"Oh. I thought you were doing the laundry when I last saw you." Karina said flatly, spinning back to the door to wait her turn.

Anne was being called now and introduced to the crowd. Karina could vaguely make out Anne answering a few questions from Penelope.

"Craftsman Caste performers often have a day job. To pay the bills... Look, it doesn't matter." Tiffany dismissed, waving her hand. "Chloe told me that she's been trying to talk to you, but she's grounded—"

"I don't want to talk to Chloe."

"I know you don't, which is why I'm her messenger."

"I don't want to hear about what Chloe's messenger has to say, either," Karina retorted.

She'd refused to talk to Chloe since her escape from the palace. Chloe could escape because she could afford to—, because she was royalty and there would be no real punishment for her. As much as Chloe complained she was trapped, she'd never be bound by the same rules as Karina.

"Well, don't shoot the messenger..." Tiffany muttered, rolling her eyes. Karina stifled a smile. She hated to admit it, but she liked Tiffany. And Chloe, too. "Look, she needs to talk to you. She says it's urgent. Please."

A man burst out of a room down the corridor. "Tiff!" He hissed. "Get your ass back in here. We're on in five!"

"And our final contestant... Karina!"

Karina ignored whatever Tiffany said and burst into the ballroom.

She blinked rapidly at the sudden lighting change. The

ballroom was enormous, with vaulted ceilings and floor to ceiling windows making it only look larger. Thick, red velvet drapes hung at the palace windows, and above her, a beautiful tiered crystal chandelier glittered in the soft light. The small orchestra playing filled her ears with sweet music. Servers offered canapes to the arriving guests, and Karina's mouth began to water at the smell of rich cheeses and chocolate delicacies.

"Karina, darling. You're a vision! Come down the stairs," Penelope called.

Karina descended the grand and sweeping staircase to a wave of applause from the Nobles watching her. The boys competing for her were lined up in a row, awaiting her at the bottom. She spied Will and immediately looked down. The way he was looking at her was... distracting.

Karina's heart felt like it was leaping into her mouth. She clutched the staircase as she descended with a vice-like grip.

"Please join the other Vessels on your podium." Penelope instructed. "Because soon we will have the royal family's grand entrance!"

Karina glanced around the room, stepping onto her podium. All the Vessels stood on podiums, similar to those in the arena. The intent was for them to be looked at. Admired. Karina just felt exposed.

She wished someone would come and talk to her, that the hushed voices of "traitor" would not echo toward her. That she would not feel so... different. The sounds of the orchestra swelled, and the ballroom doors burst open, revealing the king, queen, and an irritated-looking princess. Chloe hid it well, but Karina noted Chloe's clenching jaw and balled fists. Every moment in a place like this was an enormous effort for Chloe to stay under control. Karina's mind traveled back to the last time she'd seen Chloe like that and remembered the Shadowlander attack.

The guards... Because of Karina's recklessness, two men were dead. Karina's lip wobbled.

Karina tipped her head skyward for a second to compose herself. Her calm veneer couldn't shatter in a place as important as this. There were too many eyes on her.

"Beautiful, isn't it?" A low voice asked.

Will stood in front of her, below the podium. He wore a dark tuxedo, and Karina had to admit that it suited him well. With his square jaw, bright, intelligent eyes, and powerful stature, he looked like a Noble. Just like her, she guessed. He scrubbed up well, but they both didn't belong here.

Karina gave a half-hearted shrug in response. Now that Will had approached her, a few of the other competitors had plucked up the courage to talk to the other Vessels, too. Some gazed toward her with a hunger that she remembered from the Traitor slums. She shifted from one leg to the other. The competitors were all angling to get in the favor of the Vessels.

Karina quickly turned back to the safety of Will's dark brown eyes. He took her in too but in a way that made Karina feel... revered rather than lusted after. There was warmth in that deep brown; there were even a few flecks of green. As Will gazed at Karina, she noticed a strange kind of heat building in her belly.

"Dance with me?" He offered her a hand.

She still remembered the day that they'd met. His shocked look when he saw her identification card, his fumbling nervousness. There was a calmness to him now that made Karina feel almost safe.

"I'd love to." And strangely, Karina meant that. Truly meant it.

She didn't like dancing with anyone, yet still, Karina slipped her hand into his and he led her toward the dancefloor.

"My hands are a bit rough, sorry," she said sheepishly. "All the scrubbing toilets." Her eyes went wide when she realized that Will was probably thinking about all the disgusting places her hands had been.

She tried to withdraw it quickly, but he enveloped his hand in hers, not letting her draw away. He squeezed it a little as he looked at her with his lips curled into a wry smile.

"I don't mind." He shrugged. "They're the hands of a survivor. Hands of someone that's got grit. Someone that's been through some tough shit and has come out the other side." He moved his thumb up and down the calluses on her palms ever so gently. It made Karina's breath hitch. "I like them."

He held her gaze for a beat too long.

"Yep, they've um... literally been through some tough shit." Karina teased, one eyebrow arching, and Will guffawed with laughter. She liked the sound of his laughter, booming and without restraint.

Karina felt eyes on them, and a few cameras tracking their movement. The cameras would also be at these events, she remembered with a start. The population would want to see every detail of her love story.

When they were in their place on the dance floor, Will's hand settled on her waist. She'd only been practicing dancing with the other Vessel girls, and it was a stark contrast to have his large, warm hands gently grazing against her body. Karina bit her lip, liking the way his hands felt placed against the small of her back.

"I'm no good at dancing," she said, looking up at him as the music began to swell to a crescendo.

He towered over her. Will's sturdy body moved against hers, guiding her perfectly through the dance. As she clutched onto his arms, she couldn't help but savor the feeling of muscled arms beneath his blazer. He'd labored his whole life, and he certainly had a muscular frame to show for it. For every fumble she made—every misstep— he moved her seamlessly through it. As he cradled her body he almost lifted her, so she wouldn't fall so obviously.

"How are you so good?" Karina asked.

"My mother was a dancer, actually. That was her craft. She taught me well." He pulled her closer to him, so their bodies were pressed flush against one another.

Karina found herself picturing their lives together if he won her hand in the Games. She pictured her head tipping back with raucous laughter at something he'd said. She pictured him smothering her neck in soft and tender kisses...

He leaned forward in her ear, his breath tickling her. "Any luck with the ring?"

And just like that, Karina's illusion shattered. Of course. He was only dancing with her as a ruse, to get information. It was likely Will *wouldn't* win; he needed information about the ring to escape from the Games.

"None," Karina answered. "I haven't talked to Chloe... since I visited your Mum."

Will went rigid. "Karina, I had no idea that sending you there would..."

"Of course you didn't know. But Chloe would've, and she let me go, anyway."

"Maybe she..."

A pointed clearing of the throat next to them had both Karina and Will jumping in fright. Caleb, Lord Darfield's son, was standing right next to them. "It's my turn with the lady now, Albridge. What do you say, lady?" He grabbed Karina's hand and planted a delicate kiss.

The way he looked at her afterward seemed like he'd thought he'd made a seductive move. But all Karina wanted to do was to talk to Will. To discuss Elaine and the sigil...

Fury simmered in Will's eyes, but he nodded at Caleb, a notable tension in his voice. "She's all yours, my Lord."

"That's right. She is." An electric tension crackled between the two men, and all Karina could do was stand between them and hope she didn't catch fire herself.

Caleb took Karina in his arms with a confidence that startled her. He pulled her closer against him and they began to sway to the music. This dance was faster than the one she'd danced with Will, and Caleb's movements were more assured but less graceful.

Was it confidence or arrogance? Karina wondered.

His eyes darted behind her, and Karina knew he'd clocked the cameras on them. He tucked a tendril of hair behind her ear in a manner that seemed incredibly intimate. Karina's cheeks grew hot.

"My Lord... I..." Karina attempted to step back at the forwardness of it, but Caleb held her tight and despite her attempt to get away, his hand pressed firmly into the small of her back, keeping her locked in his embrace.

"You are the most beautiful Vessel I've ever seen, Karina. Your beauty bests everything and everyone." It sounded rather rehearsed, almost like a script. She looked up at his square face as he swallowed deeply.

Was he...was he *nervous*? Of *her?*

"T-Thank you, my Lord," she said, as he began swaying them back and forth.

"I saw how the crowd looked at you today." Caleb swallowed, his jaw working. "They are... electrified that someone like you rose above your station. You give them hope. You give...me hope. That we can do better. Think of all those young ladies looking up to you, Karina. You're their role model."

Karina didn't want to be a role model. She didn't want men to die for her.

She didn't want *Will* to die for her.

An image leapt into her mind before she could control it: Will's lifeless body on the sands of the arena. Blood pooled at his feet. Caleb, with a terrible grin and a bloody sword in hand, as he knelt down at her feet, a diamond ring in his bloody grip. Panic pressed in around her.

"Excuse me. I don't feel well," Karina muttered, turning on her heel and running out of the ballroom.

When she made it to the bathroom, Karina collapsed over the toilet, heaving her guts out. But she hadn't eaten all day, so there was nothing to give. She pressed her forehead against the cubicle wall, letting the cool marble touch her sweaty brow. The door of the bathroom creaked as someone else entered, the clacking of their heels on the tiles echoing in the bathroom.

"Karina?"

Karina gritted her teeth as she recognised the voice. "I don't want to talk to you."

"We don't have much time." Chloe dropped to the floor and gazed at Karina under the crack of the bathroom cubicle, her face pressed to the floor tiles. "Please talk to me. It's important, and I don't have long—James is just outside."

"I said to *leave me alone.*"

"You sound like my brother used to," Chloe said, a soft, sad smile etched on her face. "He always used to escape to the bathrooms. I followed him around like a puppy."

Karina rolled her eyes. "You're trying to make me feel guilty, aren't you?"

Mischief danced in Chloe's eyes. "Is it working though?" she asked, her lips upturned in a lopsided smile.

Karina sighed. "Maybe."

Chloe pressed on. "I found something. Something that might help us find Elaine."

Karina looked at the strange sight of a princess' cheek pressed against the bathroom floor. Karina sighed in resignation. She was still angry about what had happened but needed to put aside her anger at what had happened at the escape. If they wanted to find Elaine, they needed to work together. She shoved the door open, and Chloe leapt inside the bathroom stall, her eyes shining with excitement.

"Lord Dartfield was wearing the same ring as yours and Elaine's captor today," Chloe said.

Karina's mouth popped open wide in an 'o.'

Chloe nodded. "It can't just be a coincidence. He has to know something."

"Lord Dartfield, as in Caleb's father?"

"Mhm." Chloe looked at Karina with apprehension. "And... I have an idea."

"Please tell me that idea doesn't involve sneaking around," Karina said, turning the tap on to wash her hands.

"Which one of my plans doesn't involve sneaking around?" Chloe asked, jumping to sit next to the sink with a ghost of a smile playing on her lips. "I'll tell you the rest later. But here's step one of the plan: you need to make Caleb believe you fancy him. Or you at least need to appear interested in him winning your Games."

"Chloe," Karina argued, "No."

"I know. He's a little arrogant and also... looking forward to becoming a murderer. But it's the only way I see this working. It's the perfect cover to get close to him. To get close to the family."

As much as Karina hated to admit it, Chloe was right. They'd be able to get close to Darfield without suspicion.

"Your Highness?" James' muffled voice called from outside the bathroom. "Are you all right in there?" James creaked open the door. Karina's breath hitched—he shouldn't see the two of them together like this. They looked like they were... conspiring.

Chloe, as always, thought fast.

"Christ, James, I'm taking a shit!" Chloe yelled out toward the bathroom door. The door slammed shut as James retreated in horror. "Go back to the ball. I don't need you out here while I go!"

Karina slapped her hand over her mouth to stop the giggle escaping from her lips. Chloe really was nothing like what she expected a princess to be.

Chloe turned back to Karina, her voice dropping. "They won't let me out of James' sight at the moment since I told my father that I managed to sneak out of the inner-sanctum. But I do have a plan. Still, I'm going to need to rely on you to get this done. Are you in?"

Karina took a breath. She'd be risking her life; she had no doubt. Chloe might be a princess, but she'd been unable to save those Defenders. If Karina was caught, it was likely Chloe wouldn't be able to save her either.

But Karina needed to know what happened to Elaine.

She needed to at least try to find out the truth, even if Elaine were dead... because whatever had happened to her, then... it obviously involved Karina somehow, too.

"Okay." Karina sighed. "I'm in."

"That's my girl." Chloe leapt from her seat and practically bounced out of the bathroom stall without another word.

Karina listened with amusement to Chloe and James sparring as they walked away. "Can't a girl crap in peace, James?"

"You shouldn't swear like that, Your Highness. It's ungodly."

"And you shouldn't follow women to the bathroom while they do their business, sicko," Chloe huffed.

Karina gathered herself, splashing water on her cheeks. When she returned to the ballroom, Karina zeroed in on the cameras and strutted up to where Caleb stood with his father.

"Sorry about that." Karina smiled demurely. "I felt a little... ill. I've just been so excited to meet you that I didn't eat anything!"

Caleb's eyes flickered in surprise. "No problem." He offered her a tentative smile. "Karina, this is my father...."

"Lord Dartfield," she finished for him. Karina curtseyed slowly, and as her gaze dropped to his hand, Chloe had been right. Dartfield was wearing the ring.

Karina buried her shock. "It's an honor to meet you, my Lord." Karina's skin crawled as he assessed her with those same wintry blue eyes as his son.

"The pleasure is all mine," Lord Dartfield answered.

Karina made sure to dance with Caleb, to laugh at every joke. She played the part of the perfect Vessel. Karina could do this; she could fool him into thinking she liked him.

Because if Chloe was right, and that sigil ring on Lord Dart-field's finger meant that he had any part in harming Elaine...

Well, he had another thing coming, and it wasn't a new daughter-in-law.

It was a knife in his heart.

FIFTEEN

Now that the competitors and the Vessels had been introduced to New London, it was time to train for the Ranking—once the boys were ranked, the rounds would begin. Will tried not to think about the fact he'd die on these sands. He studied tiered grand-stand seating where spectators would watch him. His eyes fell on the large screen where the cameras would get their close-ups; it made his stomach turn.

The rest of the boys jogged toward the weapons—all of them wooden, of course. The previous year, some contestants killed some of the stronger or more popular competitors while they weren't prepared for it in the training ring. The ones who survived got punished. Some were still in the Traitor district. Well, what was left of them anyway.

Will jumped when the gate behind him swung open again with a loud creak. Twenty rough-looking, older men entered, assessing the sparring with a wild intensity that made Will frown. Some had tattoos etched over their powerful arms, whilst others looked smaller in stature, but all moved through the fighting with a stealth that made Will shiver.

These must have been the coaches.

Coaches had the power to make or break a competitor's Games. For an obscenely large fee, anyone could coach a competitor, even a woman. If you wished to train a specific competitor, to give them a greater chance at survival, it was no problem.

Provided you could pay up.

Coaches chose whomever impressed them most, but it often depended on their masters. Masters might have bet a large sum of money on a boy and wanted to increase their chances at winning. The Masters were the ones who truly controlled the Games. Gambling on who wins the Games was a common past-time, and some men took it to ridiculous heights.

The thought of the boys being bet on like horses made Will cringe. No one cared who paid the price if people were profiting from it. Most of the boys had already paired up, so Will pushed himself into action, trotting toward the weapons station. He assessed the wooden weapons for something that might give him his best chance. Before him: spears, swords, shields, and even tridents.

Will snatched up a sword and shield.

One competitor near him looked queasy. "Hey. You got a partner yet?" Will asked. The boy shifted from one foot to the other and shook his head. "I'm Will."

"C-Cameron." He stuttered. Cameron had sooty, black hair and hazel eyes. Just looking at his shy demeanor and tiny frame, Will thought the kid didn't have a chance in hell.

"I'm Craftsman Caste." Will smiled in a way that he hoped was comforting. "How about you?"

"F-Farmer Caste."

"Why'd you compete?"

"D-Dad said it is an honor to serve our country. He said he'd disown me if I didn't, that I'd be kicked out and become a Traitor Caste." Cameron wrinkled his nose in distaste. "I'd rather be dead."

Will's fists tightened. He thought of Karina, of her guarded, intelligent eyes. Of her kindness and her bravery in helping his mum. "There are worse things." Will shrugged.

"I guess we should fight, then," Cameron said, looking reluctant to do so.

But as soon as Cameron leapt into action, Will regretted his choice of partner. Cameron moved with ruthless intensity—moving so quickly that Will could barely keep his eyes on him.

He'd been training. *Of course,* Cameron had prepared for this opportunity, Will chided himself. He'd *chosen* to be here. Will's breath came in ragged gasps when a coach moved over to watch them. It was only Will's natural strength and athleticism that held Cameron at bay.

Will's stomach plummeted. If he was incapable of holding off someone half his size... then how would he survive hand-to-hand combat in an arena with seven other competitors? The only way he'd have a chance of survival was if he got placed in a round with weak competitors. If he got into round the stronger men, then he was screwed.

But if he got into an easier round toward the end of the Games... Karina would likely already be engaged. At that thought, Will lost his footing, and Cameron was quick to press the advantage. Will was on the ground in a second, clutching his stomach in pain.

"Dead." Cameron smirked.

Will squinted up at Cameron's sneering face in the sun's glare. His nervousness had been a ruse, so he'd be able to combat with a weaker competitor and show his skills to their full advantage. Will had been played.

A burly coach approached Cameron and assessed him with approval. "You're fast and cunning. I'll advise my Master to place his bets on you. Let's train."

"Sorry, man." Cameron shrugged and trotted off to join his new coach.

Will lay in the dirt, cheeks flushed with anger and embarrassment, as the flies buzzed around his face.

"You," a light female voice said. "Get your ass up."

Will dragged himself to his feet, wincing with the effort. a woman stood before him in a plume of smoke. She took a long drag of the cigarette that hung out her mouth, sighing in ecstasy. To Will's surprise, she wore a silky black eye patch. Silk was a symbol of wealth; it seemed strange to see such a thing in this context. Her features were sharp, her pale skin already glistening with the heat of the arena. Her golden blonde hair hung down in large, tattered chunks. It was greasy—dirty even—as if she didn't care to wash herself often.

"God, I've missed these." She sighed once more, watching the smoke like one would watch a lover. That was when Will noticed the shackles around her hands.

"You're a criminal?"

The woman gave him a saccharine grin. "No dear boy. I'm a Vessel."

"That's not possible."

"It's plenty possible," she fired back, not taking her eyes off the cigarette. "The name's Octavia. I was a Defender Caste once upon a time. Before the Lord," she spat out the word, "blessed me with being a Vessel. And here I am."

"If you're a Vessel, then why are you in shackles? And why is..."

"My eye gone?" She glowered at him, her other eye regarding him in a way that gave Will the urge to sink into the sand. He couldn't imagine the heat of the stare if she'd had two. "Well, boy. That's a story for another day. I don't repeat myself often, but I will just this once, while I'm being nice. *Get your ass up.*"

"Why?"

"Because I'm your coach." She grabbed a wooden sword for herself and moved into what looked like a fighting stance.

"But you're a woman." It came out of his mouth before he could control it. Will saw her eyes flash in anger, and a pang of shame overcame him.

He valued women, but New London often saw women as weaker, as nothing more than objects to be won. Sometimes it rubbed off on him.

"Anyone who pays the fee can be a coach. Women usually don't have the skills they need to coach anyone properly." She placed her cigarette in between her lips and leapt to strike at him, but he quickly managed to throw his sword in the way.

"And you do?" He asked, grunting with the effort of defending himself.

She swung out again, and Will was suddenly on his ass. It had taken her all but two seconds to beat him, whilst shackled at that.

Will wondered how she'd gained such skills, but then he remembered that she'd said she was a Defender Caste. Will found himself wishing he hadn't been born into the Craftsman Caste. Hammering nails into wood wouldn't do him much good in the arena.

"You haven't seen me fight properly." Will grunted, feeling embarrassed.

"Oh, I saw you with Cameron. And you suck," she said, her face deadpan and her cigarette still in her mouth. "But my Master has chosen you. He said that he wanted you, no matter your fighting skills. Which suck, by the way, if I didn't make that *crystal* clear."

She inhaled the cigarette and blew it slowly into his face. Despite his best efforts, he coughed a little. Octavia threw him a feral grin.

"No, that was clear. Thanks," Will said, sarcasm dripping in his voice.

She let out a wicked laugh. "Don't get smart with me, boy. If you want to live past the Ranking and make it into the rounds... we have our work cut out for us." Despite his dire situation, Will had to admit, it felt nice for someone to say "us." He didn't feel so alone.

"Who's your Master? Why did he choose me?"

"So many questions." She tutted, and her shackles clinked with the movement. "If I want to keep my other eye, they've ordered me not to tell you... so I choose the eye. Get up, let's start with your stance."

"How are you going to train me in shackles?"

"That, my friend, is my problem. Your problem is to stop with the questions and start with the whole wanting to live past the Ranking thing. Got it?"

"Got it." Will nodded.

The blonde woman looked at him with disdain and took another drag of her cigarette. "Let's begin."

$\approx$

KARINA'S PALMS were already slick with sweat as she knocked on the grand door.

A servant girl answered. She wore gray clothing, the only shade that Traitor Castes were permitted to wear. Despite her nerves, Karina smiled at the trembling girl. "Hello, I'm Karina. Are Lord and Lady Dartfield here? I'm looking for Caleb." The little Traitor Caste girl seemed terrified as her eyes darted between the two Defenders who flanked Karina. The only reason Karina had been allowed out was because she was "finally taking an interest in her future."

The Queen had been thrilled that Caleb and Karina had gotten along "so well" at the ball and insisted she call upon the family, playing into Karina and Chloe's hands perfectly.

"I-I'll get them, my Lady." The servant girl curtseyed and disappeared into the grand house.

"We'll wait out here, my Lady." One of the Defenders said, pulling his riot helmet up to speak to her.

The way those helmets covered their faces made Karina feel unsettled. Behind that mask, anonymity gave them the power to do anything. She nodded tightly and stepped inside, shutting the door.

The entryway was spacious with high ceilings and white marble floors. A grand balustrade led up to the second floor of the house. This place was enormous. She had no idea how she was going to pull this off.

But she had to try.

Lady Dartfield emerged from upstairs, making her jump. "Miss Roberts! You're here. Oh, Caleb will be thrilled to see you. Come with me, and let's have a cup of tea." Karina shuffled along behind Lady Dartfield, glancing at the magnificent art placed throughout the house. "You like the artwork?" the Lady asked.

Karina nodded. "It's beautiful. I wish I was half as good as that."

"You paint, do you?"

"Draw. We..." Karina cleared her throat, "We couldn't afford paints."

Lady Dartfield glanced at her with something that resembled pity. "Well, now that you're a Noble, you'll have the time and resources available to you. You can hone your craft. Once you've delivered a few children, of course."

"Of course," Karina said, trying to keep her face unreadable. They arrived in the dining room. Tea and cakes were already being laid on the table by the staff.

"Will Lord Dartfield join us, too?" Karina swallowed. "I'd... um... I'd like to get to know you. You might be my future parents-in-law."

Lady Dartfield seemed perplexed at the request, and Karina chewed on her bottom lip in worry. She hoped she hadn't been too obvious.

"He usually works in his study, but I suppose I can see if he's available to talk to us," Lady Dartfield offered, seeming unsure herself.

Caleb strode into the room and Karina dropped into a curtsey, avoiding his gaze. "My Lord." Karina addressed Caleb—he offered a small smile, and Karina tried to ignore the way his eyes roamed hungrily down her body.

"Well, I'll go find Lord Dartfield," Lady Dartfield said, exiting the suite.

Karina strained to hear where her footsteps were heading toward. If she could pick up an idea of where Dartfield's office was...

"Lady Karina, how lovely for you to drop by." His attention shot to the food on the table. "Sit and have some tea with me?"

"Of course." Karina sunk into her chair. There was an awkward silence as they filled their plates, the only sound the clink of silverware. "How was training today?" Karina tried to sound interested.

"I did very well, my Lady. The coaches practically fought over me." He announced, dunking several spoonfuls of sugar into his tea. "I'm going to have the highest skills score in the Ranking. I'll be in round one, for sure. And then you'll be mine."

"Thank you, Caleb. I'm honored." Karina lied. Karina couldn't help but feel like he was talking about her as if she were a possession rather than a person. He cared about winning in the most competitive round—round one—more than he cared about marrying her. He was just a spoiled man who wanted the best toys on his shelf. And the current, shiniest toy was Karina.

"So, Caleb," she began, "What are your hobbies?"

Caleb paused, buttering a scone. "Hobbies? I— I don't know." He shrugged, seeming a little embarrassed. "All I work on is the Games, really. Strategy, fighting, fitness. Takes the whole day. I don't know what I am without them." His eyes went far away for a moment, his scone forgotten.

Karina jumped in the air, squeaking in surprise as she felt something *soft* brush up against her ankles.

Caleb smiled, and suddenly he looked much younger than he had before. "Don't be frightened, Karina. It's just Blaze."

Karina tentatively peered under the table. A one-eyed ginger cat inspected her, it's head slightly tilted.

"You have...a cat?" Karina had never heard of such an absurd thing.

Caleb studied her. "Blaze is my pet. I keep him, look after him, play with him..."

"For fun?" Karina's brows knitted together in confusion.

Caleb nodded slowly.

"Traitor Caste's have too many mouths to feed to keep animals for fun."

Caleb gaze lowered, his shoulders hunching over. "I know I shouldn't keep him. I..." He trailed off. "I got him when I was just a kid. I couldn't imagine getting rid of him now. I know it's selfish of me, but...he's mine."

"I understand." Karina said quietly. "Once you love something, it's hard to let it go."

A soft rumbling sound came from the cat's chest.

"What's that?" Karina asked.

"It's a called a purr. Means he likes you." There it was. That soft smile again.

Karina swallowed.

"Why did you want to compete?" Karina watched him carefully.

Caleb took a breath, his eyes becoming darker for a moment as he considered the question. His body tightened, even his grip on the plate in front of him. "There was never a choice to compete – I always knew I'd have to. If our line finishes with me, then there'd be no more Dartfields. Dartfields have been Lords for centuries. The name couldn't die with me. I won't be the one to fail my entire ancestry."

Karina almost felt sorry for him—even a Noble as powerful as him didn't have a choice in whether he competed or not.

Lord and Lady Dartfield entered the room, looking decidedly uncomfortable at this impromptu family get together. Karina sprung to her feet, "My Lord. We hoped you could join us for tea."

"Of course," Dartfield said, his cold eyes freezing her to her core.

"I'm so sorry." She tried to look bashful, "may I use your bathroom before we begin?"

"Of course." Lady Dartfield let out a soft laugh, "You don't need to ask to use the bathroom, Karina. It's upstairs on your first right."

"Thank you." Adrenaline surged through Karina's veins as she ascended the stairs. She assessed the hallway, checking for any staff that might have been watching her.

She was alone. Karina stalked down the hall, quietly opening doors until she found purchase. Then, success—Dartfield's office. Karina assessed the large room, filled with large wooden bookcases and ornately lush carpets. Karina shook herself; she didn't have long, she should keep moving.

Karina yanked open draws and flipped through letters, assessing anything she could see for clues. She even tried checking for secret compartments under his desk, but the sigil was nowhere to be found. As she opened the fourth drawer, her adrenaline turned into icy dread.

Buried beneath stacks of papers was a necklace—one Karina knew very well. Elaine's heart-shaped, wooden necklace that Karina had made for her was buried there.

"Elaine." She breathed, holding the necklace out in her shaking hand.

As she said Elaine's name, Karina's head snapped around at a noise. A sound that resembled nails on wood? It seemed like the noise was coming from the grand wardrobe that stood opposite the dark mahogany desk. Karina crept closer to the closet, her heart in her mouth. The scratching only got louder.

Karina extended a shaky hand to touch the wardrobe's handle.

Footsteps ascending the stairs interrupted her.

Karina stumbled toward the office entrance in fright and clicked the door shut.

"Karina," The assertive tone in Dartfield's voice behind her made her feel like she wanted to disappear.

It wasn't until that exact moment that Karina realized Elaine's necklace remained in the ball of her fist.

The scratching had distracted her, and she'd forgotten to replace the necklace where she'd found it. Her hand burned with the jewelry inside of it. She threw her hands behind her back in panic.

"My Lord, I... " She needed to think fast, like Chloe did. "I'm so sorry to have disturbed your workplace. You see, I got lost. I don't know my left from my right, and I was too embarrassed to tell Lady Dartfield."

Dartfield assessed her for a moment. Finally after what seemed like an eternity, he spoke. "Hold out your hands." He instructed.

Karina stopped breathing entirely.

"W-What?" Karina's tone had risen a few octaves.

"Hold out your hands." Dartfield said again, impatience laced in his voice. Karina pushed the necklace from her palm and into the sleeve of her jacket, praying that it would stay hidden. When the pendant was out of sight and firmly up her sleeve, she moved her hands from behind her back and opened her palms toward the Lord.

Without breaking her gaze, Dartfield took her hands in his and tipped them, so that her knuckles were toward the sky. She shivered involuntarily at the touch. It took every piece of her self-control not to break that gaze. He pointed toward one of her hands.

"This hand," he reached forward and caressed her finger along the side, "makes a letter 'L,' see?"

"I... I can't read," Karina said, stiffening under his touch. She was going to be sick.

"Ah. Well, all the Noble ladies may learn their left from their right. How else will they tell the servants how to place decorations at their parties?" The smile he shared didn't touch his eyes. Not even a little bit.

"So, now you know what an 'L' looks like." He lifted her hand, and Karina fought not to snatch it from his grasp. He winked in a conspiratorial kind of way. "And, now, you know your left from and your right. No reason to be getting lost anymore." He smiled again, without a touch of warmth. "The bathroom is there." He pointed to where she'd known it'd been all along.

"Thank you, my Lord." Karina loosed a big breath of relief, forcing herself not to run as she turned her back.

"Karina?" he asked, as she swiveled back to him and stilled. "I do hope Caleb wins you. You two make such a beautiful couple."

CHAPTER
SIXTEEN

By the third day of training, Will half-wished they'd just kill him already. The waiting, the hoping, the wishing he'd improve—he found it so much more terrifying. But despite Octavia's barbs and taunts, he wasn't even close to being adept with a sword. She was beating him shackled, for God's sake.

After she'd put him on his ass for the twentieth time that day, Will decided that was enough. "Stop, Octavia. Let's face it. I'm not going to magically become amazing at sword combat in time for the Ranking. It's the day after tomorrow."

"That's forty-eight hours more training. They say you only need ten thousand to master a skill."

"I don't have a chance in hell." Will shrugged. He'd faced his own mortality a lot over the past week.

Even if they found Elaine, he still had no idea how he'd be excused from the Games. The king would have to admit that he'd put a criminal into the Games, in some twisted power-play against his daughter.

A few years back, one boy had discovered that he'd

fallen ill from radiation and was terminal. They'd excused him from the Games, not for pity, but if he'd lived and won, it's unlikely he would've lived long enough to put a baby in his Vessel's belly. Chloe insisted that she'd be able to convince the king to tell a similar story to the public in Will's case, with the help of Father Jeremiah. She just needed enough proof that Will didn't do it.

"Trust me," Chloe'd said in that cocky way she always did. "If there's one person my dad will listen to, it's Father Jeremiah. And he's on our side. He hates the Games."

"Training with a woman, Albridge? Doesn't surprise me at all." Caleb jeered from across the arena. He put his opponent down on the ground with a punch. Will felt an overwhelming sense of dread as Caleb swaggered toward him.

"Don't engage," Octavia instructed. "With how you're fighting right now, he'll beat you with his pinky finger."

Caleb spent most days throwing taunts toward Will, slowly grinding him down. It was hard to concentrate. That was probably Caleb's plan—to stunt Will's training as much as possible. Octavia kicked out toward Will's head, which he ducked.

"Mate, just give up now, already." Caleb was closer now. Will forced himself to continue to spar with Octavia, to not turn toward him. He wouldn't give Caleb the satisfaction. ""You're shit enough that you'll never win a round."

A few boys around them laughed. Will's face burned with embarrassment.

"Control yourself," Octavia ordered.

"You've literally got a one-eyed, traitorous, useless woman as your coach. You're screwed."

Octavia didn't falter in her fighting, "This one eyed traitor could beat you any day," she spat.

"What do you mean, beat me?" He taunted. "You're a"

criminal, Octavia, and everyone knows it. And when you dry up and stop producing babies, you'll be put to death for your crimes."

Octavia leapt at Caleb, her shackles around his neck in an instant. "I could kill you in a second," she growled.

The Defenders appeared, their guns trained on her. "Release him," one of them told her.

"What are you going to do? Shoot me?" From the crazed look in Octavia's eyes, she looked like she'd happily be killed just to kick Caleb's ass.

To Will's pleasure, Caleb looked like he was about to shit himself. Octavia loosened the chains that were wrapped around his neck, and he stumbled away. "You crazy bitch!"

"This is your last warning, Octavia." A Defender instructed her. "If you don't behave, we'll stop you from coaching, no matter how much your Master pays." Will had thought about it and figured her Master must be Chloe—who else would bother coaching him?

"As you wish." She grinned, showing all of her teeth.

"You're out of the training ring today. Return home. I'll have some Defenders escort you back," a Defender added.

Will's eyes widened in shock... she had a *home*? With the shackles, Will had assumed she went back to prison after they trained. But she was a Vessel, so she must have a husband... it was all so confusing.

"Go home to that prick? No way."

"It wasn't a suggestion, Octavia," the Defender said. "Get out of the arena. You're suspended."

Octavia paused as if about to argue, but instead, she turned to Will. "I'll see you tomorrow, kid," Octavia said and trudged back to the arena's gate.

"No more training for the rest of the day." Caleb cocked his head and said, "what a shame."

Will sighed as he connected the dots. "You baited her."

"One less competitor training is a good thing for me. Means *I'm* less likely to die, and I like evening my odds." He swung his wooden sword over his shoulder, "I'll even those odds as much as I can to get what I want. I can't wait to take Karina as my wife." He leaned in closer and whispered, "I reckon she knows how to fuck."

Thwack.

Will's fist connected with Caleb's jaw. Will might be shit at sword fighting, but he threw a damn good punch. Caleb recovered quicker than Will was expecting—the Noble flung his wooden sword out, and it connected with Will's stomach with a resounding thud.

The blow winded Will and he gasped for air, but it was too late. Caleb was upon him already, laying into him with ruthless efficiency. Caleb moved methodically as he hit every inch of Will's face. Will heard a shuddering crack. The agony overwhelmed Will, and he began to fall in and out of consciousness. "Stay away from Karina. She's mine." Caleb growled.

"Come on Caleb," one of his cronies called. "It's lunch break."

Will didn't get up. He couldn't. Maybe he'd die right here.

He would be so lucky.

Will wondered if he'd laid there for minutes or hours. A shocked gasp sounded above him and he opened his eyes, squinting in the direct sunlight.

"Will!" It was Karina. Will felt hands around him, helping him up and propping his body against hers. "We need to get you someplace. Who did this to you?"

"Take a guess," Will muttered. "Your boyfriend."

"He's not my boyfriend." Karina breathed, her voice tight. "Just hold on—"

Pain erupted as she tried to jostle him up. Darkness consumed him.

∽

BY THE TIME Will was cognizant of what was happening, he was propped up in bed. "Where am I?" He frowned, looking around the grand room.

"My bedroom." Karina said, leaning in to pat his face with a damp cloth.

Will hissed at the pain. "There's sand in that cut. I need to get it out." She said with a quiet firmness that made Will sit back and allow her to tend to him. The careful caress of her fingers made him shiver.

This whole ordeal was just ... embarrassing. His body hurt, yes. But his pride hurt more. The way that Caleb overcame him so easily...

Karina must've sensed his discomfort and placed her finger on Will's chin. She gently lifted his face to meet her eyes. "Hey," she said, her face searching his. "You have nothing to be embarrassed about. You're a good person. Him, on the other hand—."

"What will you do, Karina? If you have to marry him?" Will asked.

Karina's eyes darkened as she stood up from the bed, turning her back to him. "I'll do my duty."

"But he's a bastard!"

"You think I don't know that?" She whirled around to face him. "You think that I don't wish every day that I don't have to watch boys be slaughtered for the sake of this?" She gestured to her body. She stomped over to the bathroom sink and collected what sounded like a bucket of ice.

"I'm sorry," Will muttered. "But the thought of you with him makes me sick."

"Not as sick as it makes me. Not after seeing what he's done to you. That's why..." Her dark eyes searched his face. "You need to do well in the interview portion of the Ranking. If you can't get skill points, get popularity points. Your move at the Ceremony, that was smart."

Will tried to sit up. "It wasn't a move, Karina. I meant every word."

"Well, whatever it was," she said, her eyes refusing to meet his own, "keep making people like you. The higher you rank for personality—"

"The more likely I'll get into a lower round. I'm aware, Karina."

The more you were well-liked and voted for, you'd more likely be put into a lower round, with weaker competitors. They'd engineered it for the most liked boys to win and the most hated boys to lose. You had to choose last, but there were worse things, like being murdered and all that.

In the skills segment, the boys would have to complete a physical task, and the highly skilled fighters always got into round one alongside the least-liked competitors. The vote made all of New London feel invested in the Games.

Chloe burst into the room. She assessed Will with what looked like a mix of horror and excitement. "This... this is good." She gestured to his bruised and swollen face. "This is good. You can use this."

Will blinked. "You've lost me."

Chloe began pacing around the room. "Tell the crowd you were defending Karina's honor. That Caleb disrespected her. It'll get them on your side, and it'll move you up the board in terms of popularity."

"Fine." Will didn't want to think about the Games for a second longer.

"But as we discussed, Karina, we need you on Dartfield's side. Your special vote will need to be given to Caleb." Chloe examined Karina, who nodded fiercely. "It's the only way we can keep them unsuspecting and to give us more time to look around Dartfield Manor."

"What's the news on Elaine's necklace?" Will asked. After Karina had returned from her visit to Dartfield manor. She'd informed Chloe, who'd gotten word to him.

"We need to get back to Dartfield's house. The scratching behind the wall...it's got to be Elaine."

"Why wouldn't he just kill her?" Will asked.

"There's few places one can hide a body in New London without it being found. The walls are heavily guarded these days. He won't be able to throw her body over the wall without someone seeing. Sorry–" Chloe winced at Karina's look of horror. "These are all just guesses. But no one's found a body in New London yet. It's such a small city. Anyone that's murdered and disposed of gets found rather quickly. So, she's *not* dead. We need to go back there and get some more clues."

Karina pushed off the bed. "I'm not going back. That place is terrifying."

"You're the only one that makes sense out of the three of us." Chloe insisted.

"I'm the bloody princess, and he——" Chloe motioned to Will, "well... he's... him."

"Thanks," Will said, rolling his eyes.

Chloe assessed Will with measured calm. "You're going to need to survive the Ranking. Can you do it?"

Will gulped but steadied his shaking voice. "I can."

"Karina, after the Ceremony, you'll need to return to the manor. Your excuse to be there is that you're excited about Caleb's placement in the rounds. And then you *get to that wardrobe*."

Karina looked anxious but nodded her head.

"Right. Well. Royal duties call." Chloe turned on her heel to leave.

"Oh, Chloe?" Will asked. "Thank you for at least giving me Octavia to train with."

"You've got a coach?" Chloe stilled.

"Yes. Aren't you her Master?" he asked even as Chloe's hand remained frozen on the doorknob. "I don't have any access to any royal funds. I wouldn't be able to hire a coach even if I tried."

Chloe left the room, a worried grimace on her brow. Karina followed, throwing one last sympathetic look at Will.

Lying there, Will had one question that haunted his dreams: who had bought him that coach?

CHAPTER
SEVENTEEN

Karina shifted in her chair. Lord and Lady Dartfield sat on either side of her in the arena. Lady Dartfield tapped her on the knee, which made Karina fly out of her seat in fright. "You're jumpy." Lady Dartfield said. "You look as if you've seen a ghost... or a Shadowlander." She shivered.

"I'm just excited."

"I can't wait for my boy to rank in round one. He will, of course. Then he'll have to fight the best of the competitors to win." She looked thrilled at the thought of her own son killing others.

"Lunch is served!" The Queen said. The spread of cured meats, cut fruits, and delicious cheeses on the table made Karina's stomach heave.

"I have to go," Karina muttered.

"Good luck! Remember to say good things about Caleb."

Rachel and Sarah sat chatting about who their special vote was going to be. Both were fighting over Caleb. The other twin, Louisa, looked at Karina and rolled her eyes a little. Karina grinned back, glad to have someone that didn't hate her in the Vessel cohort. Louisa had at least been kind to Karina throughout the process.

"Good luck." Karina whispered to them both. Anne sat on the other side, looking like she was about to be sick.

Karina strode past them toward the large bench of food and forced herself to look as if she were considering what to eat. Chloe joined her, looking equally perplexed, picking up fruits.

"You understand what you have to do?" Chloe murmured, not looking away from the apple she picked up to examine.

"Show my preference for Caleb, so I can get back into the house."

Chloe plucked a piece of watermelon from the table and bit into it. "Excellent."

She swanned off to her throne with James in tow. Father Jeremiah sat near her, and Karina wondered if Father Jeremiah would pull through and convince the King to let Will go once they proved him innocent. Both tasks seemed impossible at this stage.

Karina patted her dress nervously. Today they had chosen a berry pink, gauzy gown with a plunging neckline. She couldn't help but notice they'd dressed all the Vessels much more... provocatively today.

When Karina made it through the security gates and into the arena, she frowned in confusion. A large wooden frame, as high as the top of the arena, was there. It looked like the jungle gyms she used to play on as a child but one hundred times the size. She wondered how many Traitor Castes they'd forced to make it, especially for today. Karina trudged past the jungle gym and onto her podium.

"Welcome, New London!" Penelope ran into the main area, and the crowd roared. They'd clearly plied the crowd with alcohol long before the Games had started. "Today is the Ranking. It's a day to enjoy what you've worked for. There are no rules today, as long as you don't kill one another." She chuckled.

The crowd screamed in pleasure. They'd been bound by the rules of godliness and propriety for so long. But now? They could act like sinners, and they wouldn't be punished for it.

"Let's get these boys out for the first part of the Ranking. Welcome to the popularity Ranking!" Penelope added.

The arena gates screeched open to let through the forty young men. The ones who had been lucky enough to get coaches walked in tandem with them, many of the coaches whispering in the competitor's ears.

Karina looked for Will and saw him at the back. His injuries looked even worse than they had two days ago. A wild looking blonde woman stood by Will, talking to him sternly. She clapped Will on the back and pressed a kiss on his cheek. Karina's throat tightened a little.

"The first boy we have in the interviews is Defender Caste's Aaron!"

Aaron was dressed like the other boys, in something reminiscent of Roman armor. It was almost as if they engineered every part of the Games to make sure the crowd distanced themselves from the competitors. It helped them pretend like it was a game and not a mass murder.

The Defender area of the arena roared to support Aaron. Aaron smiled and waved. Aaron did well in his questioning. He was funny and likable.

Penelope laughed and teased him. "Now, ladies." She looked at the Vessels on their podiums. "The crowd would love to know. Will anyone step forward for Aaron? Do any of you fancy his socks off? You can only step forward for *one* competitor. The Vessel's special vote will give that competitor an extra hundred points to tally in the popularity round."

Karina's eyes darted toward the other girls. Anne stepped forward with a shy smile.

"That's a girl! You like Aaron then, hey? One hundred points to you! Off you go, my boy, get ready for the skills component!" Penelope said. "Next up... William Albridge!"

Karina's heart leapt into her mouth as he hobbled forward.

"Oh... oh dear. You look worse for wear. Who did you fight with? Or did your coach lay into you?" Penelope asked.

Will looked through his swollen black eye at Penelope. "I fought with Caleb." *Ooooh's* and *aahh's* resonated from the audience.

Penelope grinned. "I think you and Caleb might have your eye on the same girl."

"I think we do, yes."

Karina's heart rate picked up. This wasn't what they'd planned. He *liked* her?

"So, why should you win the Games?"

Will looked to the floor, scuffing his feet in the sand. "I don't think I should win the Games." Hushed voices echoed around the arena. "If I win, others have to die, right? I don't want that."

"Then why did you compete?" Penelope asked.

Will paused. He glanced up at the royal box as if he were considering... as if he were considering... telling them the truth. Karina could see it in his eyes. If he was going to die, he wanted everyone to know the truth. That he wasn't doing this willingly. That he'd been caught in a much deadlier game.

Karina didn't think it through. As Will opened his

mouth to say more, she stepped from the podium and grabbed Penelope's microphone. "I... I choose Will Albridge," she said, her eyes wide. "I chose him to give my hundred points to."

Gasps echoed through the arena.

"But you've been getting on so well with Caleb!" Penelope said.

"I-I like him too." Karina said, the lie burning in her throat, "But I can only choose one, and I choose Will."

Will looked as shocked as Karina felt.

"Well, then, let's give them a round of applause." Penelope said, her shock palpable.

Karina retreated to her podium, not daring to lock eyes with Caleb. That had not been the plan. Karina was supposed to choose Caleb to give her points to, not Will.

Chloe was going to be *pissed*.

~

"REMEMBER WHAT I TOLD YOU?" Octavia said.

"Play to my natural strengths. Exactly what *are* my strengths, Octavia?"

"That you're not an asshole." She grinned, clapping him on the back.

"Octavia. I might die. I need you to give me more than that."

"Okay..." She thought for a moment. "The strength of many is greater than the strength of one."

"Octavia, quit talking in riddles."

She rolled her eyes. "Jesus, you can be a dimwit sometimes, can't you? You're not an asshole. You might be a dimwit, but you're a *likable* dimwit. Team up with people that are better than you."

167

"Right. Got it." Will said, his hands shaking with nerves. Octavia clasped his face in her hands. "You can do this. Don't die, kid." And just like that, she was gone.

Will stood waiting with the other competitors at the bottom of the large wooden contraption. His idea to tell the crowd the truth had been stupid, he admitted. He'd just wanted to see the look of shock on their faces. He wanted the King to pay for sentencing an innocent person to death.

It was like Karina had read his thoughts. As if she knew that choosing him would be the only thing to stop him. But now Caleb was looking at him as if he wanted to cut his heart out. Karina might have saved him in that moment, but she'd sentenced him to whatever lay ahead of him in this Ranking.

"Thank you Vessels, you may return to the royal box to watch the Ranking," Penelope said. The girls stepped off their podiums. Karina threw Will a worried glance before she disappeared from view. "Let us all pray that God will choose the right victors in the Games, Amen."

"Amen." Resounded from the crowd.

"Right, boys," Penelope announced. "There are forty golden arrows up at the top of this structure." She motioned to the huge, hulking wooden structure in the middle of the arena—it was as high as the arena itself. "There is also a bow at the top, if anyone chooses to use it. It's not a requirement. But remember, the fewer boys there are, the smaller each round is." She leaned in toward them. "And the greater chance you have at winning."

The surrounding boys shifted. Whoever reached the top first had a big choice to make. "The Game ends when the last arrow is claimed."

Some areas of the structure looked like he'd need to jump or swing from one bar to another. There were a few ropes to help you if you didn't reach a platform. But if you dropped from the top, then that would be certain death. This structure would be extremely challenging to scale up, and Will had been climbing up structures since he started work at twelve. At least there was a platform at the very top—that must be where the bow was located.

"On your marks."

The cheers of the crowd increased, and Will looked up at the large screen. It read, "Cheer." In bold letters. The Common Castes had no choice in the matter of cheering. Unless they wanted to be the next lot of entertainment, they needed to seem excited and follow the instructions. This seemed to increase the energy among the boys, all of them fidgeting on the starting line.

"Get set," Penelope's voice rang through the loud-speaker.

Will glanced over to Octavia, who gave him a stern nod. *The strength of many is greater than the strength of one.* But how could he team up on a Ranking task that was so dependent on individual performance?

"Go!"

Will ran toward the structure, pushing through the burn in his legs. After a few seconds of sprinting, he glanced behind him—some boys appeared to be holding back.

They clearly wanted to be at the bottom of the pack in the hopes they'd get placed into a lower round. The jeers of the crowd toward the competitors told Will it would do nothing for their popularity score with the public vote at the end of today.

Over the years, Will had watched all the tactics boys had tried to use to win. No one who didn't put everything they've got into the Ranking did well. He needed to try his hardest. And not just because of that. Listening to the way

Caleb spoke about Karina... he didn't want her to be subjected to a life like that.

He wanted better for her.

Will pushed his burning muscles on and shimmied up the first pole. He'd run further than the others, taking a route up the structure that fewer competitors were fighting for. Caleb had taken the closest route to him and was already stamping on the fingers of those below him, leaving them to drop to the floor in pain.

Will thanked God that Octavia had made him do all of those push-ups. His arms felt capable as they moved and swung on the bars, ascending the structure. It reminded him of being back on the building site. The structure was like scaffolding; it was just wooden instead of metal. Only three boys were above him in the race to the top: Adam, Aaron, and Caleb, leading the pack.

"It's just scaffolding." He breathed, climbing it. "I'm just at work." He tried to tell himself. No matter how expensive the other Nobles' training had been, it was nothing compared to hard labor for eighty hours a week.

Will's confidence faltered as his footing slipped, leaving him hanging by only his arms. Grimacing in pain, he pulled up his weight with all of his strength.

Once he was safely seated on a beam, he inspected his palms. They were riddled with splinters. Looking above him, Will surmised he was about halfway up. Toward the top, he noticed that the wood was more brittle, with more rickety nails sticking out, ones that waited to hurt him. The higher he got, the harder it would be to continue.

These weren't just any normal splinters, Will thought as he inspected them.

They seem to have been placed into the wood artificially. He pulled one out that was as long as a needle. His hands were drenched with blood already.

This was a test of pain tolerance. It was a different kind of pain to pushing your body's fitness levels. It was *grit*. He could see now that the other boys above him also had blood covering their hands. Will squinted in the sunlight toward the top of the structure. Aaron swung out to jump to a higher beam, but his grip slipped. He fell, his scream cutting through the roars of the crowd. Will had been on scaffolding this high before, and the Craftsman who had fallen, had never walked again.

Will ignored the tight feeling in his throat and continued toward the top platform. Caleb was already there. He ripped a golden arrow out of the platform and raised it high, and the crowd answered with a roar.

"Caleb has the bow!" Penelope yelled. "The question is: what will he do with it?" He knelt down, and as he stood up again, Caleb had a bow in his hand, the golden arrow notched and ready.

And he was aiming straight for Will.

Will pushed himself toward the wooden beam as the first arrow flew past him by mere inches. A Defender Caste —Jack, Will remembered—ascended to the top platform, jumping up with a flourish. Caleb notched his bow and now aimed toward Jack. Now that Caleb was distracted, Will scaled up the wooden beams. Will never saw what happened to Jack, but his shrill scream of agony would haunt him at the end of his days.

Will inched closer. He could hear Caleb now.

"Come out, come out," Caleb called.

The other boys climbing below seemed to gain on Will at pace now. They were only a few levels underneath him. He needed to move fast.

A few feet below him, Cameron scaled deftly up the structure. Cameron reached for a particularly nasty beam that was full of thick splinters and–

"Hey, don't—" Will warned.

Cameron grabbed the beam and cried out as sharp splinters protruded deeply into his hand. He let go in shock, his mouth opened wide in surprise.

But Will moved, catching the scruff of his clothing and hoisting him back onto the beam with him.

"Jesus. You saved my life." Cameron said, looking below him, eyes wide at what his fate could have been instead.

Will remembered Octavia's instructions, an idea beginning to form. "Okay, I saved you, right? Now, let's save each other. Caleb's got the bow, and he's taking down everyone that gets to the top. At this rate, he won't even have to compete. He'll get all the Vessels to himself."

Cameron grimaced. "We don't want that."

"Remember your good acting from day one? When you fooled me into thinking you weren't good at fighting?"

Cameron shrugged. "Yeah."

"You played that part well, and you're going to do it again."

EIGHTEEN

Will waited underneath the top platform, the creak of Caleb's weight on the wood mere inches above him. He didn't dare breathe, despite the wooden floor between the two of them, shielding Will from view.

Cameron nodded to Will in affirmation and launched himself onto the platform, hands already up in a sign of submission. "Wait! Wait! I can help you get Karina."

Caleb had his bow aimed at Cameron's chest. "I'm listening."

One moment of hesitation was all Will needed. Now that Cameron had distracted him from the opposite side, Will could climb up onto the platform undetected. Will lifted himself on as silently as possible, creeping toward Caleb from behind. He needed to make sure the move to restrain him was perfect, or he'd pay for it with his life.

Will took his chance.

Will jumped onto Caleb's back, locking his arms by his sides and held on for dear life as Caleb bucked and reared as if he were a raging bull. Cameron snatched the bow from Caleb's grasp in the flurry of movement.

Caleb tried to buck Will off, but he held firm. It became impossible for Caleb to pry him off or throw him over the edge.

"If you go, I go." Will grunted at the height that awaited them both if Caleb lost his footing on the platform.

Now that Caleb had become unarmed and unable to move, more and more boys jumped onto the platform and took their golden arrows, their eyes glancing to the tousle between Will and Caleb.

"I'll kill you for this, Albridge!" Caleb roared.

Cameron punched Caleb hard in the gut, and he toppled to the floor. Caleb rolled on the floor in pain, and Will removed himself as quickly as possible. They needed to leave before Caleb recovered and killed them both.

"You might be tiny. But your punches can kick ass, mate," Will admitted, remembering how painful his sparring session with Cameron had been.

"Let's go." Cameron threw the remaining arrow to Will, and as the buzzer signaled the end of the Ranking, a surge of relief overcame him. He'd *survived* the Ranking.

~

THE RANKING COMPRISED a complicated mathematical equation that no one knew or understood but the selected few: the Clergy Caste.

Chloe paced outside of Father Jeremiah's office next to her father. She'd tried to get there first, to beg Jeremiah to push Will's score lower, but the King had beaten her there. Chloe wasn't expecting Will to do so well, and she was nervous what this would mean for his rank.

Of course, he'd needed to try. If you flunked the skills component on purpose, you were at best a traitor to the Games, and your popularity always dwindled in the vote. If it dwindled too much, you might end up in round one with the best fighters.

And then you became the person the crowd loved to hate, someone they didn't mind watching lose or die. But the Ranking task this year... it's as if... they'd made it for Will. He didn't have combat skills. But he had a natural strength, speed, and balance that helped him scale the structure without incident.

After the skills component, they'd collected the votes from the crowd. As the High Priest was in Manchester doing whatever High Priests did, Father Jeremiah was the highest ranking clergy official in New London. Only he was trusted to count the votes and do the calculations necessary to rank them. Will's rank meant his life or death.

Chloe wrung her hands together at the thought.

Father Jeremiah burst out of his office, looking frazzled, his white hair sticking up all over the place. "It is done." He sounded relieved. The King snatched the paper from his hands and scanned it. His mouth turned into a thin line. "I'll hand this over to Penelope for the announcement."

Chloe would not risk him tampering with the results. "I'll go with you, Father."

The King grunted and stormed out of the church and back toward the arena. Chloe tried to read the paper in his hand as she trotted after him, but he concealed it well. She'd just have to wait, like everybody else. Chloe and her father strode back into the royal box, flanked by Defenders after he'd deposited the Ranking list to Penelope.

Karina looked like she wanted to be anywhere but here. Chloe took a calming breath; Karina's little stunt down there had cost them their visit to the Dartfields' house undetected. Thanks to Karina, Chloe's plan was useless, and she'd need to think of another. After Karina gave her points to Will and showed her clear preference for him, she'd never be welcomed back to the Dartfields' with open arms. Even now, Lord and Lady Dartfield shot sharp looks across the room at her.

"Nice little, last minute decision there, Karina." Chloe said tightly.

Karina looked everywhere but Chloe's eyes. "You didn't see it in his face. He was going to tell everyone that he's a prisoner, that he wasn't competing willingly. The King would've made sure they'd killed him then. Executed Will on the spot for speaking ill of the monarchy."

Chloe paused, shock radiating over her. "Why would Will do that? I'm going to get him out. He'd be doomed if he did that."

"Maybe he's already doomed, Your Highness." Karina muttered miserably.

Chloe understood the insinuation and narrowed her eyes. "So you don't think we can save him? Just because he's not a Noble? Why the hell did you even agree to help me anyway, then?" She hissed.

"Because... because I need to try." Karina's eyes sparkled with tears and a wave of shame washed over Chloe.

She'd pushed Karina too far.

"Good evening, New London!" Penelope's voice boomed around the arena.

The late afternoon sun had descended, leaving a bright red moon in its wake. Chloe wondered what the moon had looked like before humans had bombed it.

Anything we got our hands on gets destroyed, she thought bitterly.

"The Ranking results are here. These groups, ranked in a fair order ordained by God, will fight to the death to win their future wife, and their right for a new generation of their family. The victors will also receive large compensation for the rest of their lives, in return for fighting here today. Round one boys must compete first, and it's known to be the toughest round, so they also get to choose their Vessel first."

"Those who fight first, choose first." The crowd echoed back.

Chloe saw the words on the large screen, instructing the crowd to chime in. Chloe rolled her eyes at the stupidity of it all, of the unnecessary bloodshed. She'd become so accustomed to witnessing horror now. Other children below the age of sixteen weren't allowed to watch the Games. But she'd been forced to every year since the Uprising.

The boys lined up in the arena, awaiting the verdict.

"There are thirty boys remaining," Penelope informed the crowd, as Chloe did some quick math; ten dead, or broken beyond repair. "That means six of you will compete in each round for our five lovely ladies."

Karina's nails dug into Chloe's flesh harder. Chloe weathered the pain. Welcomed it, even.

"Round one will include: Henry, Cameron, Charles, Benjamin, Edward, and Peter."

Chloe heaved a sigh of relief. Will wasn't in the hardest round with the deadliest competitors. It was a miracle. Karina's hand loosened on hers, just a little.

But to Chloe's horror, there was another name that hadn't been mentioned.

"Round two will be Alex, Paul, Jacob, Patrick, Caleb, and…. Will."

Round two. They had placed Will in the second round.
They'd placed Will in the same round as Caleb.

Chloe looked at Karina in horror, tears sparkling in her eyes. Chloe squeezed her eyes shut and sent a prayer to the heavens that someone beat Caleb for Karina's sake. It wasn't very godly of her to pray for someone's death. But it was all she had.

They needed to work faster.

And Chloe might just have had her craziest idea yet.

~

KARINA SCHOOLED her face into neutrality as she walked down the grand marble stairs and entered the ballroom. All the Nobles were at the Ranking Ball tonight. Glasses clinked and Nobles laughed raucously at each other's dull jokes. There were performers dotted around the room, Craftsman Castes who played instruments or contorted their bodies in interesting ways.

Karina half wondered if Chloe's friend, Tiffany, was here again tonight. She hadn't seen her since she'd been so terribly rude to her. Everyone who was anyone in high society received an invitation to one of the most exclusive social events of the year. That social event also just happened to rank the young boys in what order they'd die in but hey, one knew how it went, all details, details.

Caleb stormed across the ballroom, looking as furious as he'd been when they'd first announced the rounds. Caleb would've despised the fact he hadn't been in round one with the strongest competitors and the least-liked, weaker competitors. He spoke in hushed tones to the boys who'd been announced to compete in round one, jamming his finger at a larger boy— *Henry's*—chest and then motioning toward Karina.

Karina snapped her head away from them before they could notice. She could guess what he was telling Henry to do: *don't pick Karina.*

The Dartfields were a powerful and wealthy family, and she suspected that most would heed his warning. Caleb wanted Karina all for himself. Karina gulped.

Only the Clergy knew the equations to rank the boys in their order, but Karina was sure that they'd rigged it somehow toward the more popular competitors—the crowd's favorites. Then, the crowd felt like they'd won too. The crowd could save someone they liked, even loved, from their death. People must have liked Will. Caleb was easily one of the best fighters, but he had been placed in a lower round.

Perhaps his popularity—or Caleb's lack thereof—had evened the score with his skill.

But round two meant they had *two days* left until Will competed. And round one was tomorrow.

Karina threw a panicked look at Chloe, but she couldn't catch her eye. Chloe was busy talking with Father Jermemiah again. Karina couldn't sense any worry or apprehension from Chloe, as she spoke in hushed tones to him. Chloe was a much better actress than Karina. But she'd been at this game for longer, Karina supposed.

Karina dragged her feet toward her podium, not ready to be stared at again.

Lord Dartfield stepped in her way, blocking her path. "That stunt was ...very disrespectful. Very ungodly." He inspected his fingernails casually, but Karina saw the heat in his eyes.

"I'm sorry. I had to go with my heart when I chose who

I gave the points to." Karina lifted her head high. She was no longer a Traitor—she was a Vessel. And she wouldn't let anyone tell her otherwise.

"My best friend, Elaine, always told me to follow what I believed in. And I believe in Will."

Lord Dartfield's face drained of all color. Karina could never return to Dartfield manor to check for more clues on Elaine. So, she figured it wouldn't hurt to drive the knife in a little more. She wanted to make him sweat, to let him know she was onto him. She pulled up her dress and exposed her ankle, where the wooden heart pendant now sat. Elaine's pendant had not left her since she'd taken it from his drawer.

"She'll always be with me. Reminding me of what's right. And no one's found her body in the walls of New London yet, did you hear? I think she's still alive."

"You insolent, little... what are you accusing me of?" Lord Dartfield's eyes flashed, and he flung his arm out to grip Karina's wrist. He held onto her and pulled her in closer to his ear, making her wrist sting at his tight grip. "Keep your nose *out* of Elaine's business. You don't know what powers are at play."

Out of nowhere, Chloe appeared next to Karina. "Lord Dartfield." Chloe's voice was casual as she addressed him, but there was a bite in her tone. Karina found herself thinking she wouldn't want to end up on the wrong side of it. "It seems your hand has found its way onto a Vessel's wrist. That seems like a very improper thing to do amidst our current company. I'd suggest removing it if you don't want your *own* hand removed."

Will stepped in to her right, so Karina's friends flanked either side of her. "William," Chloe said, not looking away from Dartfield, "it seems Karina wishes to dance with you. Take her to the floor, will you?"

Will's voice was icy with rage, but his exterior remained cool as he said, "It would be my pleasure, Your Highness." Will offered out his arm, and Karina settled her hand into the crook of it as he guided her safely away.

"Are you hurt?" Will asked quietly, his eyes scanning the room. "Did he harm you?"

"N-No." Karina stammered. "He was angry. He spoke about Elaine as if...as if he knew her. He spoke of her in the *present tense*. It's got to be him. Why would he take her away? Why would he want to take me?"

"I don't know, Karina." Will placed his hand on the small of her back and they began to dance. Nobles stared at them, whispering, but Karina didn't care. She moved closer to him, leaning into his warmth. She didn't even care about the camera that tracked them.

"There's got to be something bigger going on, and if we don't find out soon...You're in the same round as Caleb in the Games and he'll..."

"Don't think about it." Will smiled sadly. "I try not to."

"Right." Karina peered over Will's broad shoulder. Caleb was glaring at them. "You shouldn't dance with me, Will. You're only annoying him, giving him more reason to come for you."

"Karina." Will breathed her name as if it were a name worth worshiping. Karina had never heard it said like that.

"Yes?"

"I don't give a shit what Caleb thinks about us dancing. Because right here, right now... this dance is all I have. And I want you to know that when I die—"

"Will, don't." Tears sprang to her eyes.

"Let me finish, Karina." Will's Adam's apple bobbed as

he searched for the words, "I want you to know that if I could've won the Games, I would've chosen you." His eyes burned with passion. "I would've married *you*."

Karina didn't answer at first but placed her cheek into Will, as she savored the feeling of being pressed against his muscled chest. His heart thumped wildy, but as she placed her cheek closer to him, a tear trickled down her cheek.

"I would've liked that," she admitted quietly. "I would have liked to have spent the rest of my life with you."

A crash sounded and both of them jumped at the sound of glass skittering across the ballroom floor. The ballroom fell quiet for a moment—the violins screeching to a halt. Karina looked up to the source of the noise.

Shadowlanders were crawling through each one of them, weapons brandished and readied to kill.

CHAPTER
NINETEEN

Screams echoed around the ballroom. Nobles scattered, dropping their champagne glasses and running for the door. Shadowlanders, their entire faces painted in intricate and terrifying designs, tore through the crowd. They stabbed and slayed the Nobles.

Shouts from the Defenders erupted, "Protect the Vessels! Protect the King!"

Chloe snapped her head toward her friends. Will had Karina firmly behind him, a meat carving knife brandished. Will was desperately trying to steer Karina to safety, but he was met instead by a huge hulk of a Shadowlander. Chloe's only weapon was the small knife she always carried, at all times, in her boot. Chloe leant down and grabbed it. It was short and stubby and she had no fucking idea how to use it —she hadn't been allowed to be taught.

James grabbed for Chloe. "Where the hell did you get that?" He yelled, regarding the knife. "It doesn't matter... Your Highness, you need to come with me!"

Chloe managed to evade him by mere inches. She knew that once he got a hold of her, she would not have the opportunity to help her friends again. But if she led James to them—

Chloe lifted her skirts and sprinted for Will and Karina, James hot on her heels. By the time she got there, Caleb had joined the fray, aiding Will in fending him off. He managed to avoid the Shadowlanders ax and punched him with a deadly precision.

The man stumbled back in shock.

"Fuck off, Savage!" Caleb growled. A glimmer of surprise had Chloe pausing—Caleb might be an asshole, but he'd chosen to protect Karina rather than save himself.

That had to count for something.

"James, help Caleb!" Chloe threw her arm out and pointed at the fight. "Will, get Karina and come with me!" Chloe hated that she had to run, that she didn't have the ability to fight.

She suddenly felt utterly foolish that she'd been sneaking off for all those nights to learn something as frivolous as illusions and tricks of the eye—what use were levitation tricks when you couldn't protect yourself? When you were stuck in a sea of Shadowlanders with no way out?

A terror coiled in her gut when Chloe remembered. Chloe whirled around to meet the frightened faces of her two friends, their hands clasped together. "Tiffany—have you seen her? Have you seen her performing at the ball tonight?"

"I–I don't know!" Karina yelled. "Chloe, we've gotta get out of here!"

"I've got to find her!"

Lilian, her ladies maid, would be up in her bedchambers, and she prayed the Shadowlanders hadn't made it that far. Chloe scanned the crowd for her friend.

"Tiff!" She screamed, spotting Tiffany in her leotard,

hidden under a banquet table. "Tiff!" Chloe didn't think twice. She willed her legs to carry her faster, and to her relief, Will and Karina followed her.

Will grabbed onto her. "Get down!" He yelled to them both as arrows began to fly around the ballroom.

He leaned over both girls, his body protecting them while arrows rained down upon them.

Tiffany looked like a racoon, her dark make-up leaving big tracks down her cheeks and rings around her eyes.

Chloe flung her hand out, "Tiff, C'mon!"

Tiffany lay over another girl in her performance troop, whose eyes remained glassy and unmoving, a thin trail of blood leaving her mouth. "I can't! Marissa!" Tiffany cried. "Marissa, wake up!"

"Tiffany!" Chloe's voice was hard. "She's gone. If you don't want the same fate, come with us now!"

Tiffany seemed to see sense, blinking a few times and then nodding. She grabbed Chloe's hand and the four of them sprinted toward a shattered window. Chloe knew of an escape route in almost every room of this palace. She silently thanked God for her disobedience, even if it helped her just for this moment.

More Defender Castes had poured into the ballroom, the ear-splitting sound of bullets flying had them covering their ears in fright. "Jump onto the roof from here and follow it down until you reach my room! We'll barricade ourselves in." Chloe locked her fingers together and pushed Tiffany's feet into her hands, giving her a boost up to the window. "I'll follow soon." She squeezed Tiffany's hand. "Go." Chloe instructed fiercely.

Next, Will lifted himself up, turning back and lending his hand to pull Chloe up. Chloe winced as the sharp stinging sensation of a cut sliced across her thigh.

A shard of broken glass scraped her leg as he'd helped her up. "Karina, you're next." Will demanded.

Karina clasped her hand in his and he began to pull her up—

But a Shadowlander grabbed her waist and pulled her backward. It felt almost like déjà vu.

This was the way Will had lost hold of Elaine, Chloe thought.

"Karina!"

"Will!" Karina screamed, her hand outstretched for him.

The Shadowlander gave a disgusting smile as he locked eyes with Chloe. The man's face was weathered, with a long cut down one side of his cheek, and was missing an eye. He had an unmistakable eyepatch—red and black with a skull where his eye should be.

"Oh no, you fucking don't!" Chloe yelled at eye-patch man and jumped back down to the floor.

Will was at her side in an instant, running for Karina and brandishing the knife he'd found ready. "Give me back my Karina!" Will yelled.

"She's *mine* now," the Shadowlander said, his voice guttural, his accent strange and thick. He held a knife at Karina's throat.

Chloe wasn't quite sure how it happened.

One moment, the Shadowlander had his knife to Karina's throat. The next, his hand was on the floor, and he was screaming in agony. James stood behind him, a Shadowlander sword in one hand. The guard looked bruised and battered but alive.

The man with the eye patch took one look at the enormity of James and the sword that had just cut off his hand. He turned on his heel and ran. Chloe ran at James with force, "I've never been so grateful to see you." She said into his chest.

James awkwardly patted her hair. Chloe took her head out of his enormous chest and noticed that most of the Shadowlanders had disappeared, the remaining few left picked off by other Defender Castes.

"You're... welcome. And we're going to have a conversation about how that knife found its way into your boot, Princess," James said.

Chloe gulped.

Karina and Will embraced fiercely as she sobbed. "It's over." Will told her in soft, soothing tones. "It's over. You're safe now."

He whispered quietly into her hair. It seemed like such an intimate moment that Chloe found herself having to look away.

Her heart twisted when she realized the Games would go ahead tomorrow as they always did, and in reality, the competition had only just begun.

~

CHLOE WASN'T LOOKING FORWARD to it. But if she was ever going to be allowed to skip today's Games and considering everything that had transpired last night, this needed to be believable.

Lilian, her ladies' maid, was the only person she trusted to get the job done. Chloe exhaled a sigh of relief as Lilian stepped into Chloe's bedroom and clicked the door shut. "It's three in the morning! I told you to be back in the palace by midnight, Lil!"

"I know... I'm sorry. The guy was late."

Chloe gulped. She'd been worried sick, dreading that

another Shadowlander attack had come and hurt Lilian in their carnage. "Give it here, then. I'll need to take it now."

Lilian rustled in her pocket and produced the vial of clear liquid.

Chloe snatched it from her grasp. "Here goes nothing."

The Princess undid the topper and gulped down the contents.

"Give that back to me." Lilian instructed, yanking the vile from her grasp. "That can't be found in your bedroom."

"When you were at Hell's Gate, did you see Tiff? Is she okay after what happened?" Chloe trailed off.

"No. I got word out that you're kind of grounded, if a princess can be grounded. And that Tiffany and Tommy shouldn't expect to hear from you regarding your... *lessons* anytime soon."

"Oh, princesses can certainly be grounded," Chloe huffed, flinging herself onto her bed. "The Games will be over soon. Then I can try to get an alternative route to get to Hell's Gate."

Lilian frowned, "Don't you think you should stop doing your lessons? It seems like such a trivial thing to risk it all for. You know that illusion magic is banned. They burned every book about that sort of thing a long time ago. There are so many eyes on you."

"No. I don't." Chloe left little room for argument.

Lilian didn't push her. "Okay."

"Can you find a way to give her this?" Chloe shoved a piece of paper into Lilian's grasp. "I need her help with something. I... I have a plan for how I'm going to get Will out of this mess. I need her and Tommy's help."

Lillian frowned, looking uncertain. "She won't be able to read it, Chloe."

Chloe shrugged nonchalantly. "She can read the basics. I taught her."

Lilian's eyes bulged. "Chloe, that is *super* illegal! How did you even-–"

A thud had them both jumping. "You need to go. I'll see you at breakfast."

～

BREAKFAST WAS ALWAYS a ghastly affair in Chloe's family. But it was even worse during the Games. They said their prayers and sat in silence as they ate. Sometimes the Queen would prattle on about something irrelevant to break the tense silence. But today, Chloe slammed her fork down.

"Dad. Will didn't kill Elaine or hurt her. Why don't you trust me? Why can't you let him go? He doesn't want to compete in the Games. Just let him *go*. Surely, after what happened last night, you have more important things to be dealing with."

Her father did not look up from his oats. "You gave me no choice when you stormed into my office during that meeting. I know you did that to hold me to account. To make me do what *you* wanted. Do you think so little of me?" His lip wobbled a little, and Chloe was taken aback by his display of emotion. Then she realized what the date was today. "If you'd just come to me... if you hadn't told them you'd been prancing about outside the castle without my knowing, we could have come to an accord. But instead you made me seem weak. In my position, a weak man is a dead one. I had to reassert my authority by making him pay. Like they'd all need to pay if they ever went against us."

Chloe sat in stunned silence. It had been as simple as going to him alone? *Asking him nicely?*

189

"This was your doing, Chloe. Not mine." He stormed out of the room.

"Dad—" Chloe said, but she didn't get the rest of the sentence out. She vomited all over the table. He whirled in shock, the Queen screeching in horror. The vial had kicked in, then. "I don't feel well."

~

KARINA FELT a surge of relief as she entered the royal box, and found Chloe was nowhere to be seen. Stage one of the plan was in effect. Karina glanced around the arena. The mood amongst the crowd was more somber than it had been before the attack. Many reached for the food, but there was a bitterness to it, as if now they knew. The Games were the cost of the food and the alcohol.

The Games were the cost of the Uprising.

Karina searched the grounds for a head of black, cropped hair. For a face of olive skin. She couldn't find the one she wanted.

"Karina!" the Queen shrieked. "Today is the first day of the Games! Can you believe it? Round one is already here!"

Karina forced a smile that looked more like a baring of teeth. "I can't wait."

The other Vessels looked on edge, too. In exchange for their podiums, they all sat on thrones, one level below the queen and king.

"Nobles and Common Castes! Good morning!" Penelope ran into the arena, this time donning a lilac suit. The crowd cheered, but it sounded forced and... fake.

Defender Caste soldiers now flanked all sides of the arena, guns in hand, but Penelope continued despite the shadow of their presence. "Your King wishes to address you!"

The King stood, and everyone bowed their heads. "First, let us pray to God almighty that the boys fighting today will find their way to heaven. And let us pray for healthy children because of these Games. That is why we do this. For fairness and equality for all. You all live on— through your children." Hushed affirmations of agreement echoed throughout the Nobles, whilst the Commons remained quiet. "Remember, all of this was your choice. You were all so hungry for blood ten years ago when you tried to kill my family. When you killed my wife." The King's voice became strained. "Remember that. This is your penance. Boys, enter!"

The six boys competing for a Vessel today entered the arena one by one, each with their chosen weapon in hand. Some carried axes, others swords, and one even held a trident. Karina's stomach knotted up again—she was going to be sick. They all took their places around the edge of the circle of the arena.

The King took a deep breath and said, "Let the Games *begin*!"

~

CHLOE'S STOMACH still roiled from the poison she'd ingested last night, but she needed to push through. Getting Lilian out and organizing the vial had been hard enough—she wouldn't get this opportunity again.

The King had put minimum security around her today, as he'd need all he could get at the Games.

Chloe heard Lilian outside, speaking to James. "The

Princess has asked for me to wash her. Her body is too sore after her injury last night. It'll be a few minutes."

"Very well." James' tone was one of utter boredom. The door creaked open and Lilian darted inside.

She looked as nervous as Chloe felt. "You ready?"

Chloe nodded, taking off her robe. Underneath it lay Lilian's spare maid outfit. Thank goodness they had the same golden blonde hair and stature; they almost looked like a mirror image of one another. Chloe often wished that she could be in Lilian's position instead of her own.

Lil placed the bonnet on her. "For god's sake Chloe, be quick."

Chloe nodded, unable to even look at her old friend. She was risking Lilian's life to do this.

"Jump into bed, like you're sleeping. Turn your head toward the window, so James can't see your face. No matter what you do... pretend you're asleep. Don't respond." Chloe whispered.

"Got it," Lil said.

Chloe slipped out of her bedroom and didn't dare lift her head in greeting at James. For once, she thanked God he was so damn tall. He only saw the crown of her head from above. Chloe scuttled off down the hall. She prayed James didn't notice her slight limp from her injury last night and that she'd be back before anyone noticed.

~

THE GAMES WERE WORSE than Karina ever could have imagined. As the trumpets blared, five boys ran for the one that they'd deemed to be the weakest. The boy didn't stand a chance.

He must have lost the popularity vote, Karina assumed.

The other boys rushed toward him, brandishing their weapons. Tears sprang to Karina's eyes as she watched this frightened boy realize that he was the weakest competitor —that *he* was the easy kill. The realization of horror that his life was about to end suddenly and violently came upon him, and he wailed in outrage, jumping toward one of the boys. He attempted to defend himself from them, but they surrounded him like a pack of wolves.

He just looked so *frightened*. He went down with a scream, a trident protruding through his chest. He dropped to his knees, and the crowd was silent. The boy slid down, dropping into the sands as blood slowly leaked below him.

Next, boys picked out who they wanted to battle with, either by chance or by strategy, and peeled off into separate fights. A massive hulk of a boy—Henry, Karina remembered —held off two competitors at once with ease. He blocked and parried both boys. He was huge and hulking but moved with a swiftness that surprised Karina. Henry spun and swung his sword out in a smooth motion, slitting a boy's throat with a sick grin.

The other one he fought went down soon after.

"We... we have to marry... these people?" Anne stammered in disgust.

"So, it's just hitting you now." Rachel jeered. "Don't worry, that psycho has got his eye on Sarah. Lucky for you."

"That's my man," Sarah said proudly. "I'm so glad I voted for a winner. I'm going to be the first Vessel chosen and pregnant by autumn, mark my words ladies."

When Henry killed his next victim, when the guts of a young boy came spilling out onto the sands, Karina couldn't resist shutting her eyes any longer.

∾

DARTFIELD'S HOUSE WAS QUIET. All their servants must've left to watch the Games, too. Chloe crept through the house, a knife in her hand and at the ready. She didn't know what she was walking into. She needed to be prepared.

"Elaine?" she whispered to the empty office she now found herself in. "Elaine, I'm Karina's friend," Chloe said a little louder. No sounds came from the wardrobe. What had Karina said she'd heard?

Scratching.

Karina had been sure of it, but maybe Elaine was sleeping?

Chloe's hands shook as she pulled at the wardrobe. She held her breath—

There was no Elaine to be seen. Chloe's heart sank. She'd hoped that she would find Elaine here. That she could explain what really went on that night. That Dartfield had tried to kidnap Karina, too—

Chloe wrinkled her nose. The wardrobe...it stunk of sweat and urine. As if someone had been living there...

Maybe Karina *had* been right.

Chloe scoured every inch of Dartfield's office, desperate to find some sort of clue, some sort of idea to where he had taken her now. The whole situation seemed to grow more mysterious by the second. Chloe was about to give up, but before she did, she picked up the Bible that was placed front and center on the desk. A piece of paper fluttered out of the pages. It was a photograph.

One of Elaine.

Elaine was smiling in the photograph, but it didn't take a genius to see she's scared as hell. She sported a black eye and held a sign in front of her. She wore beautiful clothes— a gown that would envy one that any of the Vessels wore.The sign she held looked like the kind of board that criminals held in their mugshots.

The sign read: "Available for transfer."

Available for transfer?

What the hell did that mean? The date read: *August 22nd*. That was only a few days ago.

Chloe couldn't believe her luck. This was it—*this* was her proof she needed to bring to her father. Will hadn't killed Elaine, and she *was* alive. Better yet, she had proof that Lord Dartfield had abducted her. She could go to him after today's Games, and Will would be released!

But as she surveyed the bottom of the photograph, her heart sank. The sigil that had been on the ring was right there next to her father's own royal seal.

And right at the bottom of the photograph lay her father's signature.

CHAPTER

TWENTY

T t was down to Henry and Cameron. They circled one another, assessing one another's weaknesses. A bear versus a snake.

Karina spotted Will. He sat behind where Cameron and Henry fought. His coach, Octavia, whispered in his ear as she watched the fight, pointing at each competitor as she spoke. She was using the round as an opportunity to coach him.

Good.

Karina couldn't bring herself to think past today or past the moment, to think about the future that beheld Will tomorrow, so she returned her attention to the fight. Cameron was the first to strike, closing the gap between him and Henry. He struck out at Henry's knee, and Henry roared in pain, going down hard.

Henry swung his sword at Cameron, which had him retreating a few steps. Cameron struck again, nicking Henry's arm with his sword. Cameron understood he'd be too small to overpower Henry. He needed to take him down little by little.

He was smart. Perhaps he could even win. Karina dared to hope—

Then, Henry struck Cameron with such force that the smaller boy toppled over. Henry stood, limping toward Cameron. His knee looked damaged, but that didn't stop him as he punched Cameron into oblivion. The crowd wanted a show, and he'd give them one.

Henry delivered the blows to Cameron with deadly ability. He made sure that the Vessels were looking at him as he decapitated Cameron.

"I think I'm going to be sick," Anne muttered, sprinting for the bathroom.

Henry roared with victory, and the crowd cheered. He jogged over to Penelope and snatched the microphone from her.

"Sarah." He addressed her in front of the crowd. "I wanted you from the moment I laid eyes on you. I knew God intended us to be together. Consider this..." He gestured to where the bodies of the other competitors were now lying motionless. "A symbol of my love and adoration for you and for God himself. Praise him. God has blessed you with the ability to conceive children. Sarah, will you join the House of Winchester and become a Duchess as well as my bride?"

Sarah squealed with excitement. "Of course I will!"

The crowd clapped and Sarah ran down to where Henry was, and they exchanged a passionate kiss. He cradled her face in his hands, but his hands were still bloody, leaving red traces on Sarah's pale cheeks. She didn't seem to mind, though. The cameras zoomed in as far as they could.

Round one was over. It was as brutal as it was short. Karina clapped along with the others, terrified of the fate that Will would face tomorrow. She prayed Chloe had a plan.

Because right now, Karina couldn't see how Will would get out of this alive.

∽

"You're sure your... friends want me here?" Octavia sat on the dingy bed of *Madame Butterfly's*, her knees bouncing up and down. Will sat next to her, leaned over, his elbows on his knees. He didn't bother to look up at her.

"What are you gonna do, Octavia, tell on me?"

Octavia huffed out a laugh. "We should be training right now. We still have time–"

"Octavia, my round is tomorrow," Will snapped; Octavia fell silent. "My contact was trying to locate Elaine's whereabouts today. This was the only place we could meet."

"Why?"

"Her options can be limited." Will hadn't mentioned that his contact was Princess Chloe, the daughter of the man who had sentenced him to death. He figured that if Chloe showed, then Octavia would find out soon enough.

"So you say you didn't do it—what is finding this Elaine girl going to prove?"

"If she can testify for me and prove my innocence, then the King promised he'd let me go. In front of his Nobles."

Octavia blew out a breath, "I don't mean to piss on your hopes and dreams, Will, but promises from people in power... they're rarely kept."

Will gave her a wry smile. "Well, you'll see who promised to free me soon."

Both of them jumped at the rap at the door. Three hooded figures walked into the room. One had wild red hair, and the other two flanked her, both with raven hair. The former pulled down her cloak to reveal her face.

Octavia looked like she was about to shit herself. "Your Highness!" She bowed low. "I-" Octavia looked up, assessing the hair, the hoods and something clicked together in that one eye of hers. "Jesus Christ, Will. You've got the Princess involved?"

"It's my fault that he's here," Chloe shot back.

Octavia slumped down on the bed, looking baffled. "I need a cigarette."

"This is Karina and Tiffany," Chloe said.

Tiffany nodded her head in acknowledgement to Octavia, but Karina's eyes remained firmly on Will.

"Will," Karina said, sounding as exhausted as Will felt. Seeing her like this, with that Vessel necklace tight around her neck made him ache for her. She seemed wrecked. Her eyes were red and puffy, as if she'd been crying. "I-" Karina searched for the words, but none came.

Will's heart sank. "Please, just tell me you found something today, Chloe."

Chloe adjusted the hood. "I didn't find Elaine." After the Princess spoke, Will's shoulders slumped. "But I found another clue. And it's worse than we thought."

Chloe passed the photograph of Elaine over to Will. Will examined the image, trailing her fingers over Elaine's face. Octavia snatched it from his grasp, pulling it closer to her eye.

"This is evidence! We can bring the photograph to the King. It proves that I didn't hurt her. They'll let me go-" Will started.

"Look at the bottom of the photograph," Chloe interrupted. The hopeful light in Will's eyes dimmed as he saw the king's signature at the bottom. "What does this mean?"

"It means...somehow...my father is involved." Chloe shuddered. "It means we can never clear your name, and he knew it. If we go to him with this information, then it's—"

"It's treason," Octavia finished for her.

Chloe nodded, a somber expression on her face. "We'd be executed. He is God on Earth and if we accuse him of hurting her or knowing about it... then we accuse God himself."

Will's eyes darted around the room, trying to put the pieces together. "So I have to fight Caleb tomorrow?"

Chloe swallowed, not breaking her gaze from his. "You will."

"So, I'm going to die tomorrow?" he asked. The air in his lungs refused to be found.

Karina kneeled in front of him. "No, Will. You can still fight. Octavia's training—"

"Octavia's training won't mean shit in the arena. He's been training every day for years, Karina. I've been training for *weeks*." Will's head hung low, Karina's panicked expression bounced from Octavia and back to him.

His coach's silence told him what he needed to know.

It was a tense moment as Will took it all in. The surrounding women looked at him with equal amounts of pity, grief, and guilt.

Finally, Octavia said, "He's right. I've taught him enough to survive but not enough to win. We don't have enough time..."

"We might not have enough time to get you to win, but..." Chloe looked at her friend Tiffany with equal amounts of trepidation and pride, and something else. Something that Will couldn't quite place.

"But what?" Will pressed.

"But Tiffany and I have a plan. It's not going to be easy, but it might just work."

CHAPTER

TWENTY-ONE

After they'd discussed every detail of the plan until the early hours of the morning, the group finally left. Will sat alone, contemplating his fate. Today was the day he'd meet God. If he'd done enough to be worthy of that. He had never thought about death before, but now, thoughts of death consumed him like wildfire.

The door clicked open again. Will glanced up, half-expecting it to be Chloe, begging him for forgiveness that she had failed. He wouldn't hold it against her—she'd fought harder than he'd ever expected her to, and she'd been a good friend to him.

His heart thundered in his chest when it was Karina instead.

"William," she said. He'd never heard Karina speak his full name before. Her eyes were red, her cheeks tear-stained.

"Karina," he murmured.

Without another word, she sat on the bed and patted the seat next to her. "Sit with me."

Will swallowed. He obliged and sat next to her, their

shoulders brushing against one another. Will tried not to feel the shiver of excitement up his spine. He'd always felt it when he was close to her—when he was touching her.

"What are you doing here, Karina?" he asked. Their eyes met, hers a rich brown in the candlelight.

"To tell you to stay alive for as long as you can. Chloe and Tiffany's plan could really work, you know..."

Will's voice had grown gravelly at her proximity. "Chloe and her grand plans."

Karina didn't seem to notice his nervousness, "But in order for it to work, you need to make it to the last two."

Will barked a humorless laugh, "Karina. I don't stand a chance."

She moved to kneel in front of him, cradling his face in her worn hands. He closed his eyes as her fingers grazed across his skin. Her calices had softened already. He found himself leaning into her touch.

"Don't. Say. That." Her hands roamed his face, her eyes bright with intensity. "You...you need to make it to the last two. Do you understand me?"

His voice was just a breathy whisper now, "I understand."

Her mouth parted slightly. "I don't know what I'll do without you." The words hung in the air, the electricity between them almost unbearable. "Don't you dare die." And then her lips were pressed to his.

She kissed him with an intensity that made his insides burn. Will met her mouth stroke for stroke, his tongue grazing hers lightly. Her body shook, with longing or nerves, Will didn't know. Without breaking the kiss, he pulled her up from where she knelt and nestled her onto his lap, cradling her against him.

This might be the last opportunity he'd have to touch

her, and he sure as hell was going to take it. She pressed her backside into his growing length, her body responding as hungrily as his. Her hips began to rock against him as the kiss deepened. The friction made Will's toes curl with pleasure. Will's tongue lightly grazed hers, exploring her sweet, soft mouth. He hadn't dared to hope that she'd felt the same gravitational pull toward him as he'd felt for her since the day they'd met.

Karina broke from the kiss, and Will almost wept at the loss of her. He went to claim her mouth again, but instead, she said, "Just... for this one night. Just for this one moment. I want to know what it feels like to be loved. To be really loved." Her cheeks heated as she looked up through her lashes at Will. "I want you to make love to me, Will."

His eyes widened when he realized what she was asking. "Oh..." His mouth almost dropped to the floor. "I-I've never..."

"Me neither," Karina confirmed.

Will took a shaky breath. What they were about to do was risky, but Will wanted her. Every beautiful, warm, and tender piece of her. He wanted her so badly he couldn't bear it. To hell with the consequences, he'd be dead tomorrow anyway. His mouth pressed to her own, at first tenderly and then hungrily. As the kiss grew deeper, he clutched her to his chest and lifted Karina to the bed.

Will broke the kiss for a moment and assessed her, his eyes drinking in every inch before he breathed, "You're beautiful."

Karina stood in front of him, and with an achingly slow pace, she removed her dress. Even then, she refused to break eye contact. Her body was *perfect*.

He ripped off his shirt and trousers with a speed that made Karina giggle, amusement dancing in her eyes. He removed his trousers, and her eyes grew wide and heavy lidded as she took in the hard length of him.

"Come here," she instructed. He caressed her face lightly, and began to place delicate kisses on her neck, down her collarbone, and then on her breasts. Her body arched at his touch, her mouth parting, "Ohhh..." she groaned, sounding surprised at herself. "That feels...so good."

Will continued flicking his tongue in circles around her nipple, biting lightly and suckling, until she was practically writhing in front of him.

With a feather-light touch, he moved his hand further down toward the apex of her thighs, sliding a finger through her wet folds. She released a moan of pleasure, as Will began to circle the small nub that his friends had told him about. He'd never...done anything like this before, so he focused on her body, on the way she moved and the sounds she made. Will thought he might not be doing it too badly when Karina gasped out a ragged:

"Will..." She sounded almost exasperated, desperate for a release. "Please," she begged.

Will positioned himself on top of her, his heart drumming with nerves. "Are you okay?"

"More than okay." Karina's cheeks were flushed, "Will, I love you."

"I love you too, Karina." Will inched his way into her slowly, marveling at the wetness of her.

"Does this feel nice?" He asked, not wanting to hurt her.

Karina had a small frown line between her eyes. "I feel full."

His lips found hers again, the ache of desire building in Will so much that he simply had to rock back and forth into Karina's center. She began to moan again, clutching onto him, her nails digging deep, bringing a sweet kind of pain with it. Will liked that he could make her make those sounds.

"I love you." She groaned, her inner walls clenching around his length, forcing Will to let out a roar of his own release.

And as their world shattered around them, it was all Will needed to know.

TWENTY-TWO

Will sat in the holding room. Some of the boys in his round completed push-ups and stretches, as if they were about to go for a run and not die competing in a tournament.

The other coaches entered into the cell, all of them dragging the boys off to quiet corners of the room to give their final pep talks.

"You look like a man who's about to die. Snap the hell out of it!" Octavia said as she approached him.

Will looked down at his body with his caved-in chest and hanging head. He looked like a man defeated. Maybe he was already.

"You haven't got your shackles on," Will said. It was almost jolting to see her looking so...lady-like.

With her blonde hair swept up in a bun, and her floor-length baby blue dress, she looked almost beautiful. But there was a hunger in her one-eye that remained, a stark desperation that Will imagined would never leave her.

"We did a pregnancy test this morning, and I'm pregnant," she said, "My husband," she spat the word as if it were poisonous, "decided that I could upgrade to using my hands. He's even allowing me to sit in the Noble box with him to watch today. I've been behaving for the past two years after all, since my first was born."

"You have a child?"

That question earned Will a glare. "Fuck, I need a cigarette. The bastard took all my packets, but I've got one spare left." She produced the singular cigarette from the space between her breasts. Octavia sunk down the wall next to Will on the dusty floor. She seemed to care nothing for the grimy wall their backs were flush against. "Here," Octavia lit the cigarette with a lighter, pressed between her lips.

"Octavia," Will began, "I think when you're pregnant you're not allowed to..."

"Oh, shut your trap and calm your panties. I'm lighting it for you." She passed him the cigarette. "I didn't breathe in any of the smoke, I promise," she said, rolling her eyes.

Will coughed and sputtered after taking a drag of the cigarette.

Octavia cackled, "That shit is wasted on someone like you."

They were still for a moment.

"Tell me about your kid," Will said, desperate to keep his mind off the impending death that awaited him. He could hear the muffled sounds of the crowd increasing in volume. The arena must be filling up.

Octavia shrugged. "Truth is. I don't know anything about her. I didn't even get to name her. And now, she's got a shit name."

"What is it?" Will asked.

"Eve."

"As in 'Adam and Eve?' That's not so bad," Will said, as he took another drag. The motion of it calmed his nerves.

"Eve was a stupid bitch and didn't do what she was told." Octavia snapped. "I would've called her something like 'Jasmine.'" She smiled softly, her eyes far away. "She would've made a good Jasmine."

"Yeah."

"I'm nothing to my daughter. After I tried to murder my husband for...." She trailed off. "Doing things to me that I did not wish to be done, they took my eye. And they took her from me as soon as she was born. He keeps us separate in the house."

"Separated?" Will asked, horrified.

"Then I tried to run away from New London and that's...." She gulped. "That's when things got worse." She waved her hand in dismissal, "But now I'm focusing on being well behaved, on opening my legs when I'm instructed to. On taking my prenatal vitamins. He says jump, and I say how high." Octavia shrugged. "He thinks I've been tamed." She threw Will a feral grin. "Well, not completely. He still locks his door at night."

Will shivered. This Noble that caged and enslaved a Vessel like Octavia would fear her wrath. He hoped she could make him suffer for it one day.

"I'm sure as soon as I age, and I can no longer bear the children he needs from me, they'll put me down," she admitted.

Will and Octavia sat in silence on the dusty floor, both resigned to the ugly hand that fate had dealt them.

"Will you tell me then...how you came to be my coach? Who paid to get you in here?"

"I'll make you a deal. I'll tell you after you've won and proposed to Karina," she said. The smile she flashed at him didn't touch her eyes. Will could see it—his own coach didn't think he had a chance.

"Are you ready to kick some ass?" Octavia nudged him. "Are you ready to fight for her?"

"Octavia. She has as little choice in the matter as you did. Even if I somehow won, she'd never be mine."

"Oh, Will," Octavia said, passing him his armor and sword with a wicked grin on her face. "*Never* is a very big word."

~

As THEY TRUDGED into the arena, a thick fog of panic overcame Will. People shouted Will's name—some encouragement, some taunts—but Will tried his best to ignore it all. He needed to focus.

Octavia didn't stop hurling information at him since she'd suited him up in his armor. "That one over there? He's only good in defense. Without a shield, he doesn't stand a chance. Get his shield from him." She strapped the metal guards to his legs. She pushed a knife into the strap behind his leg-guard, concealing it. "For emergencies only," she said sternly, looking up at him.

The armor weighed him down, feeling heavier than it had in practice. His hands were so slicked with sweat that his sword and shield felt slippery.

"Coaches, exit the arena now."

"Look at me, Will," she said, even as Will's vision spun. "Will," Octavia insisted, grabbing his face and forcing it toward her own. "Do you want to know who paid me to be your coach?"

Things snapped into focus for Will. "Yes."

"It was your father."

The world stopped moving for a moment. "My Dad's dead," Will said, shaking his head.

"You might meet him one day, if you stay alive long enough." Octavia planted two kisses on both of his cheeks.

"Is this just a tactic to make me fight harder?" Will asked. "Or are you just lying?"

Octavia gave him a crushing embrace, whispering in his ear. "You'll have to live to find that out, won't you? Good luck, kid." And with that, she was gone.

Will glanced toward the royal box, and he caught Karina's eye, who stared back at him.

She gave him a singular nod:

You can do this, her look said.

Will breathed in.

Out.

And in.

And out.

Trumpets sounded.

The Game had begun.

A trident flew his way, missing him by inches. The competitor that had hurled the trident ran at Will. His name was Jacob, Will remembered. He was 6-foot-4 and twice Will's weight. He vaguely saw Caleb out of the corner of his eye, as he held off three other competitors at once. For a moment, Caleb was distracted.

Good.

Will ran for Jacob with equal ferocity and an animalistic roar came from his mouth. *You need to make your bark as bad as your bite. You need to look ferocious when you fight. Bare your teeth. Roar like a lion. It stuns people.*

Octavia has been right.

211

All they'd seen before today was a quiet, softly spoken boy. It stunned the competitor before him, and he slowed his run. Will struck out at his leg, the sword hitting its target. He pulled the sword, and the competitor before him screamed in agony as he fell. The boy kicked Will's hand, and Will lost the grip on his sword.

Will placed his shield up in a defensive position, but Jacob was too large. He bowled into Will, which left Will's shield out of his hand and sprawled on the sand. Jacob grabbed Will and pinned him to the ground, his fingers crushing his windpipe. Will gasped for air, feeling frantically among the sand for the sword that had dropped. He remembered the dagger in his pocket, the one Octavia had strapped to the inside of his leg guard.

Will supposed he'd better take that back-up plan. He reached down, fumbling at the strap that held his dagger. The competitor above him squeezed tighter, grinning now at the prospect of his potential first kill.

Will drove the dagger hard into his gut, and the vice-like grip he'd had on Will's throat released. The boy clutched his gut in agony. Will staggered to his feet, looking at the man bleeding out beneath him. Will had never drawn blood before. He examined the sticky substance now pooling out on the sand with equal parts terror and disgust.

He hoped to God his mum wasn't watching, that Marcus had taken her away from here. Far away. He didn't want her to see what he'd become. He hadn't entered this Game a criminal, but the Game had sure as hell made him one. Will staggered back over to where he'd lost his sword and shield. He looked around the arena to take stock of the competition, and to his horror Will found that, including the man below him, only two were dead so far.

There were still three more left. Including Caleb.

You need to make it to the final two.

That's what Karina had told him. Whatever it was that Chloe had planned, he hoped she'd move quicker. He didn't know how much longer he could last.

TWENTY-THREE

I t took all of Karina's control to sit there calmly watching the man she loved fight to the death. She pressed her lips together, willing her face into an expression of impassiveness. Will's gentleness, his kindness, was being ripped away from him in front of her very eyes. But all the same, Karina found herself praying for him to be more ruthless. To move faster and strike harder.

Her chest hurt.

Wide-eyed, she glanced at Chloe. In a way that was barely noticeable to anyone around her, Chloe shook her head. They needed more eyes on the Game and less on the Princess if the plan was going to work.

When Karina turned back to the Games, another competitor was dead. The crowd had drunken themselves into such a stupor that violence erupted in the stalls. People screamed, caught in a stampede of pushing and shoving limbs.

Will looked up, distracted for a second.

Focus, dammit, Karina willed him.

Karina forced her lungs to work. For them to move in

and out, but they would not seem to obey her command. Only when Will had driven his sword through an axe-holder's gut would they expand back out again. She gasped for air.

Another boy was sneaking up behind him, ready to pounce. *Caleb.* She realized with dread.

"Will!" Karina screamed. "Behind you!"

~

WILL SPUN around just in time to avoid an axe that Caleb had lobbed toward him. Caleb sprinted at Will, murder in his eyes as the only other remaining competitors followed him.

"Let's finish this, Albridge!" Caleb growled, pointing his sword.

Caleb lunged at him, and Will threw up his sword to parry the attack. Caleb was as ruthless as he was talented, and it was all Will could do to defend the onslaught of blows that Caleb was attacking with.

Caleb simultaneously defended against the third competitor who remained, one attacking Caleb with ferocity. He was probably hoping to kill Caleb whilst the Noble was distracted with Will.

Caleb kicked Will in the chest, and Will flew backward, losing his sword. He scrambled past a body as Caleb continued his attack. Will rolled out of the way of Caleb's sword by mere inches.

"Just stop now, Albridge and I'll save you from a painful death."

Will crawled away, blood spurting from his mouth, whilst feeling like a coward. Caleb turned suddenly, stabbing the other competitor right through his gut. The boy stood wide-eyed with shock. Caleb released the boy with a kind of grim determination that Will could almost admire if he wasn't on the other end of it. Caleb took no joy in this. Will could see in the pained expression on his face.

It was what was expected of him, and if he wanted to survive, Caleb needed to deliver it.

Thankfully, as Will crawled, he grabbed another discarded sword and climbed to his feet. Now, they were the final two, and Will knew he had only a matter of seconds left now that Caleb's full attention was on him.

Then, a voice boomed across the arena. *"I command you to halt these Games!"*

Confused, the crowd stopped fighting and tousling for a moment. No one's natural voice could be that loud. It sounded strange and distorted, not like a human voice at all. The voice sounded male—but it came from Princess Chloe— who was now floating.

Floating.

She was suspended in mid-air, her gaze toward the heavens, and her white dress and long blonde hair looking ethereal. Her eyes snapped to the crowd; they were completely white. She looked like an angel.

"This..." The raspy, strange voice said, "this man— William Albridge—is Moses. He will bring you to a new light, to a new dawn. He will save humanity."

People began dropping to their knees, crying and shaking. A cloud came across the sky, and the heavens opened above. Rain poured down in answer to Chloe.

Chloe had stopped floating now. She moved through the trembling Nobles and took up two glasses. One was empty, and one was full of water.

She said, "'But I know that the King of Egypt," her eyes went straight to her father, "will not let Moses go unless a mighty hand compels him." She moved toward the crowd. "So, I will stretch out my hand and *strike* the Egyptians with all the wonders that I will perform among them. After that, he will let you go."

Chloe poured the water into the other goblet, but it was no longer water. It was wine. Water into wine? How the *hell* did she pull that off? What she'd insinuated—the King was the King of Egypt, and the crowd was the Egyptians. If the King didn't let Will go...

Plagues would befall New London.

The King looked terrified.

"Do as I say!" The voice deepened, and again she lifted from the ground, her white eyes widening.

The crowd began chanting, "Do as the angel says. Let Moses go!"

"He will save us!"

"Maybe he'll let us all have children!"

"Do as God has told us!"

Chloe began convulsing, her whole body shaking violently. She fell to the floor. The crowd gasped and screamed.

"Chloe!" The King screamed. He ran to her and lifted her limp body up. "Get out of my way! She needs a doctor!"

Chloe didn't move, she barely looked like she was breathing.

Will looked at Caleb in utter confusion. Caleb looked just as perplexed as he was, but he'd dropped his weapons at the word of the ethereal being apparently inside of Chloe. Will didn't need to be told twice. He huffed a sigh of relief and threw down his sword. Octavia jumped from the stands above and into the arena, crushing him in a hug.

"I didn't even know she could do that," Will breathed in wonder. "She stopped the Games."

"She can't," Octavia whispered in his ear. "No one stops the Games. Not even God." The Guards reached for her. "She only got away with it because she had the crowd on her side. The King will come to his senses and put you and Caleb back in the arena to finish this. You need to leave, now."

Will assessed her. "The illusions. They worked." He ran his hand through his hair. He'd hardly dared hope that they would.

Magicians, tricksters, and illusionists were considered blasphemous. Will supposed this stunt worked purely because the King had banned "magic" so many years ago. People had forgotten that tricks and illusions could be played on others. They were all too ready to believe that it was God, as opposed to a few well-placed illusions.

"The mind can play tricks on you, if you know how to play them," Octavia said.

"But her eyes... the voice." Will shook his head.

He hadn't been at the final conversations, where the women had planned these finer details, and it could've fooled him. He knew he was not Moses. But being a God-fearing person, he'd almost wanted to believe it was real.

"A lapel microphone strapped to her chest. I attached a voice distortion equipment to it. Her eyes were something called coloured contact lenses. That's why she needed to pass out just now. Illusion magic with the levitation and water into wine trick. She'll take the contacts out when no one's looking."

"Wow," he said.

She'd done all of this... to save *him*?

"Get out of here. Once the other rounds are over, you can meet Chloe in Karina's room. That'll be in three days' time. Stay out of sight. No one escapes the Games alive, not even Moses." She winked. "Get gone."

Octavia shoved him toward the entrance, and he was running away in an instant. No one stopped him from exiting out of the gate. They all looked stunned and awed by him, a few from the crowd even followed him, begging to worship at Moses' feet. He shook his head in disbelief. He was actually *alive*. As long as he kept himself hidden for a few days, Will would get to stay that way.

~

CHLOE PEELED her contact lenses out as soon as the doctor turned away. Now, she fluttered her eyes open, as if coming to. The King appeared next to her in a second.

"Darling..." He looked like the picture of concern. His Nobles crowded around, all trying to get a glimpse of the messenger of God. "Leave us," he commanded.

The Nobles scuttled out of the room.

Chloe tried to look groggy. "W-what happened?"

The King now sat at her bedside, pinching his nose. "Oh, for Christ's sake Chloe, you can drop the fucking act now, all right?"

Shit. He was onto her. She'd never heard him swear like that. Ever. Chloe decided the best course of action was to play dumb. "I don't know what you mean."

"We banned illusionists because it is ungodly and sinful to think mere mortals can perform acts that should only be done by God." His eyes pierced her. "But you just took that to a whole new level, didn't you? Now they think you're the bloody messenger of God!"

Chloe figured there was no point pretending otherwise. "So, what if I'm not? Whose sin do you think is worse:

tricking people into believing something or letting an innocent man be put to a public death for sport?"

"I told you; I had no choice!" The king hissed.

"You always have a choice," Chloe spat back.

The King chucked a mirthless laugh. "Chloe, you don't
have any clue, do you? Maybe when you're a wife, you'll
obey. And you'll understand. You are a *woman*. You'll never
have the power that you're expecting to have when you
become Queen. And if you carry on like that, people will
soon see your trickery, and the public will execute you
themselves... they'll say you're a blasphemous witch. The
Nobles will turn against you." His eyes were wide and
manic now. "Don't you see that if anyone realized you faked
a message from God, then you'd be in danger? When they
finally come to see that Will is not Moses and cannot save
humanity from slowly dying out, or stop the acid rain from
tormenting us when it comes—and it will—then you're
dead, my daughter."

"No—"

"You've deceived them. The Nobles, the Common
Castes—all of them. But the ones who wonder, the ones
that won't dare to say anything publicly, may already have
begun. They may say your act was a defiance to God. They'll
say no future Queen should imitate the Lord like that for
her own means. That's blasphemy!" He pinched his nose
again. "You've saved William today, yes. But you've put
yourself in danger tomorrow. You've made yourself vulnerable. People are dying for us to show vulnerability. I had to
look like I believed you, or they'd have killed you right
there."

Chloe's tears came thick and fast. The King, everything he'd been doing... he'd been playing this dangerous
game to keep himself and his family safe. She'd been so

worried about Will, Elaine, Karina, and everyone else. And now she'd put her own family in danger. Even *herself* in danger.

Kings and Queens had been executed and imprisoned before. History was full of them. Her mother was just the most recent, not the only one.

He touched her face softly, "I won't lose you like I lost your mother and brother."

"Dad—"

She was dying to ask him about Elaine, about the picture of her, and why he'd signed it. Had he been forced to do it? Did Dartfield know a deadly secret and extort him for his signature? Why did Dartfield need his signature on the photograph in the first place? But nothing came out. Not a single sound.

The King paused at the door. "The higher up we are in this world, Chloe, the further we have to fall."

Hushed voices echoed around the throne room. It was packed with representatives from every Caste. They'd all asked to meet with the Queen to find out what would happen next.

The other Vessels stood by the Queen, Karina with them. The competitors all stood before her as the Queen addressed them. "God visited the Games through Princess Chloe today and forbade William Albridge from going any farther in the competition." Her shrill voice rang out, so even the Noblemen and ladies gathered on the balconies could hear her. "We cannot pretend to know God's will. All we know is that William Albridge is our Moses, and God wishes him to serve in other ways aside from the Games. Wherever he may now be."

Karina was so thrilled Will had made it out of the Games alive and disappeared into the crowd. It was all she could do to not smile from ear to ear. Maybe he'd escape. She could go with him—

"Your Majesty, if I may." Caleb was still in his Games armor, his face matted with blood and sweat.

"You may, my Lord." The Queen nodded.

"God may have called William," there was no hiding the disdain in his voice, "away from the Games. But *I* still competed. And I am the final man standing in my round. I wish to be compensated."

Shocked gasps echoed around the gathered crowd, and the cameras shot across to the Queen's face. Her countenance was impassive as she said, "I see no reason for God to not bless your union with a Vessel, Caleb. As you say, you *are* the final man in your round."

Caleb bowed low. "Thank you, Your Majesty. If I may select my prize, I will do so now."

"You may." Queen Mary nodded.

Karina gulped.

"Karina." He addressed her in front of the crowd. "You are the most beautiful Vessel I've ever laid eyes upon." The girls next to Karina shifted in discomfort, shooting daggers at her. "Even though you are a Traitor Caste, and your father betrayed this country..." He trailed off, looking at the crowd, reminding them of who she was. Karina's cheeks heated. "God has blessed you with the ability to conceive children. That must mean you, yourself, are pure of heart and can be Noble, too. Karina, will you join the House of Dartfield, become a lady, and be my bride?"

Karina didn't know why he even bothered asking. She had no choice, not if her and her family were to remain alive, despite the fact he'd just murdered other boys and almost killed Will.

Karina realized the throne room remained silent, waiting for her response. "Y-Yes."

The Common Castes erupted with cheers and hoots. It was the first time in years that a Common had been discovered as a Vessel. Someone who was like them. Even though it wasn't the ending they'd hoped for with her marrying Will and then two Common Castes ascending to Nobledom together...

Still all the crowd had been rooting for her. A fellow Common getting her happy ending. Karina's eyes stung with tears as she watched as little girls in the crowd hoot in exhilaration, hoping that one day, they might be in her position. That one day, they'd be special enough to murder for.

Karina was to be married. Married to a man whose father had likely abducted or killed her best friend. Married to a man who scared her.

~

KARINA AND WILL SAT on her bed, watching Chloe pace back and forth with a ferocity that was surprising even to her.

"You need to leave," Chloe said, eyes darting back to the door every few seconds.

The days that had followed Chloe's illusion stunt had been terrifying and painful for Karina. She'd longed to see Will, even more so now that everyone and anyone was talking about where their Moses—their Shepherd—had mysteriously disappeared to.

Karina had to watch the remaining Games at Caleb's side. She'd dreaded each day that they'd had to sit and watch the horror of it. The final three Games had passed without incident. Chloe had kept Will out of sight in case any Nobles tried to engineer him back into the final rounds. But now that he was supposed to lead New London to salvation? Out of hunger and pain and infertility and the end of the human race?

Hell, suddenly the Games were the least of his problems.

"I won't leave, not yet." Will shook his head.

"As long as you stay in New London, you'll have eyes on you, expecting... well, expecting the miracles I promised them," Chloe insisted. "It's too dangerous if you don't flee. I have a contact that can smuggle across the New London wall and get you to Manchester." Chloe said. "They'd all remember your face from the Games, so you'd need to lie low. At least they have a protection barrier from any climate events there, too. Soon everyone will have forgotten about William Albridge, the great Moses, and you can—"

"No!" It was Will's turn to put his hand up to Chloe now. "Even though the Games are over, we still need to find Elaine. We don't understand why your dad signed that photograph. Once we find and rescue her, Elaine and I can both use your contact and escape from New London together."

Karina stiffened, and Will seemed to sense her discomfort. She wished with all her heart it was her escaping to Manchester with Will instead.

But she couldn't go with him. Someone as precious as a Vessel? They'd search high and low to find her and bring her back.

But the King would gladly forget about the troublesome Moses and Elaine and let them disappear without a trace. Why else had they not found Will over the past few days? The King had had enough Defenders raid every house in the walls of New London. There was nowhere else Will could hide or flee to. Yet clearly the King *didn't want* Will to be found. He didn't want to bring any more attention to Chloe's stunt and how wrong she'd end up being.

Will disappearing worked best for his majesty too.

A knock at the door had everyone's head snapping to attention. The door handle jiggled. Had someone heard what they'd been talking about? Had someone seen Will sneak into Karina's room?

"Karina?" It was Caleb. "Can I come in?"

"It's bad luck for us to spend the night before our wedding together," Karina said in a strangled voice.

"I just want to say goodnight."

"One second..."

Chloe rolled her eyes in frustration and made for the window. She really was quite talented at climbing up and scaling down buildings. There would have been a future for her if she'd been born in the Craftsman Caste. *Perhaps a window washer*, Karina thought idly.

"Be careful," Chloe warned, disappearing out of sight in a few moments.

The door jiggled again. "Karina!"

Caleb sounded pissed.

Karina glanced at Will in a panic. It would take too long to get him out of the window. Karina motioned to the bed. Will nodded, a panicked expression etched on his face as he dove under Karina's bed, pulled the sheets down to hide himself from sight.

Karina inched the door open. Caleb was leaning against the wall, a bottle in his hand. His breath stank of liquor and cigarettes.

"Can I come in?" he repeated.

"Well, I'm not sure if..."

Karina obliged. Karina stood as far away from the bed

as she could get, trying to keep Caleb's gaze from where Will hid under the four-poster bed. He tapped the space beside him, motioning for her to take a seat next to him.

"I'm okay, here, thank you," she said.

"So tomorrow, we'll get married..." He took another swig of the bottle he was holding. "And you'll be mine."

Karina saw red at the word *mine*. "Caleb. You're a *killer* and I don't know why the hell you have this fixation with me but I *don't want you Caleb*."

"You'll not speak to me that way." he said, his voice ice cold.

Karina didn't respond.

"I... won." His face crumpled. "I killed for you." His lip quivered. "Do you honestly think I had a choice? Do you think I *wanted* that on my conscience?"

"I-I'm sorry." Karina's voice was a whisper.

He stood, prowling toward her. It took every inch of her self-control not to cower. "A beautiful traitor for a wife. Who'd have thought out of everyone, I'd yearn for you?" He said softly.

Caleb moved ever so slowly toward her, and Karina held his stare. He gently placed a hand on Karina's cheek, cradling her face. His hand was large, and warm, and not one that sought to hurt her, but Karina couldn't help but wince all the same. Hurt and sorrow lit his eyes as he stepped away from her. He wanted her to yearn for him, too.

"See you tomorrow." He muttered, sounding almost defeated, leaving the room as swiftly as he came.

He left the room, slamming the door behind him. Karina collapsed to the ground. Will appeared next to her in an instant. His arms enveloped her, holding her as if she were precious glass at the brink of breaking. Maybe she already had.

He held her there for what seemed like an eternity. His strength, his warmth, his tenderness... they all made Karina weep because she knew she would never have this. She never would have happiness. Divorce was illegal in New London, and men reigned supreme. A woman was owned by her father and then by her husband.

If she didn't want to be executed, then she could never escape from Caleb. She was glad that her father hadn't lived to see her wedding day. Will took her face in his hands and wiped the tears off her cheeks. He pressed their foreheads together.

"Come with me," he whispered.

"You know it's impossible," Karina said. "They'd find you. And when they figure out that you're not Moses—they'll kill you. You need to hide, and if you take me with you, then I'll only be a burden."

"I don't care. You're coming with me. I won't let him hurt you."

"He didn't lay a hand on me, Will. And I don't need a protector. I've been a Traitor Caste all my life. I can handle a Noble." She said fiercely. "I'd rather not become like Octavia, imprisoned in my home. That's what they did to her. They'd do the same to me if they caught me trying to run."

Karina thought of how excruciating it would've been for Octavia. To have her eye removed... The chains, the lack of freedom in her own home... it somehow seemed worse than death.

Will stood in front of her, towering over her. He stalked toward her, something in his eyes that was vengeful and desperate and—

He claimed her mouth with a ferocity that had Karina almost stumbling back. She melted into his muscled arms as he wrapped them around her, pushing her toward him.

"We can't, Will," Karina said, pulling away, feeling the heat in her belly beginning to build. "I'm supposed to be *married* tomorrow."

"Karina, I need you," Will growled, trailing kisses down her neck and leaving fire in his wake, "Please, Karina."

The desperation and grief in his voice shattered all of Karina's resolve. She grabbed his face in her hands and kissed him fervently, licking into his mouth with a ferocity that surprised even herself. He lifted her in his powerful arms up from the floor and then laid her gently on the bed.

Will stood watching her, towering over her. Karina's skin tingled with electricity as he slowly relieved her of her dress. He stalked toward her, crawling on top of the mattress and then her. "I want to make you feel the best you've ever felt."

His voice sounded like honey.

"You already do that every moment I'm with you, Will."

Will surveyed her carefully, tracing his finger across the mound of her breasts and then down toward her navel. She wriggled, his light touch causing the center of her to feel tingly and wet.

His finger pushed between her folds, soaking up the wetness before he began pumping into her. Karina's eyes rolled back, her spine arching with pleasure. Her breath came in ragged gasps,

"Will..."

But he'd already traveled down toward the apex of her thighs, his breath hot and wet. He licked her once, all the way up her center, and Karina had to press her hand to her mouth to stop from screaming at the immense pleasure of it.

He continued to pump his fingers in and out of her, in a rhythm that sent Karina's hips bucking toward the heavenly sensation of his tongue. He slowly circled her nub sending bolts of pleasure through her. Karina whimpered and moaned, lost in the ecstasy of him. By the time he was licking and pumping into her at pace, Karina felt a rush of immense euphoria overwhelm her. Every thought, burden, and worry released from her body as she bucked beneath the powerful movements of his tongue. He cradled her hips, allowing her to feel every moment of pleasure coursing through her veins. It was as if she'd touched heaven herself.

"Will...." She sighed, opening her legs for him. "I'm ready. Come here."

Will unbuckled his belt, moving toward her with a smile that seemed awed. *By her*, she realized. He was awed by *her*.

Karina opened her legs, inviting him into her.

There was the familiar feeling of opening and expanding for him as he delved into her. Her hips began to rock with his movements, savoring the feeling of having him deep inside of her. Will pushed deeper again, sending gasps of pleasure through Karina. Will increased their pace, and Karina rocked her hips in answer to him, the pressure building. He listened to Karina's body so perfectly. She couldn't feel anything else other than beautiful. It was complete and utter beauty.

And here, with him moving inside her, worshiping her body, she was finally *home*.

~

"You look... stunning Karina." Will sat on the edge of the bed, watching Karina put her earrings in. It was difficult for him to look away.

Last night had been so brilliant that Will was half-expecting for it not to have been real, like some perfect dream. But as he'd opened his eyes this morning, there she'd been. Sleeping and soft and beautiful and brilliant. *And his.* Until he remembered that today was the day she would be married. Will's chest became tight at the very thought of it. Karina placed a large diamond around her neck, struggling with the clasp of the necklace.

"I've got it," Will muttered, moving to her dresser.

He fiddled with the clasp, his fingers grazing her neck. She closed her eyes at the touch. When Will was done, he couldn't help but feel the diamond necklace looked horribly tight on her... like a collar. Will tried to distract her, leaning down to her neck, and covering it with lazy, soft kisses.

"Don't—" she said, pulling away. "It's... it's too much. Knowing that I can never have you. Knowing that we'll never see each other again."

"I'm staying in New London until we find Elaine. I'll keep working on finding her, and I'll keep working on finding us." He pulled her into him, wrapping his arms around her waist, "a way to be together. I promise."

Karina looked at him through the mirror. Her small smile was one that would shatter even the coldest of hearts. "You mean that? You'll work on finding us a way to be together?"

"Absolutely." He mustered a smile. "After all, I'm Moses, right? I can perform miracles."

That made her laugh—which was what he'd been hoping for. He grabbed the veil from the bed and placed it on her head, covering her face with the delicate material. He lifted the veil for one last, deep kiss.

"Now, go get married," he murmured into her mouth.

Karina's lip wobbled, but she nodded and disappeared out of the room without a farewell. Perhaps she hated goodbyes as much as he did.

Will took in the eerie silence for a second. Then he sat on the bed with his head in his hands and sobbed. Because even though he'd just sworn to Karina that he'd be with her... even though he'd promised her he'd find Elaine... a deep, primal fear overcame him.

Because he had no fucking idea how he was going to make those things happen.

TWENTY-FOUR

Chloe stormed into her bedroom. She'd wanted to scream the entire way through the wedding ceremonies, but she'd smiled and placed her hand on her heart and acted like true love had won out. The weddings had all been simultaneous. And filmed, of course.

Now, they took the royal carriages around the streets of New London to soak up every bit of glory possible. Chloe couldn't stand one second longer. Not after seeing Karina hide her sorrow so poorly, and now Karina would be stuck with Caleb forever.

Chloe shuddered at the thought of turning eighteen next year and having her telling. If she wasn't fertile, then the line would die with her. Then, every Noble would be out to kill off her family: Romanov style. After all, with her family at the height of its power, her mother had been murdered in the Uprising, and her brother and heir to the throne had died under... mysterious circumstances. If her telling didn't go well in a few months' time, she'd be in danger of suffering the same fate.

Chloe screamed into a sofa pillow before glancing

around her room. Her quarters were so huge that they could sleep twenty. The opulent golden, four-poster bed sat with red velvet bedding awaiting her, but it was what lay on the bed, itself, that made her freeze in terror. On the bed was a wig.

And not just any wig.

It was her red wig, the one she'd gone to great lengths to hide under floorboards, along with her lowborn clothing she'd gotten from Lilian. Chloe raced toward the discarded wig. Her breath hitched when she saw what lay on top of it: Elaine's photograph and a note.

Stop looking for what doesn't want to be found. Otherwise, other secrets that you hold may have to be revealed. Not just the illusions. We know everything.

They'd signed it with the same sigil that was on the rings. Chloe stood frozen, reading the note again and again. How had they known? Chloe was sure if they'd found the very thing she'd used to disappear into Hell's Gate so often...

Someone knew the truth about her. And not just about the illusions, they knew the *whole* truth. Her biggest and most dangerous secret.

"James!"

James' head popped around the outside of the door. Chloe blocked the wig and the rest of the contents on the bed from view. "Get me Lilian. Now."

He nodded and clicked the door shut behind him. It was only minutes, but it felt like hours as Chloe paced the room with her mind racing.

Lilian rapped on the door three times before entering. She took in the red wig, the note, and the photograph. Then, her forehead creased with worry.

"Shit, Chloe. This is bad. You need to stop looking for

Elaine. Karina's married, Will's on the run... the whole reason you started in the first place, to save Will? That's null-and-void now, and if they carry through on this threat...."

"What evidence would they even have, Lil? They wouldn't dare go against me—I'm the Princess for God's sake!" Chloe said, but the tremor in her voice betrayed her. A flash of inspiration hit her. "The ball tonight. There'll be entertainers and servers. Common Castes coming in and out of the palace."

Lilian nodded, a somber expression on her face. "I'll see what I can do."

∼

WILL KNEW that he shouldn't be doing this. He knew that returning to the palace was at best risky and, at worst, downright idiotic. But he needed to see Karina before he left New London for good. The marriage ball tonight would be the perfect place to do it; the theme was *masquerade*.

There'd be no better opportunity to hide in plain view.

Chloe insisted that he should escape New London tonight, but he couldn't go just yet. The photograph of Elaine was the only clue Will had. It was too dangerous in Chloe's hands, anyway. Over his last few days hiding in an abandoned warehouse, he'd come to see just how dangerous it was for the Princess to be working on solving this mystery. That stunt she'd pulled to get him out of the Games....

If she carried on this way, then Chloe'd be in danger.

So, Will had decided on her behalf. He'd find where Chloe had hidden the photograph and take the burden of finding Elaine from her shoulders. Plus, he'd visit Karina while he was at it. One last time. He'd stolen a server's tuxedo from the laundry in the Craftsman district; he'd seen the ones they'd used when he attended the balls as a competitor.

Will placed on the black masquerade mask that covered the top half of his face. As he looked in the mirror, he could barely recognise his own features; he was sure he'd be unrecognizable to anyone else in the crowd.

This was the last time he would see Karina. He'd be damned if he didn't make the most of it. He slipped into the night, ready to do what he needed to give Karina the peace she required. If he couldn't give her forever, then he'd give Karina her friend back.

~

By now, Will knew his way around enough to pass as one of the staff. He tried to look hurried and wide-eyed as he strode through the kitchen.

"You!" A panicked chef pointed at him. "Take this out to the ballroom floor, stat!"

"You got it," Will mumbled. He took the platter and hurried out toward the ballroom. The previous balls were lush, but they'd pulled out all the stops for the masquerade ball. Lush gold ornaments and drapery assaulted his vision.

Circus performers and even human statues, all masked and painted golden, were dotted around the room, some in hoops and material suspended from the ceiling. They did tricks that made the Nobles gasp. At the top podium sat the King, Queen and Princess, all in gold finery, complete with golden masks. Good—if Chloe was here, he'd be able to make it to her bedroom and grab the photograph of Elaine without having to convince her of his plan.

He still didn't know how he'd find Elaine. But the photograph was the only clue he had to go off. He remembered there was a background in the image. There were intricate wooden carvings, something that may be recognizable to another Craftsman Caste if he asked around. If he could just figure out that background and exactly where the image was taken, then he'd at least have a starting point to search for Elaine.

Next to the royals sat all the Vessels, still in their wedding gowns and beside the victors of this year's Games. Will's chest felt tight when his eyes fell on Karina in her wedding dress sitting next to Caleb.

He shook himself.

He needed to focus. First, the photograph. Then, he'd get Karina alone and say goodbye before he left for Manchester. He tapped another server on the shoulder and offered him the platter. The one he held was almost finished.

"Do you want to take these? Chef is in a mood back there. Trust me, going back to collect more isn't a good idea unless you want to get yelled at."

The server grasped Will's plate, not second-guessing the logic. "Chef is so pissed with me." He grimaced. "Thanks."

"Anytime," Will said, striding off back to the kitchen.

He darted up the stairs and toward the Princess's room. Will had memorized where each guard was stationed and knew when their rotation was due to end. As they moved, he moved too, managing to slip through the corridors unnoticed. He blew out a breath of relief when he spotted Chloe's bedroom and darted inside.

The humongous suite was dark and cold. About fifty

times the size of his old apartment. Being here, alone, with nothing to do...

No wonder Chloe had a habit of sneaking out. She'd be furious with him when she discovered he'd gone against her wishes and had taken the photograph, the last clue they had regarding Elaine's whereabouts. But he was doing this for *her* safety.

He rifled around her drawers, checking every hiding spot possible, but footsteps down the hall halted his endeavors. He swore. He'd just seen Chloe out in the ballroom; she wouldn't be allowed to return to her bedroom on an occasion as grand as this unaccompanied...

But the footsteps came all the same. Will sprinted for the wardrobe, jumping in and closing it. His instincts told him to leave a crack open. He peered through the crack to see who'd come to her room.

To Will's surprise, he realized it *was* Chloe as she removed her mask. She wore a server's outfit, her blonde hair tied back into a tight bun. So, he wasn't the only one making the most of the anonymity the masks brought.

"We don't have much time," Chloe said, blocking the door with a nearby chair.

In all the secret conversations Chloe had had with Will and Karina, he'd never seen her barricade her door to that extent. The girl next to Chloe removed her mask, too. She had raven hair down to her waist, giant sapphire eyes, and full, voluptuous lips. He realized with a start that this was Tiffany; Chloe's friend who had helped them with her knowledge of illusion and performance trickery.

But it was a shock all the same when Tiffany strode toward Chloe and closed the gap between them by crushing her mouth to Chloe's. His eyes widened in disbelief as he gazed through the crack. Chloe didn't recoil; she claimed Tiffany's mouth as if it were her own.

And then everything clicked into place.

It *was* her own.

Chloe *loved* Tiffany. The same way that he loved Karina.

She'd been sneaking out of the palace not just to practice her illusion tricks but to see Tiffany.

She never could have told the *real* truth to her father about where she'd been the night Elaine had been abducted. Because loving another of the same gender was a crime in New London.

Chloe would be be executed for it.

CHAPTER

TWENTY-FIVE

C hloe might've been going to hell, but Tiffany's lips felt heavenly.

Well, at least, what Chloe thought heaven might feel like. Chloe drove her tongue into Tiffany's soft mouth with a need that startled even herself. It had been too long since she'd been able to have her and all of her. Chloe needed to make up the time.

Tiffany's lips were Chloe's favorite place on earth. The thought that she might get to experience every part of Tiffany tonight made her grin like a schoolgirl.

"What are you smiling at?" Tiffany pulled back away from her, examining Chloe. "I can't kiss you when you smile, can I?"

"I've missed you. I've missed this." Chloe ran her fingers up Tiff's arms, leaving goosebumps in her wake. She loved that her touch gave Tiff such a visceral reaction. Chloe returned her mouth to Tiff's and then traveled across to the soft corners of her lips, her jawline, and her delicate cheekbones...

Tiff lifted her face toward the ceiling, her eyes closing in pleasure, and Chloe jumped at the chance to kiss and nibble at her neck. Tiff gave a soft moan. "We're *so* going to hell for this."

"If you're there with me, Tiff, I don't give a shit."

The words made Tiff snap her head back to Chloe's hot stare. As their gazes locked, Chloe remembered the first time they'd kissed at *Madame Butterfly's*, after Tommy had left, and they'd been left alone, practicing illusions together.

Chloe had told Tiff how much it meant to her to practice something forbidden. She'd thought it strange that something that so fun and harmless was a crime, something her brother had loved so very much. He would get such a thrill when he finally got a trick right, when he saw the wonder and belief in Chloe's eyes.

Chloe remembered the overbearing guilt after Chloe had taken Tiffany's perfect face in her grip and kissed her. The times that Tiff had gently guided her in the way she'd needed to, when she hadn't known how else to express the adoration she felt for her. Tiffany had taught her everything she knew: how to move, how to listen to her body, and how to pleasure her own.

It was a part of her that had never awakened before Tiff.

Every time Chloe had snuck out, she'd hoped she'd had the courage to end whatever this was but never had. Tiff had comforted her as she'd wept—cursing God, cursing Tiff, and cursing everything that she could. Because Chloe had fallen in love with her, the one person she could never have.

Tiff's steady grip roamed every curve of Chloe's body, and she lost all sense of why she'd called Tiffany here. Of what she'd intended to say. She was lost in Tiffany, lost in the ecstasy of being her true self. Chloe shook herself internally; she didn't have much time.

"Stop—" Chloe moaned into Tiff's mouth and then more urgently. "Stop. We need to talk first."

"But I haven't been able to see you. Let's just enjoy this while we have it." Tiff's hand began to slide down Chloe's trousers, where a deep ache was building already.

"Someone knows about us!" Chloe blurted.

Tiffany halted in her endeavor down Chloe's body, much to her dismay. But Chloe needed to focus anyway.

"What?" Tiffany asked.

"Listen, I don't have long. Lil and I will need to swap back soon. I said I'd meet her back in the bathroom in ten minutes." Chloe had swapped with Lilian again—Lil had been reluctant, but Chloe had convinced her.

Lilian was currently sitting on Chloe's throne, hidden only by a golden mask. If anyone found Lilian was impersonating her... Chloe needed to focus.

"I called you here, so I could tell you. Look." She shoved the paper into Tiffany's hand.

Tiff's face turned white as she read it. "But we've been so careful."

"I know, Tiff." Chloe embraced her. Six months, and their time had run out. "I don't know what to do," she said into Tiffany's hair, breathing in her musky scent.

Everything always smelt so overpowering in Chloe's world. Tiffany didn't. Tiffany's scent was subtle—it made Chloe want to take a step closer.

"The people that have Elaine... They're powerful enough to know about us. They're powerful enough to arrange for the King's seal." Chloe shoved the photograph of Elaine that she'd been carrying around since she found it in Tiff's hand. "That's my Dad's signature. I don't know how they got it. They've got something on him. Or are controlling him somehow. These are powerful people. I don't want you to get hurt." Chloe brushed Tiffany's lips again, hardly able to control the kisses that now intensified.

Tiffany broke away, breathless. "Then stop looking for Elaine. You got Will out of the Games... there's no reason for you to continue. They asked you to stop looking for her, and they won't reveal anything about us. Do what they're asking you to."

"Something else is going on here. I know it. It's bigger than Elaine. It's bigger than all of us, and if I don't find Elaine, who will?"

A low voice came from her wardrobe. It sounded slightly embarrassed but firm: "I can?"

Tiffany squealed in fright, running toward the door. Chloe stood in shock as she took in her wardrobe swinging open with William Albridge stepping out of it.

"What the actual fuck, Will?" Chloe demanded. Then, Will put his palms out in a gesture that Chloe took as, *please don't kill me.*

But she was. She was *totally* going to kill him. She rounded on him, and he began backing up, as if he were stepping away from a wild animal. "Just...calm down, okay?" Will said.

"Calm down? You... you just..."

He'd caught her. There was no hiding what she was now. A sinner. A Traitor.

She'd managed against all odds to save Will, and instead, she'd placed *herself* in danger. Chloe thought of her brother, his calm manner and his protectiveness over her. How caring he was... She hadn't been able to save her brother. But she'd saved Will. And now he'd repaid her by spying on her?

Chloe spun around, hackles raised. "So, you're sneaking around? And spying on me now? Are you collecting this information," Chloe gestured at Tiff, "to tell my father?"

Will frowned, wounded. "I would never do that to you, Chloe."

"Then, I suppose you were here to collect this." She waved the photograph of Elaine at him. "You thought you were better placed to help her right, so you'd give me no choice?" Her tone stung of defiance, of hurt.

"You said so yourself... someone knows your secret."

"And now you know my secret, too. Tiffany and I are together. If anyone knew, my head would be on a chopping block. And hers." She gripped Tiffany's hand.

"They wouldn't kill you. Would they?" Will spluttered, "You're the future Queen."

"They've done it before and for far less. My mother is one of them. They'd do it again. It would go to the next logical heir, and my father has no siblings. So, in this case that would be my step-mother."

"But your blood, and she isn't—" Will insisted.

"Stop. Just stop." Chloe held out her hand.

Tiffany gazed at Chloe, wide-eyed. "Chloe, he's offering to *help* you. It would look like you'd backed away from finding Elaine after these people's warning." She lifted the piece of paper with the threat written on it. "And then we'd be safe. Let someone else carry the burden for once."

The rattle of the door handle had them all jumping high in the air. Chloe pressed a single finger to her lips in a motion for all of them to be silent.

"It's me," Karina called.

Will ran for the door and flung it open. He pulled Karina inside, shut the door as quickly as he could, and embraced her by kissing her forehead. Chloe looked at Tiff in confusion, one eyebrow raised. Tiffany shrugged.

"Finally." Chloe said, rolling her eyes. "You've realized you're hot for one another. Thank God for that. The sexual tension brewing between you two was almost too much to handle sometimes."

Will gave a half smile and Karina nodded. "We do. I'm getting out of this marriage. Will promised he'd find a way." Karina said, smiling. "That's what got me through the ceremony."

Will swallowed.

"Chloe, Lilian sent me." Karina said. "You need to get back there soon. She's getting nervous that as the party goes on, and people get drunk, then they'll come up and talk to her. Her voice will give her away."

"Or maybe they'll be drunk enough not to notice?" Chloe said. She needed more time with Tiffany. This was the first time she'd seen her alone in over a month, and there were still... things Chloe wanted to do.

"It's okay," Tiffany said, smiling that perfect smile and brushing a kiss on Chloe's cheek that made her shiver.

Karina looked confused, but Chloe didn't care. Will could fill her in on the fact that Chloe was a Traitor and royal failure at another time. If she hadn't put two and two together already.

"Give Will the photograph. Let someone help you. And we can still see one another." Tiffany extricated the photo from her hand, but something made her pause as she glanced at it.

"What is it?" Chloe said. She was there next to Tiffany, assessing the image in an instant. She'd pored over it day and night, looking for ideas of where the photo was captured.

"That dark wooden lattice behind her. Those carvings..." Tiffany said, running her hand over the background of the image, just behind where Elaine stood holding the sign that read: "Ready for transfer."

Tiffany was the costume designer in her troop of artists. She never missed a single detail, *especially* pattern details. Chloe cursed herself for not showing her earlier. Granted, it'd been too dangerous to get the image to her, but Tiffany's eye for detail is second to none.

Will and Karina joined them, hunched over the picture. "Where do you think it is?"

"I don't think where it is," Tiffany said, eyes wide, "I *know* where it is."

CHAPTER

TWENTY-SIX

"Dartfield's been hiding her in church?" Chloe asked. "Well, that's rich."

"It makes sense." Will said, "When we learnt about that church in our history lessons at school, they always said they'd created bomb shelters under buildings in case wars happened again. There's one big one under New London, but there are private ones too. There are secret passageways under the city to get to the shelters. But those are all owned by..."

"Nobles." Karina finished for him.

"You should look for her there," Tiffany said. "Now, while everyone's distracted."

"I need to get back to Lilian," Chloe said, torn. She was desperate to find Elaine, but she wouldn't risk Lilian's life.

"I'll cover for you," Tiffany said. "I'll get some entertainers over to the royal area and start a private show. No one will talk to her while she's watching. She'll be safe for at least thirty minutes. I'll give her the signal when you're back and you can swap out back up here."

Chloe chewed on her lip. "Okay. But Karina, you need to stay here."

Karina stood. "Like hell I will."

"If Caleb or Dartfield come looking for you, we're screwed."

"So what? I won't leave Elaine again." Karina's voice broke a little.

"I can tell Caleb you've fallen ill and are being tended to," Tiffany said. "I'll say it's... your bleeding. He won't risk coming up with that excuse. It won't buy you long, but it'll buy you enough time. Get going," Tiffany said, pulling on her mask and slipping out of the room.

"Tiff..." Chloe and she looked at one another. "Thank you. Be safe."

Tiffany nodded and was gone.

Chloe looked at Will and Karina. "Let's get on with it then," she said, daring to hope that they'd be able to get Elaine out before they transferred her to God knew where.

～

CHLOE, Karina, and Will darted across the palace courtyard and toward the church. Chloe forced herself not to think of what might come to pass if Tiffany couldn't keep Lilian's presence on her throne a secret. But Tiff wouldn't fail her: she never had.

Will pushed open the door, the two girls behind him scuttling inside. "Now what?" He asked, looking around the empty church.

"Tiffany said that she recognized the carvings from the confessional door. Let's start there."

Chloe moved toward the confessional, thinking about the last time she'd been here. It seemed like such a long time ago. She opened the confessional door and stepped inside. The light of the full moon shining in from the window meant she could *just* see. She ran her hand along the doorway, along the wooden bench, feeling the rough wood. She examined the lattice detailing and couldn't believe she'd missed how obvious it was. Her hand grazed where the confessional met with the wall of the church, and Chloe gasped.

"What is it?"

"Did you bring the ring?" Chloe asked.

Karina fished in her pocket. "Here."

Chloe took the sigil ring from her and pushed the sigil into the wall. There was a gap that matched the markings of the sigil. It was so tiny, no one would've noticed as they confessed their sins. As she pushed the ring in further, she heard a click. She rotated the ring in its place, and the wall swung open to reveal a dark corridor. It was never just a ring.

It had always been a *key*.

A key to where Dartfield had kept Elaine, all this time. "Are you sure about this, Chloe?" Karina whispered, looking down the dark hallway that now lay in front of them.

"Nope. But if we want to find her, then we're going to have to get on with it." Chloe felt a chill running up her spine. Karina, you keep watch and cover for us, okay?"

"What if Elaine's down there? I'll be the only one she can trust," Karina argued.

Chloe gritted her teeth in frustration. "I liked it better when you called me 'Your H*ighness.*'" Sarcasm dripped in her voice.

Will chuckled, despite the tightness in his features. "We're well past that now."

"Fine. We all go."

"One second." Will's footsteps faded away as he disappeared from sight.

Chloe shifted. Something didn't feel right. She wished someone would stay out here and keep watch, but it was unfair to pull rank and tell the others what to do. They wanted to find Elaine as much as she did. Will returned with three long candlesticks, already lit.

He passed one to Karina, looking at her for a moment longer.

"Let's go."

∼

EVERY DOOR down the hallway was locked. All the doors were adorned with the names of the lords and ladies. Chloe imagined they didn't come down here to check on their "Plan B" too much. But instead, the Noble class slept easy, knowing if there was ever another Great War, then they'd be just fine in their shelter.

Chloe ran her hand along the thick concrete—this was a bunker. She didn't know why it'd been built after the war; that time was long over. Her family had always been well prepared.

Will called from up ahead, "Guys!"

Chloe jogged to where he stood. On the door in front of him had a sign: *House of Dartfield.*

He tried the doorknob; it swung open with ease. Chloe backed away quickly. This all seemed... too easy. Too simple. It was as if Dartfield *wanted* them to come.

"Guys," Chloe said in warning, but both of her friends had already entered the bunker.

The light of their candles did nothing to fill the large room. There were bunk beds on either side of the wall.

There was a store of food, probably enough for two years or more, if there were fewer people here.

There were Common Castes starving above their heads, but all the Nobles each had this much food stored down here? Just in case? Chloe shook her head in disgust. Then, the Princess spun around as she heard a screech of horror.

Karina stood huddled over a figure. A girl, tied up to a bunk bed, her hands and mouth bound. Tears poured down her face. The bound girl looked battered and bruised, but she was alive.

"Elaine!" Karina said, eyes wide. She ripped off the gag over Elaine's mouth.

Elaine gasped, "We need to get the others." Elaine's eyes frantically darted around the room.

"Others?" Will frowned. "It's just you in the bunker. Everywhere else is locked."

"But—" Elaine objected.

"We need to get you out of here first. You're to go with Will. We need to run from Dartfield or he'll..." Karina said.

"*John?*" Elaine said in what seemed like disbelief. "You think *John Dartfield* did this?"

Terror coiled in Chloe's gut. If Dartfield hadn't locked her down here, then who had?

"Wait here, Elaine; you're weak. You're not well." Karina stroked her hair. "You're safe now. Let's get you out, and we can talk about what happened later." Karina helped Elaine up.

"You're not going anywhere." A voice echoed from the darkness. The door slammed shut, and the finality of the click made Chloe tremble. It was a trap.

CHAPTER
TWENTY-SEVEN

"Don't move." It was a voice she recognised, but even now, Chloe couldn't quite believe.

A loaded gun made its way from the darkness, as did its owner. *Father Jeremiah* stood in front of the door, blocking their only exit. Chloe forgot how to breathe.

No no no!

This wasn't it.

This couldn't be the answer.

"No," Chloe said, backing away in horror. Father Jeremiah was her friend, her confidante. "You...you helped me. You despise the Games too."

"What has this got to do with the Games?" Father Jeremiah asked, cocking the gun.

"The fact that you're a good person," Chloe said.

"I don't like the Games," Father Jeremiah admitted. "And I *am* a good person."

"Says the man holding a gun to his Princess' head!"

Chloe's only weapon was the small knife she carried in her boot. But what use was a knife in her *boot* if she couldn't get it when she needed it the most? She was just realizing now that a knife attached to her ankle, although comforting, wasn't all that helpful in situations like this.

Father Jeremiah stalked toward her, slapping her with his free hand, sending her sprawling onto the floor. Chloe heard someone cry out. "You're no Princess of mine." Father Jeremiah sneered, "You're a sex Traitor. You're a sinner. You're *filth*. You don't deserve to be in the great royal line. People have *died* for the monarchy to live. Before the Great War, the church saved the monarchy. They warned them to escape from London before it was destroyed. And what do we get for our loyalty? Disappointing, disgusting filth."

Chloe crawled away from him.

"I agreed to help you to keep you on my side. I needed you to not suspect me. I needed to keep hold of our lovely Elaine until the Thirteenth Apostles had aligned what they needed to, and take her back. They told me about your sins, that you love a woman. They even provided me with proof, a photograph of you kissing her." He spat. "My only request to the Thirteenth Apostles when I agreed to hide Elaine for them, was that I could kill you at the end of all of this."

He kicked her onto her back and jammed his shoe into her throat. Chloe clawed at his foot, gasping for air. "The Thirteenth Apostles?" She choked out.

"A secret faction committed to serving God amongst all of you filthy sinners," the father said. Then, there was a shuffle of footsteps and a loud crack that made Chloe's ears scream in protest.

"No! Will... Will!" Karina's muffled sobs told Chloe everything she hadn't seen. Will had come to Chloe's aid, to protect her, and he'd been shot.

"Stay where you are," Chloe choked out to Karina.

"Yes. Stay where you are!" Father Jeremiah shouted. He pressed the barrel of the gun further into Chloe's forehead, and she winced at the pressure. "I am a godly man. And I will do His bidding. *Jude: 7.* 'And don't forget Sodom and Gomorrah and their neighboring towns, which were filled with immorality and every kind of sexual perversion. Those cities were destroyed by fire and serve as a warning of the eternal fire of God's judgment.'" He grinned. "My ancestors gave so much for the royals to live. My father gave his *life* to get your family out of London when the bombs came. And *this* is how he's been repaid. With perversion from the very family he died for," Father Jeremiah spat. "You who were supposed to be God on earth, but you will be destroyed by fire."

Father Jeremiah looked at the others. "Karina, Elaine— stand outside the door. I'm going to burn your princess to death."

~

KARINA FORCED herself to take deep breaths, just like her dad had taught her. In through the nose, out through the mouth. To think, she needed to breathe. She looked at Will, his blood all over the concrete floor, and whimpered in fear.

"It's okay." He said, his hand reaching up to touch her face, leaving a bloody mark. "Do as he says."

The bullet had gone straight through his thigh, so she knew he wouldn't die from the wound, but he couldn't move properly. Karina propped Will up to drag him out of the room.

"Not him. He can die with the Princess," Father Jeremiah said flatly.

"No!" Karina screamed.

"You," he addressed Karina. "The Thirteenth wanted to get their hands on you. I think I'll oblige them. I suppose I can sell the story to the public that you came down here with these two," he gestured to Chloe and Will, "to do some heinous deeds and perished in the fire. That'll bring light to the fact you," He spat at Chloe, "took the Lord's name and Moses' name and defiled it." The father grabbed Karina by the hair and pulled her out of the room.

She kicked and screamed and did everything in her power to return to Will, to return to Chloe.

"No! No!" Karina screamed, but she was useless.

She didn't have a way to fight him. She was a pawn in the game, like she'd always been. She half-registered Elaine, kissing Chloe's cheek in farewell.

"Thank you for not giving up on me," Elaine said.

Chloe nodded, her gaze never leaving Elaine's.

"Stay out here," Father Jeremiah growled. He picked up what Karina assumed to be an oil canister and began dowsing everything in the room. Elaine, still bound by her wrists and legs, looked at Father Jeremiah. "You need to untie my legs so I can move, asshole."

Father Jeremiah glanced at her, muttering, "I'll be glad to get rid of you, you know? Fucking brat." He went to untie the rope at her legs when she made her move.

Elaine launched at the priest, her eyes wild, as if she'd dreamed about this moment for a long time. Karina saw a flash of silver in Elaine's hand. *Chloe's knife.* Chloe must have smuggled it to her, as they said their goodbyes.

Elaine used it with vigor.

Elaine gritted her teeth, driving the tiny knife in and out, in and out, all over Father Jeremiah's torso. Blood pooled on his shirt as Elaine drove the stabs deeper and deeper. He stopped being able to hold her back and sank to the ground, unable to move under the weight of her ferocity.

"Bitch!" He screamed.

Another gunshot rang out, making Karina's head spin. Elaine collapsed next to Father Jeremiah, clutching her belly. Red pooled around her, seeping into the floor.

"Elaine!" Karina screamed, running toward her.

Elaine spluttered blood, "Finish him."

Elaine pushed something cold into Karina's hand. She looked down. The bloody knife. Jeremiah was clawing away from them, blood leaving a trail in his path.

"I... I can't." Karina sobbed. Karina had never taken a life. No matter what this man had done, she couldn't bring herself to taint her soul like that. She felt another hand on the hilt of the dagger. It was Chloe's. Chloe looked at her, ice in her gaze. "We'll finish it. *Together*."

Chloe and Karina pulled on one leg of Jeremiah's each. They yanked him back from the door and toward them. He was sobbing now.

"Flip him over." Karina did as Chloe instructed.

"Who were you working with?" Chloe placed her boot on his neck in an ironic twist of fate. "Who are the Thirteenth Apostles?"

The priest smiled a sadistically, blood staining his teeth, "Mother Mary herself."

Chloe looked Jeremiah right in the eyes. "I'll see you in Hell, Father." And then, she drove the dagger into his heart.

TWENTY-EIGHT

Karina and Chloe watched together as the light left Father Jeremiah's eyes. As soon as his raspy breaths were no more, Karina ran to Elaine, pulling Elaine's body up onto her lap and cradling her. "Bastard shot me." Elaine murmured. "Lord Dartfield.... Get me to him...."

"I'll get you to him." Karina whispered in desperation. Chloe had no idea why Elaine would want to see Dartfield, but she didn't question it.

Karina's sobs pushed Chloe's shaking legs into motion. Will dragged himself over to where the group of women lay. He clutched at his leg, where blood slowly seeped from his gunshot wound.

Karina's tear-streaked face peered up at Chloe. "She wants to see Dartfield. We have to take her."

Chloe examined Elaine. Her face had gone white, her eyes shuttering. The blood—there was just so much. "We can't move her like this. I need to get a doctor..."

"Don't..." Elaine said, her voice nothing but a husky

whisper. "It'll put whoever covered for you in danger. I won't have that on my conscience as I die."

Chloe thought of Lilian and of Tiff. Elaine had a point. Chloe cursed under her breath.

"You're. Not. Dying," Karina said, gritting her teeth. She held Elaine in her arms, rocking her back and forth.

"The others—" Elaine said.

"Who are the others? What do you mean, Elaine?" Chloe urged her. She needed more than this. She needed more time with Elaine.

"Tell John... that me and the baby loved him very much." Her head went slack in Karina's hands, and Karina howled, her grief pouring out of her.

Chloe couldn't make sense of anything Elaine had told them. Elaine had loved Lord Dartfield? And who were the others Elaine had spoken of?

Elaine was *pregnant?*

"Shit," Will muttered as he put the pieces together a few seconds later than Chloe—Elaine was a goddamned Vessel.

~

WILL SAT in the darkness of Lord Dartfield's study, one arm placed around Karina. She was still hiccupping, tears coursing down her face, but she sat tall in front of Lord Dartfield, who looked about as pale as Will felt. Dartfield didn't even register how tenderly Will was holding his son's wife.

The bullet wound had gone straight through Will, and Karina, although tiny, was surprisingly strong. She'd managed to support him through the back roads of the empty Noble District and into Dartfield manor. They'd found a first-aid kit in his study while they'd waited, and Karina had patched him up as best she could.

Chloe had returned to the masquerade ball, switched back with Lilian, and told Dartfield what had happened.

"I'm sorry. I loved her very much," Dartfield said, a haunted look on his face.

"You...loved her?" Karina asked, still baffled.

"I did. We were going to run away. I'd found a boat. I intended to choose an uninhabited island in the U.K. I'd fish. She would cook, and our baby..." His voice tightened. "Would play. That child would grow up blissfully unaware of the rules that our country now binds us with."

"That sounds nice," Will said, biting his lip. He hated to press Dartfield while he was full of grief, but it was necessary. "How did this all happen? We found an image of her in your desk. It said she was ready to be *transferred?*"

"I don't know what that sign she held meant, either. All I know was that when she disappeared, Father Jeremiah came to me, saying that a powerful organization called the *Thirteenth Apostles* had tasked him with holding her captive."

"Why did the Thirteenth not hold her captive themselves?"

"I don't know," Dartfield said, hand running through his hair. "Jeremiah would say nothing more. He wanted me to pay to get her back."

"He tried to extort you? To double cross the Thirteenth?" Will pressed, leaning in.

"Yes. I'd almost paid the whole thing off, and he said that if I kept her hidden that I could have her for one night. In exchange for wearing this ring for as long as he wanted.

And he gave me the image of her, a copy of the original he'd taken, to prove that she was alive." He motioned to the sigil ring on his finger.

"Jeremiah must've known we'd focus our attention on you once we saw you wear the sigil. And then we found the image..." Will said.

"And the scratching in your wardrobe?" Karina asked.

"It was her, yes. I tried to get her out of New London that night. But the King and Queen insisted I didn't leave their side during the Games and the celebrations. I only saw her for an hour, and then I asked her to hide. I thought that once I paid Jeremiah, he'd let us go. But when I returned that night to smuggle her out of New London, she was gone. He'd stolen her again."

"And what about the King's signature on the photograph?" Will said, squeezing Karina's shoulder in what he hoped was a comforting gesture. She just looked blankly ahead.

"The King is my closest friend. He's not a cruel man. He does what he needs to at court to survive. But hurting an innocent woman? He either didn't know, or he was under major duress to sign that document."

"So, you don't believe he's a part of the Thirteenth Apostles?"

Lord Dartfield put his head in his hands. "Honestly? I don't know what I believe anymore."

Will winced as he stood. "Thank you for telling us what you know. Elaine's body is in... your bunker." Will winced as Karina stiffened.

"I'll look after her," he said, lip trembling. "And I'll leave that bastard in there to rot. I'll make it look like a random attack. No one will be implicated in his death."

"Thank you," Karina said, supporting Will as they walked out of his study. "Please bury her with this." Karina placed the heart-shaped oak necklace into his palm.

"Karina?" Lord Dartfield said. She turned back to him, as his shoulders hunched with grief. "Be careful."

CHAPTER
TWENTY-NINE

Karina pulled her hood up and tipped her head down to the floor as she made her way through the Traitor district. This place used to be her home. Now it scared her.

Being a Vessel made you a precious commodity. A target, even. And as she stepped through the filth and begging, she realized with no small amount of comfort that she'd be a target for the rest of her life. Karina knocked twice on her brother's door.

He swung the door open, his nerves looking thin. "Did anyone see you leave?"

She shook her head. "Octavia is covering for me. Caleb thinks I'm at her house for high tea."

"Okay, then." He grabbed her by the hand and pulled her into his flat.

He'd moved out of their mum's house now. It was getting too dangerous for her, Marcus had said. After Karina finally came clean with Marcus about what had happened to Elaine and the Thirteenth Apostles, he'd done the same. He had indeed been part of an underground resistance group. They'd been planning another coup since the Uprising failed.

"Have you heard anything else from the others?" Karina asked.

They talked in riddles these days, never explicitly mentioning the resistance since the day after Elaine had died, the day after she'd learned of them. *You never know who may be watching.* her brother had warned.

"No one's heard about any other Common Caste girls going missing," Marcus said, his eyes darting around the small room. "And no one's heard of a group called the Thirteenth Apostles. Are you sure about this, Karina?"

"I'm positive. We need to find the records of Common Caste girls going missing over the last few years. There's probably Defenders at their headquarters burying the evidence, but they can't hide it. Not completely. Elaine mentioned *others*. She and I weren't the only ones taken. I know she wasn't confused. She seemed genuinely concerned about others she knew of who had also been stolen."

Marcus swallowed. "Okay, I'll see what I can do. If we can find someone loyal to our cause in the Defender Caste, we might just have a chance at finding the others that Elaine spoke of."

Karina folded her arms around her protectively. "Is... he still here?" Karina said, glancing at the door that led to the basement.

"Go ahead." Marcus sighed. She darted to the door before he could change his mind. "Karina?"

"Hmm?"

"You're playing a dangerous game here."

Karina nodded and turned her back to him, opening the basement's door. "You have no idea," she replied.

Karina descended the basement stairs, the squeak of each step making her flinch.

"Karina?"

"Will!" She ran the rest of the way, launching from the bottom stair and into his arms.

She held him tightly, smelling his scent. It was more sweat and grime than anything, but she breathed him in all the same, because it was *Will*. She pressed her lips to his.

"How are you?" he asked, pushing hair from her face, and a small worry line appearing between his dark eyebrows.

"I'm fine," she insisted.

"Has he hurt you?"

Karina's heart rate picked up. "Of course not." In fact, quite the opposite. He'd let Karina live and sleep in her own rooms, had given her plenty of space from him.

Lord and Lady Dartfield visited Caleb and Karina's mansion in the Noble district occasionally. She'd even been allowed to go to finishing school, where the Noble ladies learned not math, science, literature or history but dancing, applique, and deportment. They were expected to behave nicely and make their owners—their husbands—proud.

"I don't have long," Karina said. "But I had to see you." His lips curled into a smile as he pressed them to her own. He began to feel every inch of her body, making Karina's skin crackle with excitement.

"Stop," She said, putting her hand on his chest. He did so instantly. "We have a serious problem."

Will's smile dropped. "What is it?"

"Will. I'm pregnant."

Will stood there for a moment and collapsed onto his make-shift bed in a heap, as if his legs had suddenly given out on him.

"That's... that's great." His tone was dull, hurt even.

"No. Will, you don't understand," Karina said, dropping onto the bed next to him. She grabbed his face and looked into his beautiful brown eyes. "The baby is yours."

Will's eyes widened. "You mean... Caleb hasn't...."

Karina's stomach dropped; she was really going to have to explain this out loud for him to grasp this. "We sleep in separate rooms. He's never come to see me, never asked me to..." Karina had been relieved when Caleb hadn't pushed her to be with him. He knew she'd never wanted the marriage, and had tried to keep a respectful distance.

Will's eyes looked like they were about to shoot out of his skull. "Fuck." He breathed.

"I know."

Will was in pure panic mode. He knew what this would mean for Karina if anyone ever knew the truth. *Enslavement. Torture.* And as soon as she was past the age to bear any more children: death.

"Well, you need to figure out how to make him get there, uh, you know what I mean." He grimaced both at the awkwardness of everything and, worse, of thinking with his beloved Karina with anyone else.

"I know, Will," Karina snapped.

Karina had to be thinking of Octavia, as she seemed to space out and shiver there. After all rebelling—running—had not ended well for Octavia. She'd been to hell and back. Will did not want that for either Karina or for his child..

He reached over and grabbed her chin gently, gazing at her. "We will figure something out. I...I am so sorry."

They held their gaze for a long time then, but eventually, Karina was the first to break away.

"I better go. Caleb will be wondering where I am. Octavia can only cover for me for so long." She stood abruptly and turned to leave, but Will caught her hand in his.

"Karina," he breathed the word like it was a prayer, he chewed on his bottom lip as he searched for the words. "Again, I'm sorry you have to live like this. I'll find a way. I'll fix this. But now... you need to protect yourself, too. Do whatever you have to do."

Karina had to see with the sincerity he was projecting that he meant. Didn't she? After all, if she couldn't make it look like it was Caleb's child... He wanted her to protect herself before the baby that grew inside her. Karina nodded in assent.

Karina shrugged her shoulders and looked around the tiny basement that Will was confined to for now. He'd refused to run on her account. So, he was stuck in hiding in her big brother's basement for the foreseeable future. It was ironic, but he suspected if they could both be together, then Karina would rather live hand-to-mouth in a room smaller than this than have to go back to that mansion for one second longer.

But that was not the way this worked.

"I have to go," Karina repeated, "I'll bring more food whenever I can get away. I love you, Will."

She bolted out the door before Will could see if her eyes were welling with tears.

He sighed, thinking of how trapped they all felt and of the false lies of the Games.

After all, if being a Vessel was the top of the food-chain, then they were all trapped, no matter the Caste.

CHAPTER
THIRTY

Chloe laid with Tiffany in her arms. She'd have to be up for church soon but fuck it. She never knew when Tiff could get into the palace unde-tected, or when she could leave again. Lil stood watch outdoors, sure to knock if anyone came into her bedroom unannounced.

"I missed you."

"I missed you, too." Tiffany smiled, tracing her delicate fingers over Chloe's bare breasts. Chloe closed her eyes as the shiver of desire trickled down her spine and landed somewhere deeper.

"You can't do things like that. You'll make me want to..."

"Want to what?" Tiff lifted a brow, mischief dancing on her stunning features.

"Want to miss church," Chloe confessed.

Tiffany continued her work on Chloe, her hands now cupped around Chloe's breasts. She took turns with them, fondling, stroking, and caressing them with her fingers. Then eventually, those talented fingers were replaced with her tongue. Chloe felt a soft nibble of Tiffany's teeth and a flick of Tiffany's tongue around her nipple that both sent her trembling.

Chloe groaned with pleasure.

A sharp but quiet knock at the door had both women jumping.

"I should go." Chloe swallowed, leaping out of bed. "Thank you for protecting Karina the other night. And me but now, it's my turn to protect you."

"What do you mean?" Tiffany asked, her gaze narrowing.

"We can't keep doing this, Tiff. If anyone found out—"

"I know what they'd do," Tiffany snapped. "And I love you enough to take the risk. We're not the only people who have this problem in New London, you know."

Chloe paused in her dressing for a moment. There were others like them? She hadn't even thought to ask. "I know, but I'm the only *Princess* who has this problem. I'm constantly watched, scrutinized, and the fact that the Thirteenth Apostles knew about us... I'm just... " Chloe ran her hand through her hair, searching for the words. "Frightened."

Tiffany slid from her place on the bed, her naked body in full view. Despite Chloe's terror at someone bursting through the doors and spying them like this, she couldn't help but admire the soft curves of Tiff's body.

"I know you are. But I'll be fine. We'll be fine. Trust me." Tiff grinned. "Now go to church and hunt. Do whatever else it is that princesses do. I'll be waiting." Tiffany tossed Chloe the reg wig. "Keep that safe, you'll be needing it to see me outside the walls again soon."

Chloe's lips curved into a smile as she took the wig and pulled Tiff toward her, embracing her. But when she was sure Tiff couldn't see her face, she let the smile drop and the worried crease between her eyes returned yet again.

~

CHLOE STOOD in her stirrups and waited for her father and her step-mother. "Come on, you two!"

They'd taken a day trip on their large, private boat to an island that lay just above New London. The King had insisted she accompany them. These days, what once had been cities, concrete roads, and buildings had been laid waste by weather events, like the acid rain that came every summer. Now, moss and grass covered them completely.

They were, in fact, wonderful places to hunt for rabbits and deer that remained. The place was scoured for any rogue Shadowlanders by a small army of Defenders, and once it'd been deemed safe and uninhabited, the King, Queen and Princess had descended from the large boat and jumped onto their horses.

Dogs yapped and barked at the horses' hooves, ready to hunt down their prey.

"Oh, I've been meaning to ask. Have you heard anything about the Shadowlander attack on Father Jeremiah?" Chloe asked.

Once Dartfield had taken Elaine's body, he'd sent in some of his best, most loyal men to make Father Jeremiah look like the victim of a savage Shadowlander attack. They'd plundered all the gold and jewels available in the church to make it look as legitimate as possible.

"No. Don't worry though, darling; the Shadowlanders won't get to you." The King shrugged.

Chloe followed suit, mounting with a rather unladylike

grunt. The King looked at her sharply. They were not the sounds a princess should be making. She shrugged.

"We will have to do something about them, dear heart." The Queen said, mounting her black horse with ease, "These unbelieving savages are getting out of control. I've heard the High Priest in Manchester has also seen an increase in attacks in their city. With how sparse food is with the crops this year, we can't afford to be losing anything of more value."

"Don't tell me how to do my job," the King snapped.

The Queen bowed her head in subservience. "I'm sorry, Your Majesty. I only worry for your and Chloe's safety. These are dangerous times..."

The King nodded in assent, and he took her hand in his and kissed it, his gaze never leaving her eyes. Chloe glanced behind her, and her eyes widened in disbelief.

It couldn't be.

She gazed at what lay on her father's finger and tried to pull in air that didn't want to be found. It had been haunting her. The signature she'd found on the photograph of Elaine—her father's signature.

She didn't want to believe that he would knowingly hurt women. But Chloe had to ask him. She had to look into his eyes and know the truth. If this was more complicated than just Father Jeremiah. If her *own* father was also a monster. If the rings... if they meant something more.

"Dad, I just wondered," Chloe started, "that ring you have on. I noticed Lord Dartfield wore the same one too, a few weeks ago. Do you know what the sigil means?"

The King frowned. "That's strange for you to remember such a detail about Dartfield, Chloe." He smiled at her in a way that was carefree and without deceit. "This ring?" He wiggled his finger, inspecting the ring in the sunlight. "I have no idea. I never asked Mary. She gifted it to me a few days ago for our wedding anniversary."

"Is that so?" Chloe nudged her horse a little too hard, and it moved forward into a trot.

She slowed the horse once again, trying to keep her emotions in check. It did not seem of any significance to him. Her father was clever, yes, but Chloe could read his emotions well after years of practice.

"Darling?" the King called behind them. "What does the symbol on the ring mean?"

The Queen rode up next to them both. "It's the Eye of Providence. The all-seeing eye of God. It represents Divine Providence. Everything we, as the divine on earth, do is God's Will. He controls us all."

The King nodded and moved the symbol of the cross across his torso with his hand. Chloe knew in that moment he was not connected to the Thirteenth Apostles. Chloe looked at the Queen. He didn't seem like he cared about the origin of the symbol of this ring. But the Queen now assessed her with an intensity that burned.

"Everything you do, Chloe, is watched by God. Everything." The Queen leant across on her horse and plucked a singular long hair off Chloe's jacket. It was red.

"You've got red hair on you, darling. That's strange. It's so long, too." The Queen looked at her with an innocent gaze that could've fooled Chloe. "What have you been up to that would get red hair on you?"

The King looked over at Chloe, with curiosity etched on his features. "I was appliqueing before I came out on the hunt." The lie rolled off Chloe's tongue, despite the shaking of her legs. "It must be a thread from that."

"Strange." Mary tilted her head. "It feels coarser than a sewing thread. Almost *hair-like*."

Chloe did not miss a beat. "I'm trying a new type."

The smile she shared was for show. Mary continued to look at Chloe with such an intensity that even the horse underneath her began to shift, as if he could sense a threat to his rider. What had Father Jeremiah said before they'd left him there?

He was on a mission for Mother Mary herself.

The only way for her father's signature to get onto the photograph...

Will had said Dartfield had mentioned it could've been under duress, or he didn't know what he was signing. But what if it was *neither*? What if someone else had access to the royal seal, all royal stationery, and knew her father's signature as well as *her own*?

"Of course, my darling." The Queen plucked the red hair from Chloe's wig and sent it flying into the wind. "May God's Will guide you safely to our throne." Mary placed her hand on Chloe's cheek, as she had done many times before.

But this time, it felt different. This time, it felt like a threat.

END OF BOOK 1

*****

Want more drama? More mystery? And more excitement?
Order book two of the series, Rebel Rising on Amazon
today!

Do you want to join my Facebook group and get a BONUS CHAPTER (that I must admit, gave me ALL the feels when writing) in Caleb's POV? You'll also get the opportunity to compete in monthly giveaways. (I promise there will be no fighting to the death for the prizes. At the moment.)

Join my Facebook group, "The Edenites - E.J. Eden book lovers" or sign up to my mailing list at ejeden.com. (Both will get you the giveaway opportunities and the Caleb chapter.)

******

Reviews are the lifeblood of an indie author career, so I encourage you to leave a review if you're able to!

E.J x

ACKNOWLEDGMENTS

Thank you to my team: Ali at The Book Brander Boutique for my cover, the Zero Alchemy team for my editing, Rebecca Hamilton. I want to also thank my beta readers: Kathryn Rose, Alicia White, Jessie Feyen, Renee Evans, and Renee Green and everyone else in my street team and ARC reader team.

Thank you to AK Mulford and Anne Kemp—who are authors local to me and open and lovely enough to meet with me and let me pick their brains about all things authoring. These ladies have been a great source of inspiration for me.

Thank you to my amazing newsletter readers, ARC readers, and TikTok friends; it has been so amazing to see you share your excitement for my work and gave me a final push to do this thing. Thanks a bunch also to my real-life friends who have been nothing but utterly supportive.

Thank you to my family, particularly my mom who has to put up with me talking about books on almost every phone call; I love you so much. You'll always be the first to read my books. Except the smut bits. My dad has always told me to follow my dreams and supported me no matter what. I love you!

And lastly, thank you to my Craftsman Caste, my inspiration for Will; my Pete. Thanks for being everything I could ever want in a human. And thanks for forcing me out of bed every morning at 6am to write. Love you.

Printed in Great Britain
by Amazon

26622041R00159